DANGEROUS DECISIONS

B.B. CRUZ

CRIMSON
ROMANCE

F+W Media, Inc.

Published by
Crimson Romance
an imprint of F+W Media, Inc.
10151 Carver Road, Suite 200
Blue Ash, OH 45242. U.S.A.
www.crimsonromance.com

ISBN 10: 1-4405-9090-7
ISBN 13: 978-1-4405-9090-0
eISBN 10: 1-4405-9091-5
eISBN 13: 978-1-4405-9091-7

Cover art © iStockphoto.com/jandrielombard.

This book is dedicated to my family, whom I love with all my heart. Your never-ending support gives me the courage to keep reaching for the stars.

Acknowledgments

Words simply can't express my gratitude for all the encouragement I've received from my family and friends. Special thanks goes to my wonderful husband, who is the most patient and loving man I've ever known. Your unwavering support is the wind beneath my wings. Thanks to my two beautiful daughters, who are the brightest stars in the sky; keep shining. Thank you to my #1 fan— my mom—for tirelessly taking notes and for falling in love with Ramon. You helped breathe him to life! Thanks Dad, for enduring multiple manuscript readings, as romance is certainly not your genre of choice. Your input and ability to catch even the tiniest of errors was invaluable. To my sister, thanks for always believing in me. Without you and your great ideas, I'd still be trying to figure out what happened next! To my friends who volunteered to read my drafts, even at their roughest, thank you for your patience, kind words, and precious time.

Thanks to everyone at Crimson Romance for all of their hard work and support, especially Tara Gelsomino for recognizing a diamond in the rough and Jess Verdi for polishing that diamond.

Finally, thank you to all those who've chosen to read my writing. I'm eternally grateful.

Chapter 1

"Get out of my way!" Carino Montgomery wrenched the wheel, swerving in front of the car next to her, barely making her freeway exit. The driver flipped her the bird, which was to be expected; she truly was driving like a jerk, but it couldn't be helped. Today, she had one of the most important meetings of her career, so, naturally, she'd overslept.

Her tires screeched as she pulled up to her parking garage. Swiping her gate pass, she gunned the engine of her pint-sized Mazda3 hatchback and frantically sought out a parking space. Blasting out of the garage's elevator, unwelcome beads of sweat forming at the edge of her hairline, she tore down the block toward her office building.

Glancing at the time on her phone to see how close she was cutting it, she realized that she'd made up some serious ground in her haste and had nearly ten minutes to spare before the workday began. Due to meticulous planning, she had everything ready for the big meeting at 8:15, aside from laying the presentation binders on the table in the conference room. Figuring she now had the time, she ducked into the coffee shop across from her building for some much-needed caffeine. Plus, she wanted to catch her breath.

The line moved quickly, in spite of the pretentious jerk in front of her who ordered a venti, half-caf, skinny, sugar free, vanilla soy latte. Carino wasn't fluent in "Starbucks," as she didn't frequently splurge, so she kept it simple by ordering a tall spiced chai.

She crossed the street, gingerly tipping the cup to her caffeine-deprived mouth, only to discover the lid was not secure. She immediately stuck her butt out and hunched her shoulders forward, mimicking the *I just spilled scalding liquid down the front of my shirt* pose.

Oh holy shit, that's hot.

"No, no, no, this cannot happen today!" Her loud rant caused several pedestrians to take a wider berth while passing on the sidewalk.

She pinched the scalding, soaked fabric and held it away from her skin with her fingernails. While she let the brisk morning air cool the hot liquid, she prayed there was a spare white tee shirt in her gym bag, which was thankfully still stowed away in her office credenza. If not, she was definitely screwed—unless someone wanted to swap clothes with her, which was *so* not likely.

Shoving the circular glass doors of her building into action, she popped the plastic lid on her cup correctly, in an effort to save the last few tablespoons of liquid.

"Good mornin', ma'am." Sammy, the head security guard for the building, always had a pleasant smile. "Need a napkin?" He glanced down at her outfit. "Or, how about a few?"

"Thanks, Sammy." She accepted the tissues, which quickly became soaked as she sopped up the mess on her shirt. "It's morning, but not a good one." She tossed the tissues in the trash bin and rushed over to the bank of elevators that serviced the upper twelve floors of the building. A throng of impatient people waited, sighing loudly and tapping their feet as they raced the time clock.

"Spilled your coffee." A man holding a weathered briefcase rocked back and forth on his heels while nodding toward her stained shirt, acting as if he'd just solved a cold case.

"Really? Where?" Carino leveled her icy gaze on him. He turned away very quickly, and she didn't feel even a tiny pang of regret at her harsh tone.

Ducking in as soon as the elevator doors opened, she pushed the button for the twenty-third floor and sandwiched herself into the far back corner to make room for the others. By now it was 7:58 a.m., so the elevator car quickly filled to capacity with harried workers, most of them glancing repeatedly at their watches. The wall was lit up like a Christmas tree, which meant they'd be stopping on nearly every floor between twelve and twenty-three. At this rate, she wasn't even going to make it to work on time, much less early enough to set up the conference room and attempt to salvage her appearance.

This is so not happening! *Raj is going to be pissed!*

Carino was on a mission as she entered the law firm's lobby through the big glass doors etched with the name Franklin Everly, LLC: Change. Her. Shirt.

Abby was at the receptionist's desk, masterfully manning the phone tree, writing with her left hand while transferring a call with her right. More than once, Carino had imagined she was hiding several extra arms behind the ergonomically correct array of computer monitors, document holders, and cordless headsets.

Briefly looking up, Abby flashed a smile that quickly faded as her eyes drifted to the brown stain on the front of Carino's shirt. "Raj is going to be pissed!"

Rolling her eyes, Carino turned and continued down the hall to the entrance of the labyrinth. She swiftly navigated the beige and green cubicle walls with practiced expertise until she reached her teeny, tiny office. Sure, it was buried within the center of the floor—hence, no windows—and was the visual representation of the word "drab," but she didn't care; it was hers. And she could close her door, which made her feel like she was someone important.

Even though Franklin Everly handled various types of commercial transactions, ranging from new business formations to bankruptcy, their client roster read like a Forbes list of real estate moguls. Not only had they made a name for themselves as leaders in domestic and international real estate law, but they were good to their employees as well and had been voted one of the "Top Ten Best Places to Work in Denver" several years back. Carino felt pretty great about being one of their senior paralegals, especially at her young age of twenty-five, and the only one with her own office to boot.

She'd been terrified walking through this place on her first day nearly three and a half years ago but had quickly worked her way into Raj Gulati's good graces by demonstrating a knack for handling complex, international real estate transactions. It normally took at least a year to be considered for a position on a special projects team, but as it was, less than six months after being hired Carino joined forces with Raj, a third-year associate, and two legal secretaries working for Raj's biggest client: Sebastian Emerson.

Over time, Carino had strategically integrated herself more and more into Emerson's business transactions and had become quite an indispensable asset. But regardless of how hard she worked, some of the more seasoned employees still made her feel as if she constantly needed to prove herself.

Generally speaking, Carino liked Raj. Abby had heard he'd fought hard to get her on his team, which helped take the sting out of being treated like his personal assistant at times. And somehow, he was able to make even the toughest sales happen, although he didn't share his trade secrets and did all the "heavy lifting" on his own. But it was obvious that he recognized Carino's talents, and she was thankful he'd taken her under his wing—especially since working under him gave her direct, unadulterated access to all of Emerson's files, not to mention she was pretty sure being a part of his team had helped her survive two rounds of heart-wrenching layoffs. Outwardly, she'd displayed the appropriate level of horrified indignation, but inside she'd been doing back-handsprings because she'd kept her job. Even the guy who'd hired her had abruptly left the firm, after being the office manager for nearly six years. Carino was glad he'd brought her on board before his time was up. She'd been inexperienced in the paralegal field, but with the proper incentives in place, anything is possible.

She paused for a moment to soak in the atmosphere, since today was different than most. It seemed as if the entire office was buzzing with anticipation, everyone hustling and bustling to avoid getting caught sitting around on the clock. It was no secret their team had been working through a brutal real estate negotiation on a piece of land in Costa Rica that Emerson wanted to purchase, and just last week Raj had announced that the seller had miraculously decided to come down to a price Emerson should be happy with. It was also common knowledge that today was the day Emerson decided whether or not to accept the offer.

Naïveté ran rampant through Franklin Everly, especially when it came to Emerson. Either that, or people had simply made the conscious decision to look the other way. The amount of money Franklin Everly would make off of today's transaction was significant; Carino's motivation was much more personal.

This is one of the most important days in my career and I look like a filthy hobo.

No sooner had Carino turned on her office light did she hear Raj coming down the hall. She'd recognize his walk anywhere; his steps were quick and measured, like a man with a serious purpose. Or it could've just been the fact he was only 5'4" and his legs were super short.

Raj appeared in her doorway looking dapper, as usual, in his tailored suit and manscaped facial hair. "Why are you not in the conference room for the final setup?"

"I literally just walked in."

His face twisted in horror as he looked her up and down. "Carino, please tell me you are joking. You knew I would be pissed!"

"That's weird, I thought you loved my sense of fashion." His dark eyes narrowed at her sarcasm. "I have a clean shirt in my gym bag, but I need two seconds to catch my breath, okay?" Carino was careful to fine-tune her attitude; she didn't want to risk her position with Raj by being too much of a smartass.

I really need that shirt to be in my bag. And he really needs to leave so I can check.

"Pull it together, Carino. I need all hands on the deck!"

Normally, she would've laughed at his slight misuse of the common cliché, but not today. Never on a day like today.

As he walked off with short, clipped stomps, Carino snatched up the black cardigan still draped over her chair, and furiously dug through her credenza, relieved beyond measure when she saw the white fabric. Hurriedly retracing her steps, inwardly cursing that her office was the farthest away from the bathroom, she dashed through the waiting area in front of Abby's desk and sprinted down the hallway.

In her frenzied rush, she plowed into the man exiting the bathroom. Well, more specifically, her sternum ran into his elbow, so hard that his arm rocketed forward causing him to punch the bathroom door, while simultaneously knocking the wind out of her.

Cursing under his breath and rubbing his injured knuckles, he turned toward the freight train that had hit him. She was dumbfounded. He was truly the most gorgeous male specimen she'd ever seen. Drop-dead, love-at-first-sight gorgeous, in fact. His eyes were melted milk chocolate, deeply set and framed by thick, inky lashes. She wondered if his jet black hair was as silky as it looked, and just barely managed to restrain herself from checking. The hard set of his cleanly shaven, chiseled jaw was softened by his adorable lopsided grin, and the way he wore his suit over skin kissed with a golden tan could have easily landed him on the cover of *GQ*. He was so perfect, it almost hurt to look at him.

"Are you okay?" What an accent! Carino could only guess it was from some Latin American country.

Sputtering, both from the sight of him and her sudden lack of oxygen, she waved her right hand in the air. Coincidentally, it was the same hand that was holding her replacement white shirt.

He smiled, flashing a mouthful of perfectly straight, gleaming white teeth. "I accept your surrender."

Struggling to catch her breath while not passing out from the massive amount of blood rushing to her flaming cheeks, Carino's words came out in a sputter. "S-s-sorry, sir." Turning abruptly, she continued down the hall and into the ladies' room, desperate to flee the humiliating situation.

She cringed, as her reflection confirmed she was a total mess. Her barrette had been dislodged during the hallway collision and was now hanging from several loose strands of curly hair, and knocking the wind out of her lungs had caused her eyes to water, smudging her mascara.

No, I'm not crying!

And of course, there was her shirt. Upon closer inspection, she could see that the lace border of her bra was no longer white but dingy, chai brown. Carino quickly swapped clothes, praying her plain white tee would provide sufficient coverage. She made a lame attempt at fixing her barrette and swiped at her under-eye area to remove the lingering black smudges. Her face twisted into a grimace. She hated how her dark hair brought out the shadowed circles under her green eyes, and her skin seemed sallow under all her freckles.

Glancing quickly at the overhead clock, Carino realized she had exactly three minutes to get to the conference room, finish setting up, and help the team pull this off. Abby had warned her months ago of the deep-rooted jealousy that smoldered within a few of her co-workers, especially those who believed they were more qualified than her to be on Raj's special team; they constantly sought to exploit any mistake she made. All the more reason she had to bring her A-game today and not strike out.

Wow, I've stooped to cheesy baseball references for this pep talk. Rock bottom, nice to meet you, I'm Carino.

In full-blown tunnel vision mode, Carino raced out of the bathroom, focused squarely on getting to the meeting. With as much poise as someone wearing a tee shirt to a million dollar negotiation can have, she strode into the conference room. To her immense relief, someone—probably Abby—had already set everything up. She had seemed a little distant recently, so Carino made a mental note to profusely thank her later, complete with coffee, chocolate, and possibly jewelry.

She refused to look directly at Raj, but sensed his gaze burning a hole through her. He'd kept the seat to his right empty, and Carino quickly sat down, reaching for one of the presentation binders stacked on the table.

Raj's voice was hushed. "Much better."

Carino scooted slightly away from him, since his incessant leg bouncing was rocking her whole chair. His hands shook lightly as he took a few gulps from his water bottle. She found his unexpected twitchiness odd—and slightly disturbing; Raj never got nervous. She figured he must've been just as affected by the magnitude of this deal as she was—but for different reasons, obviously. There was a lot riding on their client's acceptance of the offer. So much more than the firm—or Raj—realized.

The intercom buzzed and Abby's voice filled the room. "Raj, your 8:15 is headed your way."

Raj nodded at Carino, and she took a deep, calming breath. This was *the* landmark day in her career, provided Emerson accepted the deal and signed the paperwork. Standing with her colleagues, she once again reminded herself that Sebastian Emerson was just a man. A rich, powerful, and ruthless man, whose mere finger snap would incite a frenzy of activity around him—but a man, nonetheless.

Carino figured Emerson could smell fear, so she sucked in her gut, threw her shoulders back, and stood up tall. Of course, her resolve began to melt the moment Emerson entered—no, dominated—the room. Carino's previous interactions with him had never been face-to-face, and were extremely brief and totally impersonal; this was completely different. She was worried that her brittle confidence would begin to crack under the pressure, exposing her true purpose.

She took a moment to really look at him, the man who had unknowingly controlled her life for the past several years. Emerson was imported luxury on a stick. His charcoal gray suit that screamed Savile Row and the Patek Philippe gleaming on his wrist were stark reminders that he was in a completely different league. Wealth radiated from his every pore, and a furtive glance around the room told her everyone else noticed as well.

She wouldn't call Emerson good-looking, but he wasn't exactly sleazy either. His salt-and-pepper hair was thinning but wasn't combed-over, and he kept a well-groomed mustache. He was fairly tall and very trim, and carried himself with an air of dignity. His most arresting feature, by far, was undiluted confidence. But underneath the façade, Carino clearly sensed his lethal edge.

"Ladies. Gentlemen." Emerson spoke calmly, looking around the room and making eye contact with each person for a few seconds. Carino resisted the urge to look down at her hands as their eyes met. "I appreciate your hard work and I'm looking forward to hearing some good news."

As captivated as she was by Emerson's presence, Carino nearly missed the person standing behind him. Of course, with her luck today, she didn't know why she was surprised to see the man from her hallway crash. Her mouth ran dry and she heard a strangled noise. To be honest, she couldn't tell if it came from her or Raj, because immediately he cleared his throat a little too long and a little too loud.

"Please, Mr. Emerson, have a seat." Raj's composure was once again intact as he motioned toward the empty chair at the opposite end of the conference room table, directly in front of a large presentation binder. "We also have an extra chair for your colleague."

"Thank you, Raj. Actually, Ramon prefers to stand."

Well, shit. Of course the sexiest man alive would have to be part of Emerson's entourage.

As everyone took their seats again, Carino stole a glance at Ramon and caught him looking directly at her. His lips curved into a sexy smirk and he winked; her cheeks were instantly on fire.

Thankfully, she didn't have much time to focus on her blossoming embarrassment as Raj promptly began the presentation, which meant her speaking points were next and she didn't dare screw this up.

Carino and Raj fell into their practiced rhythm and the audience faded into the background—everyone except Emerson—as they deftly communicated all aspects of the transaction and the effect the acquisition would have on his financial position. They reviewed each clause of the lengthy purchase and sale agreement, from payment terms to the proposed revisions to the legal description of the property.

"In conclusion, the seller has agreed to reduce his asking price to an amount that is in line with your offer, so the resulting ROI—if you decide to subdivide the property—is much better than we had initially projected." Carino directed him to the final page in the binder.

"Yes, I can see that." Emerson flipped through the agreement as he ran his finger down the page of data, clearly comparing the information presented in each document.

Sign it, Emerson. Just pick up your Mont Blanc *and sign the damn thing. You already know you're going to anyway so stop grandstanding and be done with it already.*

Carino realized she was holding her breath and quietly let it out, tamping down her anxiety as best she could and refocusing on the present. If Emerson signed the papers, things were going to kick into overdrive and she needed all her faculties intact so she could recall every detail later for her notes file.

"Do you have any questions before making your final decision?" Raj asked.

Emerson pressed his lips together and closed the binder, while the room's occupants remained poised on the edge of their seats, anticipating his next move. He fiddled with his pen, twirling it around his fingers, before he finally turned to the last page of the agreement.

•••

Hours later, when Carino finally made it back to her office, she glanced at her phone and realized it was already afternoon. The presentation was over, and as hoped, Emerson had accepted the offer. Of course, she'd known he would; the land in Costa Rica was too choice to pass up. His transaction with Franklin Everly involved purchasing several huge tracts of land and subdividing the massive acreage so he could sell it off in smaller chunks for future development. But she figured Emerson needed to expand his cocaine processing operation to meet rising demands, so Carino knew if he did sell the parcels, it would most likely be to other members of the cartel or to businesses he silently owned.

She'd been engrossed in Emerson's business practices long before she'd accepted the assignment at Franklin Everly; therefore, she knew precisely how he operated. He was dirty and violent and relentless and needed to be stopped, which was actually why she'd taken the job in the first place. The fact that it was classified as a "Sensitive Circumstances" assignment had deterred her at first, but once she'd fully realized the kind of person he was, she wanted to be part of the operation that took him down. And with each passing year that she was isolated in Denver, segregated from her family and cut off from having personal relationships that threatened her phony cover story, the drive to nail him to the wall intensified.

She flopped into her chair and released a tremendous sigh, feeling boneless now that her adrenaline had been depleted. Emerson didn't typically come into the office, which had definitely added to the overall intensity of the morning. Even Raj seemed to have been affected, since he'd definitely seemed off his game, although he seemed to relax a bit after Emerson and Ramon left.

She wished she hadn't been tied up with Raj and the team after the meeting concluded because she hadn't even been able to say anything more to Ramon. But, since he was there with Emerson, it was probably better that she stayed away from him anyway.

Raj was off assigning some follow-up tasks to the secretaries, so she realized if she wanted to sneak in a lunch break, this was definitely her chance. Feeling like she could use some non-recycled air, Carino grabbed her windbreaker and opted for a quick walk down Champa to 16th Street. She planned to catch one of the free shuttle buses that ran every few minutes and head several blocks over to Market Street for a slice of pizza.

The eclectic mix of people waiting for the bus never ceased to amaze her. The Armani-clad stockbrokers were standing shoulder-to-shoulder with homeless people who were riding the buses to either get warm or cool down, depending on the season, and neither seemed to mind each other's presence. It was also one of the reasons she loved working in Lower Downtown Denver, aka LoDo.

The bus ground to a halt in front of the group of lunchtime travelers, its air suspension hissing like a scalded cat. The doors opened and the synthesized female voice wafted out, announcing the intersection's name. People filtered on and off the bus with practiced ease, and she quickly carved out a small space to stand toward the back.

Caught up in her self-satisfied splendor, several moments passed before Carino saw Ramon sitting against the opposite side of the bus. He was reading the newspaper, so she was pretty sure he hadn't seen her yet; she took the time to really look him over. His skin reminded her of creamy caramel, and she noticed that his thick, dark hair had a slight curl to it. She zeroed in on his left hand, which was very clearly lacking a wedding ring. Carino didn't think he was much older than her. If she had to guess, she'd say early thirties. She wondered how he'd gotten himself wrapped up with Emerson—and what exactly his work for Emerson entailed.

"Gorgeous, eh?" An elderly, mostly toothless woman in a dingy, flowered smock effectively interrupted her ogling session. Carino glanced down at her, noticing that she looked like she was chewing something; Carino was quite certain she wasn't.

Yucky.

Realizing she'd been publicly salivating over Ramon, Carino cleared her throat, smiled wanly at the woman, and quickly turned her entire body in the opposite direction.

"*Mi Cariño?*" crooned a smooth voice behind her.

Carino swung around and saw that Ramon had stood up and was leaning against one of the metal poles in the middle of the bus. She immediately recognized that he had put a Spanish twist to her name, which she knew translated as "My Love" or "My Everything." And she also knew that he knew exactly what he was saying.

Blushing, as usual, she adopted her best *I didn't see you there* expression and smiled.

"Hi, Mr. Ramon, I didn't see you there." Her words sounded phony, even to her own ears.

"I'm glad we've run into each other, since I didn't get the chance to tell you that I liked your presentation. You're very knowledgeable about Emerson's business needs," he purred.

Wait, am I the one purring?

"Thank you! And I'm sorry about running into you, by the way. In the hall. Before the meeting. By the bathrooms." Carino hated that she was rambling. And really? Had he run into multiple people that morning?

"No apology necessary." His voice reverberated deep in his chest. "It was the most fun I've had since arriving in Denver."

And then he just smiled and stopped talking, raking his eyes over Carino's form. The driver must have turned up the heat because it suddenly became hot and she couldn't wait until the next stop so she could exit the bus.

"Next stop, Market Street Station." The bus abruptly slowed down and Carino lost her balance. She fell against Ramon as he reached out to steady her. She looked down and the lady chewing her cud was smiling up at them, her eyes twinkling.

I have got to get out of here!

"Well, thanks again, Mr. Ramon."

She pushed off of his rock-hard chest and hurried onto the sidewalk, praying she wouldn't trip and make an even bigger fool of herself. Stealing a glance over her shoulder as the doors closed, she found he was still watching her, that sexy smile never once leaving his face.

Chapter 2

Ramon Terrones didn't get worked up over a woman; he could have his pick of any that he wanted. But, as the bus drove away, he couldn't seem to tear his eyes off of Carino. All he could think about was how thankful he now was that Emerson had contacted him about helping out with the situation that was unfolding in Denver—even if it did mean working with Raj again. The last time they'd seen each other was several years back when a heated argument had led to Ramon pulling his gun and pointing it in Raj's face. Things hadn't exactly been rosy between them before that, and certainly hadn't been any better since.

Ramon's instincts about the situation Emerson described warned him to refuse his request for help. He knew if the Feds were sniffing around Emerson's business dealings, eventually they might find out about his own role in some of Emerson's more difficult transactions—and murder carried a lengthy prison sentence. But he was a "fixer" and was Emerson's go-to guy whenever he needed a problem to go away. If there truly was a mole inside Franklin Everly, the issue needed to be resolved quickly, especially considering the measures Emerson had taken to secure the Costa Rica property, which alone were enough for him to be arrested.

Nevertheless, Ramon went ahead and dug out one of his passports and bought a plane ticket to America, breezing through customs without a hitch. His flight out of the Caymans had been on time with very little turbulence, a beautiful woman had occupied the seat next to him, and a driver was waiting when he arrived at DIA. His hotel was appropriately luxurious, which was to be expected with a name like Brown Palace. He'd woken up the following morning on time after a restful night's sleep, and had a delectable breakfast of perfectly poached eggs and expertly cooked bacon, complimented with freshly-squeezed orange juice and dark-roasted coffee. His shower was hot and the staff had pressed his suit to perfection. The rental car he'd ordered was promptly delivered, with plenty of time to spare before the meeting at Franklin Everly. Everything was perfect. Too perfect.

When Emerson had suggested he attend the meeting, Ramon had agreed, thinking it would help him get a bead on who'd been exposed to the details of Emerson's business dealings before initiating the server lockdown. He intended to start digging deeper into the various members of Raj's team, since the phone calls to the Feds had been conspicuously close to Emerson's last few transactions. Most of the calls on the phone records Emerson had provided to him for review had come from an untraceable burner phone, but one had actually originated from inside Franklin Everly.

Even though the work Emerson transacted at the firm was legitimate, everything else about his empire was illegal. He ran one of the largest networks of cocaine producers, suppliers, and dealers in South and Central America, not to mention his money laundering operation, and had kept the authorities off his back because they were either in his pocket or too scared of him. Ramon had to determine if someone working on Emerson's account was really fool enough to attempt exposing him, as they were putting their life on the line to do so.

He'd arrived at Franklin Everly about fifteen minutes early, mostly because he'd been too jittery to stay at the hotel, and not just from the excitement of getting to see Raj squirm. Something was just different about this trip. He couldn't put his finger on it yet, but could feel it in his bones.

And then it had hit him.

Literally.

She had a face like an angel and a body made for sin. She was incredible. But before he could ask her name, she'd disappeared.

For a fleeting moment, Ramon had even considered following her. He'd envisioned locking the bathroom door and taking her against the wall. Considering how she'd detonated his desire in less than ten seconds, which had never happened to him before, he figured he would've had no problem being done in time for the meeting.

Even as he'd thought it, he'd known he was being utterly ridiculous. What kind of woman would want a quick screw in the bathroom by a perfect stranger first thing in the morning after she got to work? And anyway, there was never a shortage of women for him to choose from—even though he'd suddenly wanted no one else but *her*, and he didn't even know who she was. Yet.

Ramon had paced the lobby at Franklin Everly while wrestling his urges into submission. He had actually been thankful for Emerson's arrival, flanked by two large men in black suits, since he'd needed a distraction from the beautiful stranger he'd just encountered.

After exchanging brief pleasantries, Emerson had sent his bodyguards away and questioned Ramon about his analysis of the phone records. The clenching of his jaw had been the only visible sign of anger at hearing Ramon's confirmation that there was most likely a traitor in their midst. But, to a practiced observer like Ramon, Emerson's calm appearance became infused with a deadly coldness and his blue eyes had frozen over.

Falling into step beside him, the two men had entered Franklin Everly's lobby at precisely 8:13a.m. The receptionist's demeanor had immediately changed, once she'd laid eyes on Emerson. "Good morning, sir."

"Raj is expecting me. And I know the way." Emerson had turned and strode down the hallway with Ramon in tow.

Ramon had remained in the background as Emerson greeted everyone. As suspected, Raj was not at all happy to see him, though he did a fairly decent job of pulling himself back together. Ramon knew his presence was disconcerting; he never showed up unless it was to "solve" a problem. Based on Raj's reaction, he was fairly certain Emerson hadn't mentioned he was coming to Denver. Maybe Raj would now become worried that Emerson suspected him as the mole, a notion that didn't bother Ramon one little bit.

And then he'd seen *her*. He had to stifle a gasp as he'd been struck by her beauty once more. He couldn't remember ever being so captivated by a woman at first sight. And his luck! He couldn't believe she was working on Emerson's account. Now he had a legitimate excuse for getting to know her better.

He'd learned her name was Carino Montgomery, and not only was she beautiful, but she was smart too. Her sultry voice had mesmerized him, and he was impressed at her level of composure while presenting facts and figures to Emerson. It wasn't hard to find out that Carino's life had dramatically changed a few years back, since Ramon's Google search was fraught with online obituaries featuring her name in the "survived by" section. He'd even found a newspaper article with a picture of her receiving a folded flag from a man in a Class A uniform. From what he could tell, her parents had died in a car crash with a drunk driver, and very shortly thereafter her brother had been KIA in Afghanistan. Carino was only twenty-one when she lost all three of her family members, and only a few months after she'd moved to Aurora, Colorado. Yet, even after everything that happened, she'd stuck around and hadn't moved back home to Wyoming. Ramon figured it was because she didn't have anything to go home to, really. It would seem that she'd thrown herself into her work, which helped explain her quick ascent at Franklin Everly.

All in all, Ramon hadn't really been able to find much information about Carino, with the exception of college transcripts, a couple of credit cards that she paid on time, and a rental agreement she kept renewing. She didn't even have a speeding ticket. He wasn't troubled by her lack of history, considering she was still just a kid.

Even though she was now twenty-five and only six years younger than him, his life experiences had weathered him well beyond his age.

Ramon was more surprised Carino wasn't married, considering what a catch she was. Maybe it was due to all the long days she put in at Franklin Everly. Or maybe it was the result of lingering trauma over losing loved ones. Either way, he knew he shouldn't be this happy that she might be unattached, but couldn't seem to help himself. Her being single would definitely uncomplicate things if she wanted to stay the night with him.

Oh, she'll end up in my bed. There's just no way around it.

Thoughts of Carino had continued to invade Ramon's mind until he could think of nothing more than her flushed cheeks and pouty lips, and how her sexy, emerald-green eyes contrasted interestingly with her dark brown curls. He wondered how good she would feel underneath him when he explored all of her fine points in much closer detail.

It was those thoughts that had led him to board the shuttle bus and head back to Franklin Everly. He'd needed a surefire deterrent to keep his mind from wandering into places that he knew were better left alone—well, at least for now—and could think of no easier way to douse the flame of his growing desire than to pay Raj a little visit.

Ramon wanted to remind him of who was in charge, should Raj decide to start any shit while Ramon was in town, and planned to do so by assigning him a ridiculous task. Ramon wanted to see if Raj would actually comply with his orders, because if so, that would mean Raj still recognized him as a serious threat.

But, instead of getting his desires under control, he'd actually noticed Carino at his intended departure point, waiting to get on his very shuttle. His heart had leapt in his chest at the mere sight of her. She hadn't noticed him at first, but once she did, her entire body had lit up. Or maybe that had just been his wishful thinking.

There was something about her that Ramon found absolutely irresistible. Maybe it was because he hadn't quickly gotten a read on her, which was something he usually excelled at; it was his job to decipher what people were hiding. But either she wasn't hiding anything, or she was really good at keeping it hidden.

As he rode the elevator up to Franklin Everly, he replayed every moment of their brief shuttle encounter in his mind. She'd seemed anxious to get off the bus and away from him, which was a much-needed reminder that he'd have to be extremely careful with her. She obviously spooked easily, which was understandable, given her history. And since he was only in town for a few days, he didn't want to waste any opportunity to get with her.

Abigail recognized Ramon the moment he entered the lobby, but was clearly puzzled about why he'd returned without Emerson.

"Good afternoon, sir. Back again?"

"Mr. Emerson thinks he left some paperwork on Raj's desk when he was here earlier today, and asked me to pick it up." The lie rolled off of his tongue.

Raj is so *not going to be happy to see me. This is going to be fun.*

"Let me see if he's available." She skillfully punched buttons on the switchboard next to her computer. "Hi, Raj, Mr.—ah, sir, what's your name?" She stopped mid-sentence and looked up at him.

"Ramon." He made sure Raj heard his reply on the other end of the line, and relished the fact that he'd probably just shit his little boy pants.

"Mr. Ramon is here to pick up some paperwork Mr. Emerson accidentally left behind." She listened to Raj's reply and ended the call. "Raj will be out momentarily. Would you like something to drink while you wait?"

"A bottle of water please." He knew full well Raj would keep him waiting for a while. It was his way of wielding a small amount of imaginary power, however childish it may be.

Ramon sat down in one of the plush leather lobby chairs and took out his phone, surfing the Web to pass the time. He wasn't a patient man, but would never let Raj have the pleasure of seeing him sweat, no matter how long he had to wait.

Raj, the perpetual pain in Ramon's ass. Emerson had first discovered him about eight years prior while in Manila for a meeting with a prospective buyer. By that time, Ramon had already proven to be invaluable, so Emerson had brought him along as his personal bodyguard. Emerson's business had begun growing faster than he could handle, especially with Ramon doing his dirty work behind the scenes, so he'd decided to invest in a legitimate front-man: Raj Gulati.

Raj had been struggling with his meager salary as an immigration attorney for the U.S. Embassy, which was why he'd started working both sides of the law. He'd been running a fairly lucrative underground business of doctoring papers, creating fake identities—the list went on—but had been caught red-handed in a sting operation. Emerson heard about the situation from one of his informants inside the MPD and had negotiated the price necessary to make the whole situation go away before shelling out the hefty sum without so much as a second thought. To Emerson, the cost had been worth it, since he'd ultimately bought Raj's permanent loyalty.

Raj was exactly what Emerson had been waiting for: a smart, unattached, dissatisfied lawyer with a proclivity for illegal activity; they were the perfect match. Ramon remembered Raj's confusion when he'd first seen them waiting patiently as he emerged from the police station. He didn't understand the lengths to which Emerson had gone to free him, nor did he understand why, until Emerson explained it all over dinner. If Raj came back to the U.S. as Emerson's employee, he could choose where to live and would never want for anything. Raj agreed without hesitation, and the trio was on Emerson's private jet heading back to his main estate in South Carolina within a couple of days.

Raj was beyond grateful, and Ramon had actually been able to relate to how he felt; Emerson had saved him too. But many times over the years, Ramon had wondered if Emerson had truly *saved* them from anything.

Raj had stayed with Emerson for a few weeks, getting a feel for the organization and Emerson's needs, and determining where he wanted to set down roots; essentially, Raj had the entire country at his disposal. He eventually selected Denver as his home base, due to the central location and high demand for minority lawyers with immigration experience.

Emerson waited until Raj had passed the Denver Bar and became an established attorney at Franklin Everly before they set it up so Raj could "land" him as a client. The entire process took well over a year, but they both knew the return was well worth the investment. Since then, Raj had helped Emerson launder millions of dollars through multiple legitimate real estate investment companies, and had made a fortune for himself in the process.

The minutiae of how Raj managed to keep everything legal was beyond Ramon's scope, but doing so had proved quite lucrative for both Raj and Emerson over the years. Reluctantly, Ramon admitted that Raj's efforts had also worked out well for him too, since he wasn't rotting away in some hellish prison cell right now.

At first, he and Raj got along decently well. But that all changed several months later, the night Raj showed up unannounced at his girlfriend's house and found Ramon warming her bed. In Ramon's defense, she'd come onto him and he didn't even know she was with Raj. He wasn't entirely sure that knowledge would have mattered, since he wasn't exactly scrupulous back then, but still—he hadn't known. Of course, Raj didn't care about anything Ramon had to say; the irreparable damage to his miniscule male ego had been done.

Over the last several years, Raj continued to be a thorn in Ramon's side. He knew it was because, after witnessing exactly what he did for Emerson, Raj had grown to be afraid of him. Frankly, Ramon had never possessed any real intention of harming Raj—physically, anyway—as long as Raj didn't screw with him. But that had all changed after the last time they'd worked together, which was when he'd gone off the deep end thinking Ramon was plotting to jeopardize his position with Emerson; Ramon was doing no such thing. But Raj kept pushing the matter, trying to get him to discuss the details of the private discussions Ramon had been having with Emerson—which had nothing to do with Raj at all—until Ramon finally drew his weapon and promised to end his life if he didn't back off.

Ramon was jolted from his reverie by Raj's sudden appearance in the hallway, his miniature hands resting on his hips. "Come with me."

Ramon smiled pleasantly and stood, noticing from the corner of his eye that Abigail was much more observant than she let on. She seemed to track every aspect of their brief exchange, and easily picked up on the underlying current of mutual unfriendliness. More than likely, she'd never heard that level of hostility in Raj's voice before, which wasn't surprising; Ramon brought out a side of him that he rarely displayed in public.

Slowing his pace to match Raj's tiny, childlike strides, Ramon followed him into his office. Raj roughly closed the door, making no attempt to hide his disdain as he rounded his desk and sat in his enormous leather chair.

"Yes, thank you, I'd love to sit down." Ramon was smug as he pulled out one of the guest chairs facing Raj's desk. "How's my favorite fun-sized attorney? Business must be good, since you kept me waiting for over twenty minutes."

"What the fu—" Raj caught himself and cleared his throat before continuing. "What do you want, Ramon? That *is* still the name you're using these days, isn't it?"

Ramon quickly leaned forward in his chair and Raj flinched, ever so slightly. "Listen carefully, Raj, because I'll only remind you of this once. It's because of your extreme value to Emerson that you haven't already found your way into a small, shallow grave. And you know damn well why I'm here. I'm sniffing out the mole." He sniffed in Raj's direction, earning him a hateful glare.

"I've examined everything. Twice. There are no holes. No issues. No loose ends. Emerson doesn't have anything to be worried about, even if someone is creating a stir. So you can just go home and crawl back into the hole you slithered out of. There's no need for you to be here." Raj was clearly confident. "And, surely, no one on my team would be foolish enough to participate in whatever lunacy you've dreamed up."

"It's not up to you to decide whether or not Emerson should be worried. If he said one of his men heard a rumor about an informant and potential investigation, then clearly he still has reason to feel uncomfortable. And until he's comfortable, I'll be here *adjusting* things. Oh, and a piece of advice: stay out of my way. I won't warn you again…and I *always* keep my promises."

Raj's Adam's apple bobbed as he swallowed deeply, revealing a crack in his outward demonstration of confidence.

"I assume you came here simply for the purpose of intimidating me. So, are you finished now? Because I have work to do."

"No, that's not the reason why I came. Well, not the only one anyway." Ramon chuckled, causing Raj to narrow his beady eyes. "I want full personnel files for each person on your team."

Slapping his hands on his desk, Raj shook his head vigorously. "No. Absolutely not. You know that I can't just give those to you."

"What I know, Raj, is that it wasn't a question. You have until Tuesday morning to get me the personnel files for each person on your team." Ramon hated repeating himself.

"Those files are confidential and I don't have any way to get to them!"

"I've told you what I want and when I want it. The rest is your problem. I'll be around, and you've got my number. I'll be expecting a call when the files are ready." Ramon abruptly stood, signaling the conversation was over.

"I don't have your number."

"Yes, you do."

"Oh, really? And when do you presume to have given it to me?" Raj's tone was dripping with poorly concealed anger.

"I wrote it in the address book you keep in the top drawer of your nightstand." Ramon winked at Raj, enjoying the look of horror plastered on his face, before striding out of his office. He was pleased at his foresight to stop by Raj's house, after picking up his car from the valet earlier that morning.

As Ramon approached Abigail's desk, he pulled a small envelope from his inside coat pocket and handed it to her. "Would you mind giving this to Carino, if it's not too much trouble?" Ramon had decided the best way to get to know more about her would be over dinner and drinks.

Abigail's face lit up as she took the letter. "Of course. I'll make sure she gets it."

"Thank you." He flashed his best smile. On cue, she blushed and looked down at her hands.

"Ha...have a nice day, Mr. Ramon."

Ramon had invited Carino out that evening, but was fairly certain she wouldn't agree to meet him so soon. But he wanted to know how badly she wanted to see him, which he would gauge by how long she postponed his invitation. Because she would eventually accept; she was too curious not to.

Chapter 3

"Monday, we hit the ground at a run, so be ready." Raj stood in Carino's doorway mere seconds after she returned from lunch. Without waiting for a reply, he walked away, indicating he was still not back to his usual self.

Raj was tough and driven, which had helped him become so successful so quickly at Franklin Everly. Well, that and the fact that he'd single-handedly landed the firm's largest client: Sebastian Emerson.

Even though being on Raj's team meant early mornings and late nights, Carino didn't mind; working the extra hours gave her something to do. Shortly after moving to Denver over three years ago, she'd almost packed up and left out of sheer loneliness. The only friend she had really made since moving was Abby, who hadn't started working at Franklin Everly until after Carino had already been employed there for a while. So, mostly she'd become a homebody, dare say a recluse, and over time had grown quite accustomed to being alone.

Carino chuckled to herself, remembering how awkward it had been the first time Abby had asked her to hang out after work. She had been nervous answering questions about her past, as it was the first time she'd tested out her backstory on an actual person. Thankfully, a few shots of liquid courage and Abby's probing personality were all it took to loosen her up.

"So, your older brother is named James, but you got stuck with the name Carino?" Abby had guffawed. "No offense, by the way."

"Trust me, I'm used to it. Apparently the Montgomerys tapped into their creative side, once I came along." Carino had chuckled along with her, partially due to the way her family had helped her decide her cover name. "Mom and Dad honeymooned in Milan,

Italy, and I was born almost exactly nine months later. Apparently, Carino is a common name for little Italian girls, and they thought it would be a crafty way to have a part of them with me at all times. Clever, huh?"

She'd gone on to explain how James had enlisted in the army right before graduation, and shortly after glimpsing the outside world, had started hounding her to get out of Casper before she got sucked in and did something crazy like buy a pickup truck. Or cowboy boots.

"I didn't need much convincing really, since Wyoming was definitely not where I called home." She punctuated her words with a full-body shudder. "I mean, finding out you're moving from the only home you've ever known when you're a freshman in high school? It was devastating. And James was a sophomore, so he felt the same way. Our household was the epitome of teenage angst, let me assure you."

"No kidding! I would've absolutely died!" Abby had scrunched her face in abject horror.

"Yeah, when Dad had rounded us up for a family meeting, James and I both figured he'd finally heard about us sneaking out and getting wasted at the Homecoming after-party. If only we'd been so lucky. Instead, he told us that after fifteen years, he'd gotten laid off from the Red Wing factory, and we were moving to Wyoming so he could help at my uncle's construction company."

"I'm pretty sure your life was a bad afterschool movie I saw on LMN a while back."

"I know, right? Don't get me wrong though, it's not like Red Wing, Minnesota was the mecca of excitement. I mean, the town was named after a boot. Or was it the other way around?"

"Does it even matter?"

"So true! Well, we moved and survived—just barely though. After James graduated and left for Basic, I counted down the days until I was finished with senior year. If I thought Casper had been mind-numbing when we first moved there, it was even worse after he left."

"I must say, that's a lot different than my senior year. I was too busy sampling every new drug on the market to notice how bored I was." Abby's eyes had taken on a distant look as she'd recalled her past.

"You know, going through senior year in a constant fog might have actually helped me!"

"Nah, then your parents would've felt responsible for your addiction because they forced you to move to the dullest place on earth, and you'd still be in therapy to this day."

"You're probably right," Carino had agreed. "As it was, Mom knew I wasn't happy there, and she definitely didn't want me making a career out of my waitress job at the Corner Diner." Abby had signified her agreement with a dramatic eye-roll mixed with the vigorous nodding of her head. "I'd also made it crystal clear there was no way I was going to Casper Community College, so instead Mom just kept hounding me about taking some online college classes. But I'm really glad she did because I graduated with my Bachelor's right before my twenty-first birthday."

"That's really great, Carino!" Abby had appeared genuinely happy for her. "I wish my parents had encouraged me to do something more with my life, but I probably wouldn't have listened to them anyway. So, that's my excuse for ending up as a twenty-four-year-old receptionist."

"You're not just a receptionist, Abby; you're the Administrator of First Impressions."

"Haha, yeah that's what it says on my business cards, all right. But you and I both know I'll never climb the ladder like you have."

"Abby, you could totally go back to school. Even an Associate's would help."

"You're right, but all of that takes money, which is something I'm fresh out of. Sometimes there's still a lot of month left when the cash runs out, if you know what I mean. What I really need is a big payday and then I wouldn't have to worry about anything!" Abby had tried to joke, but Carino had sensed the strain behind her words.

"Maybe you'll get lucky and hit the Powerball!"

"Yeah, something like that."

"Well, anyway … " Carino had wanted to break the sudden tension. "When James came back from his first tour in Afghanistan, he got stationed at Fort Carson in Colorado Springs, and asked me to move out here."

"And the rest is history."

Abby managed to thaw Carino out a bit, and it didn't take long before they began spending a lot more time together. She was the only person from the office that Carino ever hung out with. For that matter, she was pretty much the only person Carino hung out with, period, even though they couldn't be more opposite. Abby liked quaint and cozy shabby-chic, and Carino liked plain, clean, and simple. Abby lived in a cute, cottage-style house in Golden and Carino lived in a master-planned community with an HOA. Where Abby was creative, Carino was scholastic. Abby was a sleek, raven-haired beauty with tanned skin and Carino was a freckled, ultra-white, curly-headed mess. Abby laughed at Carino's ridiculous jokes and Carino put up with Abby's bossiness—or bitchiness—however one wanted to phrase it. But they were both single, in their late twenties, and had definitely bonded with each other. Generally speaking, they were a match made in Gen Y heaven.

About a year ago, shortly after Abby's father had unexpectedly passed away, she'd confided in Carino that she was overwhelmed with debt from helping to pay for her sick mother's medical bills and was even considering getting a second job. To her knowledge, Abby hadn't actually done that and seemed to still be hanging in there, but Carino constantly worried about her.

Carino had grown to really care about Abby, but didn't know how to help her, besides being a shoulder to lean on. Lately, she'd noticed Abby was having a few more bad days than usual though. She had no doubt Abby's financial stress was taking a toll, and while she generally managed to hide it under a mask of sharp wit and general evasiveness, Carino still noticed.

"Hey girl!" Abby strode into Carino's office with a flourish, snapping her back to the present. "You look extremely too deep in thought for a Friday afternoon. Is everything okay?"

Carino crooked her mouth into a wistful smile. "I was actually just thinking about the first time we went out for drinks, and how much has happened since then."

"You've got that right! But are you sure that you don't have a concussion from running into that hottie's rock-hard abs?" Abby covered her mouth.

"Isn't it funny how the only one who thinks you're funny is you?"

"Ha! You love me and you know it!" She dropped a stack of papers on Carino's desk, spun on her kitten heel, and headed back toward her command center. "I'll expect some girl time over drinks very soon!"

Carino glanced toward her in-basket, noticing an envelope on top of the paperwork Abby had just deposited. It had a single handwritten word: Carino. The handwriting was neat and small, but she didn't recognize it, which instantly piqued her interest. Slicing the top edge, she extracted the single sheet of paper and began to read the note.

Mi Cariño, I enjoyed our encounters today. Please afford me the opportunity of another. Have dinner with me tonight? With anticipation, Ramon / 914-555-1999.

Carino dropped the letter like her hand had been scalded, as myriad questions ran through her mind. What the hell did his invitation mean? Why did he want to meet with her and not Raj or another member of the team? Did Emerson put him up to this? Did they suspect her as working undercover? What was she going to wear?

Checking the time, she saw that dinnertime was quickly approaching; she'd have to make a decision, and fast.

Wait, don't I seem like a woman who'd already have Friday night plans?

Of course she didn't have any, but he couldn't have known that. Who was he to put her on the spot? It was situations like these when she desperately wished for motherly advice, because this had the potential to become highly problematic, for a number of reasons.

Picking up her phone to call Ramon and decline proved to be an impossible task, mostly because she found herself wanting terribly to accept his invite. In the end, she sent him a text that she couldn't go that evening, but was free on Saturday; his favorable response appeared on her phone within moments.

Sleep evaded Carino most of Friday night, and while she tried to chalk it up to overdosing on caffeine, she knew it was because she was anxious about seeing Ramon the next day. She was unreasonably attracted to him, so she'd desperately needed the extra time to get her wits about her, before spending hours in his company.

It had been an inordinate amount of time since Carino had been out with a member of the opposite sex, and Ramon had trouble written all over him in bold, permanent marker. Since he was here with Emerson, she should be treating him as off-limits, but he surely possessed information that would prove valuable to her investigation. Plus, his visit should be fairly quick and before she knew it, he'd be headed back to wherever it was he came from. No harm, no foul, right?

Famous last words.

Ramon's text had informed her he'd pick her up at 7:00 on Saturday evening. Carino was fairly uncomfortable about Ramon knowing where she lived, but sent him the address anyway, against her better judgment. And only after convincing herself that the gun she kept in her purse, her self-defense classes, and somewhat functional security system would do the trick, if Ramon turned out to be a serial killer. Or a rapist. Or a burglar.

On second thought, maybe I shouldn't have given him my address.

Finally, after lying in bed for hours contemplating the various ways Ramon could break in, Carino dozed off. Mercifully, she didn't wake up on Saturday morning until after nine a.m., so the luggage that normally resided under her eyes was reduced to small carry-on bags. And she knew some strategically placed concealer and smoky eye makeup would take care of those.

It had been an extremely long time since she'd been this excited to see someone. Normally, her walls were firmly intact, so her adult dating history was virtually non-existent. She liked it that way; bad things could happen if people got too close. Especially at this point in her life.

But something about Ramon was different. Yes, he was absolutely gorgeous, but it wasn't like he was the first good looking man Carino had ever been around. It was much more than that, something that had mesmerized her within seconds of coming in contact with him. He was the quintessential bad boy, complete with a ruthlessness that appeared to simmer dangerously close to the surface. Couple that with his devil-may-care swagger and panty-dropping smile, and it was a small wonder she hadn't fainted from the sheer emotional overload.

There was absolutely no denying that he was a vortex and she was being sucked in at warp speed. Even though she desperately needed to put the brakes on her out-of-control fascination with him, she had to admit she felt a long overdue and much needed thrill from having such a sexy, powerful man chasing after her.

Okay, he wasn't really *chasing*, since he'd only asked her to have dinner. And, more than likely, she was reading way more into the invitation than she should; they had literally met less than forty-eight hours ago. Nevertheless, Carino was going to put forth some major effort into transforming herself from the spastic klutz Ramon had met yesterday to a very professional—and desirable—woman.

• • •

Fifteen minutes and counting.

"If only Mom could see me now." Carino felt a wave of melancholy, as she prepared to mentally go through her pre-date checklist one last time.

New outfit, check. Mani/pedi, done. Hair salon, finito. Legs shaved, yep—but not above the knee.

She needed some guarantee that she'd end their night at an appropriate time; there was no doubt in her mind that she would be tempted to invite him in.

Carino had found the perfect dress at Nieman Marcus, the emerald green being the exact same shade as her eyes. It also looked amazing against her fair skin. The forecast had predicted a chilly evening, so she'd opted for a sheer black shawl to drape over her shoulders, since the spaghetti straps didn't provide much in the way of coverage. The three-inch heel on her black, peep-toe slingbacks caused her long legs to look even longer, but the calf-length of her dress still left plenty to the imagination. She loved how the slightest of movements would cause the soft, draping fabric to twirl and dance around her slender body, and the thin belt really accentuated her small waistline.

The Aveda Salon had worked miracles on her mop of hair, and now it was piled high on her head, with several tendrils curling delicately around her neck. Both her fingernails and toenails shone with polish, French manicures all around. She'd also splurged a little, having one of their techs do a mini-makeover. Her skin looked flawless, even in her overly critical opinion, and her eyes were perfectly shadowed. She had to admit, she looked fantastic.

"I hope Ramon likes tall women." She examined her backside to ensure she didn't have VPL.

Thank you, Spanx!

At precisely 7:00 Carino's doorbell rang, causing a Pavlovian response; her stomach lurched into her throat. Swallowing profusely, she stole one last glimpse at herself in the full-length mirror. She grabbed her black leather clutch from the side table, took a deep breath, and opened the door.

She was momentarily struck speechless at how amazing Ramon looked—even more gorgeous than she'd remembered from yesterday. And he was definitely over six feet tall, as she still had to look up at him just a little bit.

Sweet mother, he is so freaking good looking.

He was dressed in dark-washed, designer jeans and a white sweater that looked soft enough to curl up in and take a nap. His jet-black hair made her fingers itch with the need to run them through it, and his face carried a hint of stubble that she had to physically restrain herself from touching. He had just the right amount of cologne on, and it created a powerful blend of sweet and spicy—and red-blooded male.

"*Mi Cariño.*" His face broke into a wide smile. "It's such a pleasure to see you again."

Uh oh, he has dimples too.

She matched his grin. "Ditto."

Ditto?! What is this, a scene from Ghost?

Carino's gaze focused over his shoulder and took in the shiny black Mercedes S-Class parked in the driveway. Her poor little Mazda was cowering in middle-class shame. But really, she shouldn't have expected anything less than extravagant; it seemed that everyone in Emerson's inner circle was dripping with money. Ramon was certainly no exception.

Having never ridden in a luxury car before, Carino had to admit she was practically giddy. She also had to admit that her biggest fear, when she'd accepted his invitation, was quickly becoming reality; it was definitely going to be much harder than she had anticipated, keeping herself safely distanced from this man. To say he was irresistible was the understatement of a lifetime.

Realizing she was gaping at him like a mental patient, Carino twisted abruptly and latched the deadbolt on her front door. When she turned back around, Ramon was holding his hand out.

"Allow me, please." His tone demanded her compliance and caused her stomach to flutter.

Carino felt like a princess as he escorted her to his car and opened the passenger door.

Two minutes in and I'm already a total mess!

She shamelessly ogled Ramon as he walked around the front of the car to the driver's side and had to keep reminding herself that this wasn't a date. It was simply a professional meeting. A professional meeting she'd dressed to the nines for and obsessed over for hours on end. But it couldn't possibly be a date.

Could it?

Her job had to remain her first priority, and truthfully, she was not at a place in her life where she could become involved with someone. Much less someone who worked with Franklin Everly's biggest client—not to mention the one she was currently investigating. She was breaking all the rules by going out to dinner with Ramon, but at this point she knew she could still brush it off as simply business.

Note to self: reread the office fraternization policy.

Her palms were getting sweaty and her fight-or-flight response was ramping into high gear. Her thoughts were becoming jumbled, but the main theme was that she should just tell him she didn't feel well and end this fiasco before it even began. It wouldn't even really be a lie, since her stomach was in knots and one lurch might send her meager lunch flying. But before she could solidify her plan, Ramon entered the vehicle and threw it into reverse.

As he zoomed out of her driveway, he gave her a look so hot it could've melted butter. "*Eres bella*. You are beautiful."

Well, shit.

•••

The duo arrived at Shanahan's Steakhouse on Syracuse in about fifteen minutes, mostly due to Ramon's expert ability to thread between vehicles on I-225. Conversation was minimal and consisted mostly of small talk about the weather and traffic. Carino mentally cursed herself for not meeting him at the restaurant, because she found it increasingly difficult to keep her eyes from wandering to the corded muscles that rippled in his tanned forearms as he gripped and turned the wheel.

As they walked through the restaurant, she felt all eyes on them. The men wanted to be Ramon and the women wanted to be with Ramon. Honestly, she couldn't blame them. After being seated at the most secluded table, she knew she was about to discover something about herself. Would she cave to Ramon's devilish sex appeal, or not? It emanated from his very pores, and she knew he could tell the effect he had on her, no matter how hard she tried to hide it.

"I hope you're hungry, because I heard the food here is absolutely fantastic." Ramon broke the silence before it became awkward.

"I'm looking forward to trying it." Carino wished her stomach weren't turning somersaults like it was on the Olympic gymnastics team. Nevertheless, she opened the menu and began scanning the various selections.

"Good evening, sir, madam. My name is Victor and I'll be taking care of you this fine evening. May I interest you in something to drink from the bar?"

Before Carino could answer, Ramon cut in.

"If my lovely lady doesn't mind, we will decide on dinner first and then perhaps choose a nice bottle of wine." He shot her a questioning look.

"Yes, that sounds very good." She noted the flutter in her stomach at hearing him call her *his* lady, while simultaneously tamping down the need to assert her feminist rights. He was probably just trying to impress her anyway with his skills as an aficionado.

Well, it's working!

"Very wise decision, sir, as our wine list is sure to contain a pleasing selection. I will return shortly to take your order." Victor efficiently produced a wine list for Ramon's review.

After some deliberation, they decided on the Coconut Shrimp to share. Ramon chose London Broil and she ordered the Filet Mignon—sans onions, because one never knew when fresh breath was needed. Carino enjoyed Ramon's accent as he ordered a bottle of Petite Sirah. She didn't know what it was, but he sure made it sound delicious!

With the distraction of ordering their dinner out of the way, there wasn't much left to do except get down to the business of learning about each other, which was the part Carino was most nervous about. She took a sip of water in a lame attempt to calm her raging nerves, somewhat frustrated that Ramon remained completely unruffled.

It wasn't like she had never been on a date—or, professional meeting—before with a dazzling male specimen. It's just that it had been a really, really long time and she was rusty. Plus, she was worried about him finding a chink in her armor.

"I hope you didn't have to cancel any Saturday night plans for me." Ramon leaned forward in his chair. Instinctively, Carino leaned back and he smiled, noticing her behavior.

"It was no trouble. I simply pushed my plans out one more day." She smiled right back. This man was positively predatory and there was absolutely no reason for him to know the plans she referred to involved putting on her fat pants and curling up with a giant bowl of popcorn to watch a marathon of *The Walking Dead*.

"So, does that mean I should be looking over my shoulder for an angry boyfriend?"

"Mr. Ramon, you certainly get right to the point, don't you?"

"Please, just Ramon. And I'm merely assessing the situation, which is what I do. But really," he gestured toward her, "can you blame me?"

Blushing, in spite of herculean efforts not to, Carino shook her head. "No, you don't need to worry about any of that."

"I must say, I've never met anyone like you, and I've worked for Mr. Emerson many times over the years. The management at Franklin Everly made a very wise decision bringing you on board."

She shifted in her seat. "Thank you for the compliment. I've enjoyed working at Franklin Everly."

Carino couldn't help but notice how intently he looked at her when she spoke. It was unnerving, to say the least. Like he was measuring the amount of truth in her every word.

"So, you've been on Raj's team for about three years now, yes?"

She nodded. "My anniversary is next month."

"You must have become quite familiar with Mr. Emerson's businesses and various associates over the years."

Carino's hackles instantly rose.

Where is he going with this?

"Raj involves me as he sees fit." She shrugged.

"What did you do for the first several months of working for Franklin Everly?"

It didn't take a rocket scientist to figure out he had already checked her out. He even knew how long she'd been with the firm before Raj had asked her to join his team.

She held his gaze, fighting against his passive intimidation. "Well, Ramon. It sounds like you might already know more about me than I thought."

Damn, I need to watch this guy more closely, and not just his hot ass either.

"*Mi Cariño*, it's my job to know who Mr. Emerson does business with, at all levels." His voice was as smooth as glass and he never broke their stare. Or lost his Cheshire grin. His eyes were warm, but any fool could recognize the hard glint as well.

Their rapidly intensifying conversation was interrupted by Victor bringing the wine, which gave Carino time to mentally recalibrate. A date, this most certainly was not; it was an interrogation.

I'm supposed to be getting information from him, *not the other way around!*

Taking a sip of the dark red liquid, which was surprisingly good, Carino heaved a deep breath. "Well, obviously I would've preferred getting to know each other the old fashioned way, but nothing about you seems old fashioned."

Chuckling, Ramon raised his glass. "I'm looking forward to getting to know you, *mi Cariño*, one way or another. To uncharted territories."

Smiling, she raised her glass and delicately touched it to his. She still wasn't sure if there was more risk to Ramon than reward, but regardless, there was no refuting that she was the moth and he was the smoldering flame.

"So, since you know so much about me, I think it's only fair that I get to ask you a few questions." She needed to regain some control over the conversation.

"I'm an open book." He opened his hands and leaned back comfortably in his chair, his face a portrait of trustworthiness.

Yeah, right.

She imagined he could beat a polygraph with ease. He definitely knew how to use his alluring attributes to his advantage, and more than once since they'd met Carino had been knocked totally off guard. She had to remember he'd spent years perfecting this charming persona. And behind those pearly whites, perfect dimples, and sexy brown eyes, he was dangerous and calculating as well.

"So, you said you've worked for Mr. Emerson several times. What type of work do you do for him?" She took another sip of wine, which she noticed was going down very easily. She'd have to be careful that she didn't drink too much and end up eating a bowl of regret for breakfast tomorrow morning.

"Whatever needs to be done, really."

Evasive? Please, Ramon, that's child's play.

"Then what brings you to Denver?"

"Well, as you already know, Mr. Emerson is an extremely wealthy and powerful businessman. He must proceed with utmost caution while conducting his business endeavors, especially considering that he deals with equally powerful businessmen. Arrangements can turn sour unexpectedly, and I'm here to make sure things stay … sweet."

Even though Franklin Everly only dealt with Emerson's "legitimate" transactions, Carino knew he maintained his status by capitalizing on the lucrative business of the drug trade. He dealt with ruthless and dangerous people, and obviously Carino had known someone did his dirty work. She just didn't want to envision that person as Ramon. But Emerson's intimidation tactics were working, as all of his companies were thriving and his global footprint seemed to know no bounds.

"Is something happening with the Costa Rican transaction? Are you aware of something I should know?" Carino hoped he might provide something useful, but was careful not to mention any specifics of the transaction. Even though he'd been in the meeting with Emerson, she was mindful of maintaining confidentiality—except when working through official channels with the Bureau, of course.

"Not specifically, no."

"Well, the meeting yesterday seemed to go fine. Hopefully it stays that way." She kept fishing, but he kept his infuriatingly sexy smile fixed in place. "So, then you're here until … the Costa Rica deal closes?"

"Would you like me to stay until the deal closes?" He leaned forward, placing his hands on the table close to hers.

Carino's brain instantly registered the contrast between his dark skin and the pristine white tablecloth underneath, and she suppressed a shiver as she blocked out the mental image of his hands against her own alabaster skin.

"I'm not sure yet." Her answer was honest.

She'd definitely have to pay attention to his pendulum swings. One minute he was all business and the next he was chipping away at her already weak resolve.

"Understandable. So, are you ever going to tell me how you came to have such an interesting name?" He lightened up the conversation and redirected the questions her way. It didn't escape that he'd never answered hers though.

"My parents were interesting people."

Heh, look at me being evasive too.

"And you were close with them?"

She looked at him, knowing that if he had checked her out—and she was sure he had—he already knew full well about her parents. Well, her fake parents, anyway. "Yes, I was."

"I'm sorry, it's not my intention to dredge up painful memories."

"It's okay. I'm able to talk about it now, but if we had met a few years ago—well, I don't know." She wanted to get this discussion out of the way, since she felt most vulnerable when answering specific questions about her "past."

"The loss of family members is something you never really get over."

"Are you speaking from experience?" He pressed his lips together in a tight line and nodded curtly in answer to her question, before she continued. "The driver who hit them was so far over the legal alcohol limit, he most likely blacked out behind the wheel. Mom and Dad didn't even have a chance. They were pronounced dead at the scene."

He grimaced, clearly troubled by the topic. "That's horrific. And your brother passed away only a few weeks later? That's enough to send anyone over the edge."

"Yes, he was serving his second tour in Iraq, and several weeks after he got there, his convoy was destroyed by multiple IEDs while out on a routine mission."

What am I even doing here with him? I should not be risking my cover, cavorting with the right-hand henchman of the very person I'm hiding myself from.

"He died honorably, I hope you realize."

"Yes, but thank you for saying so." A fissure of anxiety ran through her about misleading him, when he was very clearly being sincere.

This is precisely the reason I never get too close to anyone—especially someone this dangerous ... and appealing.

"I know we've just met, but I can tell you're an extraordinary woman. I'm greatly privileged that you were willing to share your story with me, and will never ask you about these heartbreaking memories again."

"Thank you." She felt a mixture of pleasure and relief from his words. "Enough about that anyway, I want to hear more about you." Carino waved her hand in the air in an attempt to clear the emotion that had suddenly grown quite thick, as she redirected the topic away from her sad, phony family history.

"There's not much to tell, really. I was born in Mazatlan, Mexico and my mother brought me to America at age ten to try to keep me away from the Mexican gangs. We couldn't afford much and lived in places I wouldn't dream of letting you venture into alone—night or day. Of course, I got involved with some of the local Cholos anyway, and by the time I was age thirteen, I was running drugs and making quite a name for myself."

Carino's eyes went wide, and she knew she was actually seeing the real Ramon. She paid rapt attention to his every word, because he didn't give her the impression that he opened up and revealed his feelings very often; this was probably her one and only opportunity to hear his story.

"I did that for several years and managed to graduate high school too, although I'm not really sure how. Looking back, it's a miracle I wasn't killed. Unfortunately, my *madre* was not so lucky."

Pain flashed briefly across his face and Carino resisted the urge to reach out and grab his hand. She also noted he didn't elaborate on his mother's death, and she wasn't about to pry.

"After that, I left the U.S. and moved down to Venezuela to be closer to my boss. I was in really deep with one of the cartels at that point, and after a few more years, I knew I needed to get out. Problem was—I couldn't. That is, until I met Mr. Emerson. And ten years later, here I am having dinner with one of the most interesting, beautiful women I've had the pleasure of running into." He paused. "Literally."

"Well, as collisions go, it was definitely one of my better ones too." She flashed what she hoped was her best seductive smile, knowing in that moment that no matter how hard she tried, there was absolutely no way she was going to be able to stay away from this man.

• • •

Ramon pulled into Carino's driveway a pleasant two and a half hours later, and he killed the engine before walking around to her side of the car and opening the door.

They walked the distance to her front door with his hand on the small of her back which, no matter how hard she tried to convince herself otherwise, she didn't mind one little bit. She'd already fished her keys out of her clutch, because she didn't want to be tempted in any way to dawdle. She needed to say goodnight and get inside. Alone. She wanted to get to know him, but not like *that*.

"Carino, this has been one of the most enjoyable evenings I've had in quite some time. Thank you for allowing me the pleasure of your company."

Oh boy, there are those dimples again.

"And thank you for treating me to such a lovely dinner, Ramon." She looked down at her keys—anywhere but at his gorgeous face.

"Hey, there's a basketball game at the Pepsi Center on Monday night. Would you have any interest in going with me?"

Carino's head snapped up at the mention of basketball.

Oh yeah, he definitely checked up on me.

"You mean the Nuggets and the Mavs?"

"My tickets are decent." He shrugged, as if it was no big deal.

"Yes. Yes, I definitely would be very much interested in going with you to the game!" She all but jumped up and down. For Carino, NBA = crack, and it was the one aspect of her real life she'd been unwilling to give up.

"It's a date then. Tip-off is at seven p.m., so how about I pick you up from work and we grab some dinner first?"

She hesitated, but Ramon misunderstood why. "It's just a saying. It doesn't have to be a date. I didn't mean to pressure you. So we can just meet at the stadium."

"No, that's not it at all! I definitely want to have dinner first. It's just that my job is—well, I have to be careful about how much personal time I spend with one of our clients. The bosses don't really go for that sort of thing."

"Ah yes, of course. Well, it's a good thing I'm not one of your clients then."

No way, she wasn't about to get suckered in on a technicality. "How about we meet at the restaurant instead?"

"Sounds perfect. Call me with details on where to go and I'll be waiting."

"Okay, I'll call you on Monday then." Carino was barely containing her excitement.

Good grief, get ahold of yourself!

Reaching for her empty hand, he brought it to his lips and planted a soft kiss, all the while holding her gaze with his own. "Unless, of course, you'd like to call me before then."

Walk into the house, NOW!

Smiling delectably, he released her hand and sauntered back to his car. Carino, at least, had the sense to turn around and put her key in the lock before he saw her gaping mouth. And the drool.

After entering her house, she closed the door behind her and leaned back on it. Her cheeks hurt from smiling. She had enough energy to run a marathon. She was also glad the evening, while wonderful and invigorating, was over.

After tossing her purse on the side table and locking the dead bolt, Carino recounted that as the conversation—and the wine— kept flowing, it became increasingly easier to forget that Ramon was forbidden fruit.

Yep, I'm in big trouble.

Chapter 4

Tickets. He needed to find some. And not cheap ones either.

As luck had it, earlier that day when Ramon had been researching Abigail, he'd come across a picture of Carino in a basketball jersey. He'd known the picture had to be fairly recent, because it was posted on Abby's—as her friends called her—Facebook page, and they'd only known each other since she began working at Franklin Everly. Since it was a Timberwolves jersey, not the Denver Nuggets, Ramon assumed Carino was a long-time fan—a tidbit that proved very convenient, since the newspaper had mentioned a game on Monday. It had been the perfect segue into a second date.

As Ramon walked back to his car, he recognized that had this been any other woman, he wouldn't have nearly suffered a nervous breakdown trying to plan the perfect evening. He also would've suggested continuing their night in a more intimate setting, once back at her place, but he was painfully aware that Carino deserved better than that. Better than him pawing all over her and taking what he had no doubt she would freely give, if he persisted. Ramon could tell she was into him, despite her struggle not to be. So, before they even pulled into her driveway, Ramon had already resolved there was no way he was going to ask to come inside. Instead he said goodbye, which was actually much more difficult than he could've ever imagined.

In a matter of hours, Carino had effortlessly dominated his consciousness. And after spending the evening with her, Ramon had grudgingly accepted that she was much more than just a passing fling. If he wasn't with her, he was thinking about her. When they were together, he was planning ahead for their next encounter. It was clear that she was quickly changing from a mere sexual conquest into someone who was of actual importance to him. She was far from being a mere stateside distraction; she wasn't someone to be toyed with and discarded when the Emerson job wrapped. No, she needed to be wined and dined and treated like the lovely, classy lady she was, and he knew he was just the man to do it—if she would only allow him the chance.

All the more reason to hurry up and prove that she isn't the mole.

Although he started his car, he couldn't seem to put it in reverse and drive away from Carino's homey little abode. It was simple and unobtrusive, blending into the background, which seemed to mirror how she conducted her life. She had plain, white blinds covering the front picture window, which matched the light exterior paint. In fact, the only real color Ramon could see came from the smattering of flowers lining the perimeter of the front and right side of the place, since the light powder dusting of snow that had briefly fallen on Friday evening muted the green of her small front lawn. But it made him picture it all with her: the 2.5 kids, the family sedan, and the white picket fence. He'd never wanted that before in all of his life. He'd never been a relationship kind of guy at all really, but since meeting Carino, he'd found himself contemplating future plans with her—more than once—in spite of how outrageous that seemed.

After tonight, he knew he wanted more evenings with Carino, but it hadn't taken long for him to figure out that she'd built a fairly sturdy wall around her heart. She was uncomfortable speaking of her family, which was to be expected, and she was proud of her accomplishments on Raj's team, and rightly so. She also seemed to be aware that Emerson had a dark side, but appeared to have made the choice to ignore it.

Will she ignore mine too?

Ramon knew he'd have to be careful not to scare her, like he was most certainly scaring himself with these out-of-place feelings; coming on strong was definitely not going to be part of his game plan. Everything should happen naturally, once he showed her how much of a gentleman he could be.

If I even remember how.

Chapter 5

Carino woke up on Sunday morning with unmanageable levels of excitement about her prior evening with Ramon.

She jumped out of bed and took a super-fast shower before throwing on some sweats and a hoodie. After spinning her hair into a quick, messy ponytail and brushing on mascara and lip gloss, she headed to Golden, calling Abby on the way.

"Hullllo?" murmured a sleepy voice.

"Abby! Wake up and get ready!" Carino paused to take a swig of her Sugar-Free Red Bull. "I'll be there in fifteen minutes to pick you up!"

"What time is it anyway?" Abby stifled a yawn.

"It's nearly 8:15! Get up! I've got lots to tell you!"

"Fine, but you need to cease and desist on the caffeine. You're stressing me out."

"What? I've barely had any!" At that point, Carino realized she was shouting at Abby through her car's Bluetooth connection, while darting in and out of traffic at a speed that was certain to carry a mandatory court appearance.

On second thought, maybe Abby was right.

"All right, I'll be ready. But don't expect much."

"See you in a few!" Carino knew she was still yelling, but couldn't seem to help it.

Abby was scowling on her front steps when Carino pulled up. Even though she'd been out of bed for just a few minutes, she was lovely. She had a natural beauty that no amount of makeup could ever compete with. Her pixie haircut showcased her big, brown eyes and prominent cheekbones. She was wearing a pair of black yoga pants, Uggs, and a Rockies sweatshirt, and looked casually fabulous.

"This had better be damned good." Abby flopped down into the passenger seat before making a show of putting on her dark, over-sized sunglasses.

Carino smiled. "So, where do you feel like going?"

"Back to bed."

"To eat!"

"You know I don't make important decisions before nine a.m."

"Ok, then we're going to Mimi's!"

She could sense the eye-roll behind Abby's dark shades, but knew her outlook would improve as soon as she swallowed her first bite of buttermilk spice muffin.

• • •

Even though Abby and Carino hadn't really spent much time together as of late, they naturally fell back into their normal, effortless rhythm.

"Wow, so you're seeing him again tomorrow night?"

"Why, do you think it's too soon?" Carino was suddenly paranoid. She'd been out of the dating scene for so long that she didn't really know what was considered normal anymore.

"No! I just think it's fantastic that he asked you out again so fast. And it's been a really long time since you've been out with anyone. And we both know how that ended."

"Yeah, thanks for the reminder."

Nearly two years had passed since the last time Nathan had contacted her, and to say the whole situation had ended badly would be a definite understatement. As her handler, he was only supposed to get in touch with her through official channels, as anything else could risk her cover—such as he'd done when Abby had seen them together. Of course, Carino hadn't told Abby who he really was, instead fabricating a story that he was her stalker ex-boyfriend.

Since the "Abby Incident," as she'd labeled it, Nathan had been formally barred from communicating with her, but it still took a very long time before Carino stopped looking for him, expecting to see him following her like he had during the early stages of her assignment. She could handle herself and didn't need a babysitter, which was actually the reason she'd decided to report him to the director. Deep down, Carino knew that something would eventually trigger his overly-protective, borderline obsessive behavior and he would attempt to make contact with her again, even though he knew full well he wasn't allowed to.

"I'm just glad Ramon was up front with you. Most guys make you sweat by the phone." Abby's voice was laced with disgust. "Nothing but game-playing bullshit, if you ask me. And they aren't even worth it in the end anyway!"

Carino knew Abby was still bitter about her latest ex-boyfriend—well, if he could even be called that. He didn't like "labels." And apparently he didn't like exclusivity either, considering she surprised him at his office last week with brown-bag lunches and found him otherwise engaged with one of his office temps. Such a loser.

"Well, if you want him to ever ask you out again, you'd better leave your big foam finger at home!"

They both laughed, recalling how horrified Abby had been when she picked Carino up for a game a couple months back. Abby said her outfit looked like a cross between the Timberwolves mascot, a cheerleader, and a homeless person; she'd nearly driven off and left.

"Ok, fine! I'll save it for the third date then."

"In all seriousness, just be careful with this one, okay? There's no doubt he's ultra-gorgeous and I'm sure he's every bit as wonderful as you described, but I just don't want to see you get hurt again."

"He didn't ask me to marry him, Abby, just to go to a basketball game." Carino's deadpan look complimented her sarcastic tone.

"I know! It's just that you don't really know him."

"Thanks for looking out for me, but when it comes down to it, how well do we *really* know anybody?"

Case in point: how well do you really know me?

"That's true, but you might feel differently if you'd seen Raj after he met with Ramon on Friday. He was so mad, he was nearly frothing at the mouth!"

"What? When did Ramon come to see Raj?" This was definitely news to her. She wondered what business Ramon had with Raj, especially when Emerson wasn't around.

"While you were at lunch. That's when he dropped off the booty-call letter for you too." She grinned from ear-to-ear.

"What did they talk about?" Carino was immediately anxious and completely ignored Abby's attempt at humor.

"I don't know; they went back to Raj's office." Abby frowned, most likely because of Carino's sudden intensity.

"How long were they together?"

"I guess for about ten minutes. Geez, counselor! What's with the cross-examination?"

"Sorry!" Carino realized she was coming on pretty strong. "It's just that Raj was acting really strange on Friday afternoon, but I thought it was because of stress in general. Now I'm dying to know what happened!"

"I don't know what went down between the two of them, but I do have some dirt on Ramon ... " Abby trailed off, casually inspecting her flawless fingernail polish.

Carino shouldn't have been surprised that Abby had already checked him out. In fact, Abby had seemed more curious about *all* of the firm's large accounts lately, including Emerson's.

"And? Spill it!"

"Well, I had trouble finding much, but he currently lives in the Caymans, and is single with no kids. He doesn't have any public court records that I could find. He's staying at the Brown Palace under the name Ramon Terrones. He hasn't had any visitors, but has left quite a few times. He hasn't rented any hotel movies—you know, the kind you can buy straight from the TV." She paused her story to wink knowingly. "Oh, and he likes poached eggs." She grinned, bouncing up and down in her chair, clearly pleased with herself.

"Ok, what else?" Carino had been hoping for something more substantial, since she hadn't contacted the agency to have his name run through the system. She knew it was foolish, since that's what she should've done, pursuant to the operation's protocol, but knew as soon as she reported him he'd officially become part of the case. She would then be prohibited from being around him, unless it was specifically related to the investigation. She also knew that if Nathan found out they were spending personal time together, he would have a shit fit. No more dinners, no more basketball games … and definitely no sleepovers. Not that she was planning any.

"What do you mean, 'what else'?"

"He already told me where he lives and about his childhood, and I asked him where he was staying while he was in town. So, the only new intel is that he isn't into porn and if he stays over, I'd better learn how to poach an egg."

"Well, damn. I thought I had some good stuff!" The corners of Abby's lips pulled down into an arch.

"I'm sorry." Carino tried hard to rein in her disappointment. "Of course you found some good information and if we hadn't been together last night, I wouldn't have even known all that stuff. I was just hoping to find out more about his involvement with Emerson, that's all. If Emerson brought him into the meeting on Friday, he must be a trusted associate. I'm just interested to know why I've never come across his name or any information about him in all the years I've been working on the account."

"Well, why didn't you say so?"

Carino cocked her head to the side as she regarded Abby across the table. "Tell me again why I hang out with you?"

"Because I'm awesome, duh!" Now it was Carino's turn to roll her eyes. "Honestly, I don't have a lot more information on Ramon, but damn, have you seen how loaded Emerson is? The man is a whale! He literally pays cash for everything. Down payments, wire transfers, legal fees. It's crazy!"

"Yeah, I've noticed that too." Carino also wondered who had noticed Abby's file-surfing activity on Franklin Everly's server.

"Raj was sure lucky to hook up with him. The firm too. He's the epitome of 'Cash Cow.' I could live happily-ever-after on just a quarter of a percent of his net worth!"

"Okay wait, how do you know Emerson's net worth?" Carino was instantly wary.

"When I was looking through some of the files to see what I could find out about Ramon—for your sake, of course."

"Of course."

"I happened upon one of Emerson's old financial statements," she tried to minimize the extent of her completely inappropriate snooping, "right before I found a document with Ramon's name in it. But then my computer froze up and I had to reboot. Not before I printed a copy of it though." She dug in her purse and produced a folded up piece of printer paper, which she extended across the table.

"What's this?" Carino unfolded the document.

Abby was nothing if not nosy. Carino made a mental note to talk to her about curbing her self-imposed sleuthing through Emerson's files, lest someone get the wrong idea. Franklin Everly was extremely protective of their top clients, not to mention Raj's hyper-sensitivity when it came to unauthorized file access.

"I didn't really get a chance to look at it too closely, and then I kinda forgot I had it until just now! Maybe you can make something out of it?"

Quickly skimming the document, Carino thought it looked like the summary of a conference call Raj had with Emerson about five years ago. The document indicated that a person named S. DeSilva had been the owner of a warehouse in San Cristobal, Venezuela that had been a regular storage facility used by one of the well-known, South American criminal regimes. In parenthesis next to the owner's name was one word: Ramon.

"Well, I can't tell what this means. Is DeSilva the same person as Ramon? If so, I can't tell if it's my Ramon or not." Carino refolded the paper. She was frustrated by the lack of detail, but also confused about how she hadn't remembered the document— or Ramon's name—from her searches before.

Probably because the name Ramon has only become significant in the last forty-eight hours.

"*Your* Ramon?" Abby wiggled her eyebrows up and down.

"Oh whatever, you know what I mean!"

"All I'm asking is that you please be careful. At least until you get to know him a little bit better, okay?"

Carino nonchalantly tucked the folded paper under her leg before Abby could speculate any further or ask for it back; she wanted to look at it more closely later. "Okay, I will! Now please help me figure out where we should go for dinner tomorrow night."

Even though Carino didn't really know what the document represented, she'd have to be a complete fool to ignore the fact that Ramon's relationship with Raj—and with Emerson—was much more complex than he'd let on.

Chapter 6

Ramon's phone buzzed, jolting him awake. The GPS tracker he'd circled back to stick under Carino's car before he'd driven to his hotel last night had notified him that she'd traveled out of the perimeter he'd programmed for her daily schedule.

Even though Ramon was merely following S.O.P., which he'd developed eons ago when he'd started doing this type of work for Emerson, he'd nearly talked himself out of this invasion of Carino's privacy. But he never deviated from procedure, which he felt was what had kept him successfully under the radar, and out of trouble, all these years. In the end, he'd justified it as a method by which to quickly find her, in the event she was ever in danger. Right then, the tracker indicated she was on I-70 West. If he had to guess, she was visiting with Abby.

Sitting up, Ramon threw his legs over the edge of the bed, untangled the sheet that had wrapped itself around his waist, and rubbed his hands vigorously over his face to stimulate some blood flow. Groaning, he chastised himself for staying up so late to research the last several transactions Raj's team—including Carino—had worked on. But, he'd known it was going to be a long and grueling process to identify the mole at Franklin Everly, especially considering Emerson hadn't given him anything more to go on than the phone records that indicated the calls to the Feds.

He'd hacked into the mainframe on Friday, so he had full, unobstructed access to everything—including personnel files. He'd never *actually* needed Raj to produce hard copies for him, but it was fun having him scamper around anyway. Ramon had spent hours sifting through years of electronic notes, documents, phone conversation and voice mail transcripts, trying to find anything that stood out to him.

The firm's phone system layout indicated the phone call from Franklin Everly to the Feds had originated from a small interior file room, which probably meant most, if not all, employees had access to it. Unfortunately, since there were no existing video cameras, Ramon wouldn't have any way to view historical access. It would also, no doubt, prove difficult to install a camera, since the room was in the middle of the floor. But he definitely needed to figure something out, which would most likely involve trying to get a view of the doorway from one of the neighboring office computer webcams, at the very least.

Ramon, unintentionally, found himself focused heavily on Carino's work, reviewing anything of Emerson's she had worked on with a fine-toothed comb. He knew he was trying way too hard to prove that she wasn't the informant, but he couldn't seem to help himself; he had to know she was fully in the clear. Thankfully, no immediate red flags stood out, but it was still too early to completely rule her out.

The fresh standout had been Abby. She definitely saw everything that happened at Franklin Everly, was one of the newest employees, and was street-savvy. She'd spent a few months in rehab—instead of behind bars—about four years ago for a meth-related issue, but from what Ramon could tell, had managed to remain clean ever since. Her father had recently passed away, but she had a sick mother in another state, whose treatments ate up most of her disposable income.

Since Abby had successfully evaded jail time, Ramon assumed she'd turned state's evidence on someone, and therefore was familiar with the system. That troubled him, especially because she seemed to have become really intense in the last year or so, even participating in several anti-drug rallies that resulted in numerous injuries and multiple arrests. Ramon could tell she had been picked up at least once, but never was formally arrested. In any event, he definitely felt Abby was ripe for being picked by the

Feds, if she wasn't already a narc. And she snooped through client files, including Emerson's. A lot. Of course, she had access to the file room, so she easily could have made the phone call.

Ramon knew she'd printed something on Friday before he could restrict her electronic file access, and after searching his own name in the server, he came up with only one file that referenced his name, or any of his aliases; he assumed that was the document she'd printed. It appeared to be something Raj had written, so Ramon figured it was the start of his attempted retribution for the gun pointing incident. In hindsight, Ramon realized it probably would've been wise to review Franklin Everly's files every so often, just to make sure Raj wasn't trying to sabotage him, since that seemed to be his intent now.

Luckily, after quickly scanning the document, Ramon determined it wasn't too disparaging. Raj's narrative referenced the warehouse in Venezuela that Ramon had owned in his previous name—his birth name—as well as a one-word reference to his current alias. But Ramon was on the wrong side of Emerson's business, and therefore his name and everything associated with him was strictly black bag. Raj knew that, more than anyone involved in Emerson's inner circle, and shouldn't have formally tied Ramon to Emerson in any way. His name was never to appear on anything. Ever. And for that, Raj would pay.

Ramon had been making money renting his warehouse to one of the cartels as a temporary storage facility for, well, whatever they needed to store large quantities of. But when Emerson had blown into town and started taking over, Ramon had recognized his chance to break free from the cartel, prompting him to approach Emerson late one evening as he was leaving the boss's compound. Emerson had immediately brought him into the fold, established his new identity—Ramon Terrones—and wasted no time capitalizing on his brawn and apparent lack of morals, mainly using him when difficult problems needed to "disappear."

Once the cartel got wind that he was on Emerson's payroll, they began making waves about their pre-existing rental arrangement. So, to resolve the issue, Emerson brokered the sale of Ramon's warehouse to the very men he'd been renting it to. Emerson made Ramon a ton of money on the deal, but the real value was that it had allowed him to make a clean break from the stronghold of the cartel; the warehouse had been the last official tie between Ramon and his old life.

Knowing full well what the cartel was capable of, the fear and respect they showed Emerson caused Ramon concern that he'd left a bad situation for something much worse. Obviously, he knew Emerson was extremely dangerous, and he should have walked away from it all right then. He would have had a pleasant nest egg that he could've lived on comfortably until the day he died, but instead felt a sense of indebtedness to Emerson that wouldn't let him break free. In his heart, he wasn't sure Emerson would have let him go, but he'd never even tried, since Emerson was one of the only people who had ever been able to intimidate him. And if the cartel was afraid of him, he was more hazardous than Ramon could truly know. So, he'd stuck around.

When Ramon had reviewed the document earlier, the information seemed to indicate that Emerson had actually been the one to purchase the warehouse, not the cartel. That didn't make any sense to Ramon, especially since he knew the cartel still used the property. He guessed Emerson had just rented it back out to them, the same way Ramon had been doing for so long, but he'd never mentioned the arrangement before. In hindsight, Ramon realized he should've actually read the paperwork he signed.

There's no question about it now—he owns me.

Ramon had long suspected that Raj had tried multiple times to convince Emerson that his services were no longer needed, and this document served as confirmation that he was starting to take matters into his own hands. It was also another reminder that Raj was a conniving little SOB, and Ramon shouldn't trust him any farther than he could throw him. Well, maybe that wasn't true—Ramon could probably throw him pretty far; Raj was fairly small.

While he didn't think it would be a big deal if Abby showed Carino the document, he didn't like to leave any stone uncovered. Which was why, instead of reviewing each and every document in Raj's electronic file on Emerson, he'd dressed in a tattered baseball cap, green hoodie, and jeans, and headed over to Abby's neck of the woods.

On his way out of the hotel, he'd caught a glimpse of his reflection in one of the lobby mirrors; he was unrecognizable. One of the many benefits of dressing the way he normally did and driving the cars he normally drove was that he stood out, which made it easier for him to blend into the crowd when he needed to. No one looked too hard at the average guy, and that was exactly how he looked: average. In the event anyone at the hotel had been keeping an eye on him, he'd wanted them to think he was still lounging around in his room.

Knowing at times he was going to have to travel incognito while in Denver, he'd purchased a separate, less conspicuous, vehicle than his rented Mercedes. He'd found the perfect nondescript, beige 2004 Toyota Camry on a Craigslist ad, complete with several dents and chipped paint. He'd met with the owner on Friday evening, who was more than happy to accept an extra-large sum of cash in lieu of a name, and Ramon was pleased at how well he blended in with the hoard of other faceless commuters.

He'd been parking the Camry in one of the pay lots down the street from his hotel, making sure to change spaces once a day, so it wasn't long before he'd headed west on Colfax Avenue in search of a building numbered 14265, which was where the blip had stopped on his tracker. As soon as he'd seen the restaurant that corresponded to that address, Ramon had spotted Carino's bright blue Mazda hatchback in the lot.

Parking in the adjacent row, he entered the foyer and saw Carino and Abby sitting near the far side of the main room. He'd asked the hostess for a specific table near theirs, which allowed him to sit close enough to make out a few snippets of their conversation, but far enough away that he wouldn't be made.

No sooner had the waitress delivered his coffee and a plain bagel with cream cheese did he see Abby pull some paperwork out of her purse. Discreetly zooming in on the document with a small camera, thankful he'd upgraded to an internal telephoto lens a few months ago, Ramon was able to recognize the document's layout. It was the definitely the one he'd reviewed earlier.

"Well, shit."

Abby was definitely turning out to be a problem.

• • •

Ramon parked his car on the curb around the corner from Abby's house, utilizing the time she was out with Carino. Based on his previous drive-by on Friday night, he'd calculated he would need no more than five minutes to get inside. She was obviously far too casual about her personal safety because, as it turned out, it took him less than one. Once he'd been satisfied there was no one around, he had simply walked through her unfenced, slightly wooded backyard and tried the latch on the back door; it opened.

With practiced expertise, Ramon inserted a bug into her home phone, and stuck another one under the small dining table. He then placed a nearly invisible, cordless, motion-activated camera in the lamp at the far corner of her living room facing the access areas from both the front and back doors, and another one in the lamp on her desk in the master bedroom. It looked like she did most of her paperwork there, so he'd be able to see if she brought anything home from Franklin Everly.

A quick scan of the easily visible documents she had laying out didn't reveal Emerson's name or any of his business entities. Glancing around, Ramon made sure he didn't leave anything behind and headed out the same way he entered. A cursory look told him there still wasn't anyone nearby, so he walked briskly to his car, removed his blue surgical gloves, and headed back to the hotel to complete the surveillance setup on his laptop.

Ramon really hoped Abby was clean, because he could tell she was important to Carino, and he didn't want harm to come to anyone else she cared about. But Emerson was merciless and Ramon was fully aware of his expectations regarding the informant; it wouldn't matter one iota to him who had to be eliminated.

He could feel the day quickly approaching when he would reach a crossroads with Emerson. He knew he needed to get out, before it was too late.

How foolish of me; it already is.

Chapter 7

Carino dropped Abby off at her house and headed back to her own, feeling an equal mixture of excitement and uneasiness about seeing Ramon after work tomorrow. She was still confused about how she'd missed the document Abby found, because she had reviewed each and every one of the closed transaction files on Franklin Everly's server, and hadn't come across it before.

And what the hell was Abby doing snooping around in the files anyway?

Carino thought Abby knew better than to do something like that. Even though she'd said she was looking out for Carino's best interests, she didn't even have a clue about what she was getting herself into.

Once home, Carino opened her wall safe, which was hidden behind an old, invisibly hinged bookshelf, and removed its one and only item: her laptop. She powered it up and connected her iPhone through the USB port.

The wall safe was an incredibly attractive—and practical— feature of her house. And she kept her laptop in it, but who wouldn't? One couldn't be too cautious when it came to Emerson. She knew he had countless people on his payroll and wasn't willing to take any chances on the wrong person realizing the true extent of her involvement when his wretched empire came crumbling down.

Knowledge was power, and where Emerson was concerned, Carino intended to be omnipotent. She'd amassed quite an extensive catalog over the past few years, in spite of the firm's steely control over his account. Several times she had requested files to be retrieved from Archives, but had never actually gone down to the basement on her own; it was generally a request she reserved for the newest intern.

She hadn't dared to download documents straight from the server onto her portable flash drive, and since she wasn't in Admin she had to put in a client code each time she used the printer. Those charges were then billed to the client each month, so she'd had to devise a different method. Thank goodness for technology because she'd meticulously used her iPhone, which was not connected to iCloud, to take photos of her monitor once she had each document open and visible.

Carino figured that a man like Emerson had someone permanently situated on the inside at Franklin Everly who updated him on any activity pertaining to his account, and she wasn't fool enough to think electronic file access wasn't monitored too.

She'd obtained copies from most of the early files within the first few months of joining Raj's team, and was prepared to explain her activity as simply trying to get fully up to speed on the client she was working for—which was actually true. The only one who had asked her about it was Raj himself, because he'd been trying to access a document on the server that she inadvertently had open at the exact same time. But he'd totally understood when she'd provided her explanation, and actually commended her on being conscientious. That was also the day she'd placed Raj in the "Not an Accomplice" file. She wasn't totally sure her analysis of his involvement with Emerson was accurate, but he'd always appeared to conduct himself with veracity and she hadn't found evidence to the contrary.

The last step of her file-capturing process was to upload the photos to her laptop from the phone's camera roll by USB connection. There was no way she was going to email the photos to herself! Email could be hacked by the everyday bargain-basement criminal, and she was certain Emerson's support system was staffed with top of the line computer gurus who viewed email hacking as child's play. In fact, she didn't even have her laptop connected to the Internet at all, so as to not provide any opportunity for unauthorized remote access. Her only period of exposure was from the time she snapped the photos until the time she got home, but that had been a calculated risk she was willing to take.

So, to recap, the process was: Inefficient? Check. Time-consuming? Check. The only way to secure and safeguard the evidence she needed to take down the international criminal she worked with, so it was totally worth it? Check and double-check.

Keeping consistent with her file storage methodology, she snapped a photo of the paper she'd taken from Abby, then uploaded and saved it to her computer. Once finished, she deleted the photo from her phone's camera roll, powered down her laptop, and returned it to the safe, spun off the combination lock, and righted the bookshelf.

She planned to destroy the hard copy after she had a chance to read it word-for-word, which she would do after a quick power nap. For now it was going to remain untouched on her coffee table.

Carino's caffeine and adrenaline high had long since worn off and had left her more than exhausted. With heavy eyelids, she curled up on the couch, covered herself with the cushy microfiber throw, and was asleep within seconds.

When she awoke, it was still light outside but it was definitely dwindling. She slowly sat up, not immediately sure if she felt better or worse, and grabbed her phone to see what time it actually was. That was when she noticed the text message.

"Looking forward to seeing you again."

It wasn't a number she had programmed into her contacts, but she instantly recognized it as Ramon's. Her stomach did a backflip and she felt tingly all over. But then she saw it was already four p.m., so he'd sent it well over an hour ago. Since her phone had been in silent mode, its arrival hadn't woken her up.

Great, he probably thinks I'm ignoring him.

Carino added Ramon's number to her contacts, noting that she needed to get a picture of him to add to his record, before replying, "Me too! Meet me at PF Chang's on 15th? I'll be there around 5:30."

Seconds later, her phone vibrated.

"With pleasure."

Envisioning Ramon's perfect lips curving into a sultry smile as he typed the word "pleasure" sent shivers down her spine. She instantly knew tomorrow night was going to be simultaneously amazing and draining. He was chocolate cake dripping with decadent icing and she was the salivating diabetic. Oh, how she craved a taste. Yeah sure, she could indulge, but at what cost?

Ugh, now I really won't be able to sleep tonight.

Carino rolled her eyes and, in doing so, caught sight of the paper Abby had given her, which was still lying on her coffee table. Figuring now was as good of a time as any, she grabbed it and started from the top.

Even though she already knew Ramon had been involved with unsavory folks in his past, not to mention his steady employment with Emerson doing who knows what, her heart still sank when she read the words.

Raj had summarized a conversation with Emerson where he strongly advised him against purchasing a warehouse in Venezuela. He had described the property as a dilapidated, drug-infested shell, located in a severely run-down neighborhood in San Cristobal. He indicated the place had been the site of several unsolved murders, as well as various other sinister events, such as missing persons reportedly last seen on the premises. Raj had insinuated that the owner of the property, a man named S. DeSilva—maybe the same person as Ramon—was a very dangerous criminal who was suspected to hold a power position within one of the cartels, and firmly cautioned Emerson about getting involved.

In the end, Emerson hadn't taken Raj's advice, and had purchased the building anyway. Raj had helped draft the paperwork, for a sum of money that told her the property couldn't have been as bad as he'd described.

She vaguely remembered reading about this transaction, but hadn't registered the name 'Ramon.' If she recalled correctly, the file indicated that Emerson had helped to clean up the area by purchasing the warehouse and converting it into a location for a textile manufacturing company, effectively removing the cartel's presence in the area.

But now that she knew how integrated Ramon had been with the cartel, Carino wondered if Emerson had actually cleaned it up. And murders? Disappearances? She now understood Raj's reaction to seeing Ramon. Obviously, Raj was fully aware of who Ramon was, and old friends they certainly were not.

Carino had never been able to confirm if Raj simply ignored Emerson's shady dealings, or if he was actually involved with any of the illegal stuff. She hadn't seen anything that would cause her to take Raj at anything except face value, and this latest discovery made it seem even less likely that Raj would participate in Emerson's illegal activity. He was trying to keep Emerson from getting too close to cartel property.

But no matter what, there was definitely more to the Raj/Ramon/Emerson triangle. One thing was certain: Ramon was hazardous. If she had any sliver of a brain at all, she'd tuck tail and run in the opposite direction. But clearly she didn't, since she was longing to see him, and tomorrow night couldn't seem to get there fast enough!

Once Carino finished reading the document, she walked into the kitchen, grabbed her lighter from the junk drawer, and stepped out the back door onto her small concrete patio. She opened the cover of her barbeque grill, laid the document directly on the rack, and lit it on fire. Flames tore through the paper with lightning speed.

While she watched to ensure it had fully disintegrated, her stomach began growling, reminding her that it had been several hours since she'd last eaten. She knew there was a strip steak in the fridge that was going to spoil if she didn't cook it soon, so she closed the lid of the grill, went back inside, and set about prepping her dinner.

In spite of what she'd just read, or of her burgeoning opinion of who Ramon truly was, Carino had to put aside all negative thoughts and focus on tomorrow night. He was potentially a fount of information and she was in a prime position to tap that.

Maybe not the best choice of words?

Truth be told, Carino couldn't wait to go to the basketball game. Having only been in town for a few days, she was sure Ramon couldn't have gotten very good seats, but it didn't even matter; she would be there with the most attractive man she'd ever met. She knew she was flirting with disaster by even spending time with him, and the fact that she hadn't had him formally investigated was most likely career suicide.

But she was just so lonely. She had been by herself, rattling around in her empty house like a marble in a box for years. She couldn't stand the solitude anymore and Ramon was so tempting. He was gorgeous and dangerous and exciting, and no matter how many times she chastised herself for breaking the rules, she couldn't seem to keep herself from counting the minutes until she saw him again.

So, even if only for a short time, she planned to live a little. She was going to forget about Emerson and Raj, ignore the investigation, and suppress the images swirling around in her head of Ramon with blood on his hands.

Chapter 8

Initially, Ramon wasn't uneasy about not hearing back from Carino. He was nearly certain that her discussion with Abby hadn't changed her mind about him, and he was sure she wasn't waiting by the phone for him to contact her.

Disappointingly, he realized he was.

He paced his hotel room as the minutes turned into an hour, and then closed in on a half hour more. It took all of his willpower to keep from driving out to her house to make sure she was okay. He reminded himself this was precisely why he'd always kept himself unattached.

Ramon had never allowed himself to truly get close to anyone over the years because he knew no good could come of it. He didn't have a regular job, and how was he supposed to tell his woman that he was on-call for a dangerous criminal whose needs required him to leave on a moment's notice for weeks, or even months, to another continent? Not to mention the type of work he might actually be doing. Add to that, he was afraid that at some point he'd be discovered by one of the many powerful people who would love to get their hands on him—and anyone he cared about.

In spite of all his years of rigid discipline, Ramon definitely had it bad for this girl, and he couldn't quite isolate why either; she had so many appealing qualities. He certainly wasn't sappy enough to believe in love at first sight, but he'd known her all of three days and she'd effortlessly dominated his every thought. Somehow, she had drawn him in on a visceral level, and he couldn't turn away now, even if he wanted to. Ramon felt like he'd known her for years, which he supposed was due to obsessing over every detail he'd been able to uncover about her since Friday.

He hated that her parents and brother had died in such an unexpected, gut-wrenching way, leaving her all alone at such a young age. In spite of the heartache he was certain she still felt on a daily basis, she'd done fairly well over the past few years; she lived in a nice house, had a decent car and a good, steady job.

Raj definitely seemed to like her too, judging from the annual performance evaluations Ramon had read in her file. He remembered Raj falling for an employee once prior, many years ago, and it hadn't worked back then either. If Raj believed that Carino would give him the time of day, he was an even bigger moron than Ramon gave him credit for. Anyone could see that Carino took her job very seriously, and would be devastated if she thought her advancement within Franklin Everly was due to anything other than her superior work performance. Ramon had reviewed all of the contracts she drafted and the transcripts of the negotiations she had co-anchored; she was razor sharp. Even if Raj hadn't lobbied to get her on his team, she still undoubtedly would have risen quickly through the company.

Ramon was fully aware that it would be a monumental task building a solid foundation with Carino, but surprisingly enough, realized he was up for the challenge. In fact, she had awakened a primal need within him that had long since been dormant. It was as if her very essence had leached into his veins, and without her he would surely cease to exist.

From what Ramon could tell, Carino was nearly as closed off to the rest of the world as he was, and if he was going to have any glimmer of a chance with her at all, he had to first earn her trust. Even with the mammoth obstacle of his past hampering the way, it was still worth it to him to try.

Ramon had done some unspeakable things that still haunted him most nights, but he'd come to terms with his sins and knew he alone would pay the price for them later. He'd told himself he was done with the hardcore dirty work, and was pretty sure

Emerson had to know this was his last job, even though he'd never actually come right out and said as much. In light of the new information he'd learned about Emerson buying his warehouse—and essentially his freedom—all those years ago, Ramon wondered if Emerson was going to let him go without a fight, or if he felt that Ramon still owed him after all these years.

Emerson was getting too ballsy and Ramon knew it was only a matter of time before he got busted. Ramon figured Emerson's insatiable greed would eventually get the best of him, and he was going to implode so spectacularly that everyone around him was sure to get sucked into his black hole. Ramon planned to be long gone when that happened, but first he had to make sure Raj wasn't going to deliver up his first class, one-way ticket to Club Fed.

Emerson's business ran like a well-oiled machine. In fact, had he continued to operate sufficiently under the radar, he'd have probably been able to carry on indefinitely, sans interference. But there was never enough for him; he always had to have more. About five years ago, he'd gotten involved with several high-octane Central American radicals who reportedly had a number of treasonous U.S. military members on the payroll. These soldiers were supposedly on-call wet workers, a brute-force insurance policy against any obstruction of Emerson's budding international drug commerce.

It was absolutely not Ramon's style, and he had strongly cautioned Emerson about getting involved with them. Much to Ramon's surprise, Raj had openly agreed, also providing an adverse opinion. It was no secret that certain countries were hyper-scrutinized for any kind of suspected illegal activity, and just a mere conversation with the wrong person could land a person on the Federal Watch List.

But in true Emerson fashion he'd plowed ahead, despite their shared warnings. It was almost as if he had become bored with how easy he was able to pull off such complex, high-dollar scams.

Ramon figured Emerson considered himself so wealthy that money was no longer the measure of success—power had become his new crowning achievement.

Raj had reluctantly become involved in merely an off-the-books advisory role, refusing to become heavily associated with the particular group Emerson was hooking up with. Ramon wasn't sure if Emerson had ever finalized any dealings with them, but it was the only time he could remember Raj standing up to him.

Ramon's phone dinged, disrupting his reverie. He picked it up, letting out a deep breath he hadn't realized he'd been holding. "Finally."

He was simultaneously relieved that she'd responded and annoyed with himself for being such a sap. But she still wanted to meet for dinner, and Ramon couldn't hide from the happiness he felt because of it.

Chapter 9

As usual, Carino was running late because she couldn't get her lazy ass out of bed when her alarm went off—for the fourth time. Excitement had kept sleep at bay until well after two a.m., which hadn't helped matters either. Luckily, she knew herself pretty well, which was why she'd selected her game-day outfit last night, and had already put her bag in the trunk of her car. She'd opted for dark skinny jeans, layered white and coral tanks with a thin black jacket and silver sparkly Toms. Of course, her North Face jacket too, in case it was really chilly after the game. And, as much as it pained her to say, no big foam finger.

By the time Carino was showered and dressed for work, she had no choice but to throw her hair up in a messy bun and toss her makeup into her purse to apply later during the day. Again, she'd have to speed to even have a remote chance at being on time. Luckily, there wasn't anything of importance going on that morning, so even though Raj would probably chastise her for being late, he'd get over it.

Traffic turned out to be unusually light for a Monday morning, which momentarily had her freaked that she'd forgotten a holiday or something. In retrospect, she realized she was probably so late that she had actually missed the big rush.

With less than a minute to spare, Carino plowed through the glass rotating doors into the main lobby of her building. Sammy was standing post, as usual, with a wide smile plastered across his jowly face.

"Good mornin', ma'am."

"Hi, Sammy. How's it going today?"

"Never better, Miss Carino." His standard response always made her smile, even on her worst day.

Abby had recently told Carino that Sammy's wife just completed her first round of chemo for a tumor the doctors had found in her brain, and his daughter had just gotten accepted into one of the Ivy League colleges—Brown, if she remembered correctly. She figured he was burning the candle at both ends, so she knew he'd been better.

"Well, that's good to hear, Sammy." Carino turned toward the elevator bank before it got any later.

"You have yourself a good day now."

She turned and waved at him, saying a quick, silent prayer that his wife pulled through.

Carino stepped out of the elevator and immediately saw Abby involved in a heated conversation with Jason, one of the other admin assistants. They stopped talking as soon as Abby caught a glimpse of her through the glass doors, and Jason hurried off down the hall toward the restrooms, glancing sheepishly at Carino as he passed by. She frowned and shot Abby a questioning glance as she approached her desk.

"Oh, it's nothing." Abby waved her hand in front of her face, as if to clear the air. She appeared flustered, which was a look Carino didn't often see on her.

"It didn't seem like nothing. In fact, it looked like *something*."

"Really, it's no biggie!" Abby's reddening cheeks gave away her lie.

"If you don't tell me what's going on, I'll be forced to assume you're sleeping with him and having his illegitimate baby, which you just told him you were keeping but he wants you to have—"

"Okay, enough!" She abruptly stood, causing her chair to shoot backwards and bump noisily into a filing cabinet. "It's nothing like that! Jason is married!"

"Duh. That's why I said *illegitimate* baby!" Carino hadn't seen Abby this rattled in a long time; pushing her buttons was actually quite amusing.

"Carino! No, you don't understand!" She finally met Carino's gaze. "Word somehow got out that you were going to dinner with Ramon, and Jason was asking me for more details—which I didn't give him, by the way."

"Okay, not what I would have guessed." The hairs on the back of Carino's neck stood up. "How did anyone even find out? You're the only one I told and *I* didn't even know I was going to have dinner with him until after I left work on Friday!"

"Well, I might have accidentally let one harmless, itty-bitty piece of information slip when me and a few of the girls from Admin met up for drinks after work on Friday night … " Her voice trailed off as she concentrated on wiping an invisible smudge off of the countertop.

"Abby! What the—? Why?" Carino's nervousness rapidly converted to anger.

"I know and I'm so sorry! I really didn't even say anything specific though." Her brown eyes became impossibly wide. "I just agreed when one of the girls said Ramon was super-hot, and said we should be jealous because we never have super-hot guys asking us out. I never even said you had decided to have dinner with him. I swear it!"

Abby's eyes began to fill with tears. Carino knew she was telling the truth and hadn't meant to start any trouble. But still …

"It's ok, Abby. I'll figure it out if anyone says anything. But you know that I'm trying to avoid people thinking I'm in my position for any reason other than my skills! I definitely don't need them to think I'm dating one of the top clients now!" Since some of the people at Franklin Everly were already bothered about her quick advancement, the last thing she needed was for rumors to start spreading that she was sleeping her way even farther up the chain to really get them worked up.

"I know, Carino! I can't tell you how sorry I am." Abby slumped back down into her chair.

Carino did her best to placate Abby before heading to her office, fully expecting a chorus of "Ramon and Carino, sitting in a tree" to break out at any moment. She carefully avoided making eye contact with anyone, and prayed this situation would blow over quickly, once something more interesting came along to feed the gossipmongers. She should be focusing on staying under the radar, and seeing Ramon was obviously not the way to accomplish that. And yet, she still couldn't bring herself to cancel on him.

She exhaled a relieved sigh upon entering her office unscathed, and sat down at her desk to boot up her computer. She should've known her reprieve would be short-lived; she'd only been able to read one email when the shit hit the fan.

"What do you think you are doing, Carino?" Raj barged into her office, arms akimbo.

Carino jerked her head around toward him, completely startled. "Reading my emails."

What the hell does it look like I'm doing?

"You know full and well that's not what I'm talking about." His petite frame vibrated with ill-contained fury.

Patience already paper-thin, she turned her chair fully toward him and clasped her hands together on top of her desk. She could only guess he was there because of the Ramon rumors, so she mentally geared up for a confrontation that she'd never envisioned having with Raj. Someone higher up? Possibly. But not Raj.

"It sounds as if you have an issue you'd like to discuss with me. Please, come in and have a seat." Carino calmly motioned toward her guest chair, hoping to diffuse the mounting tension before the rest of the staff latched onto yet another juicy encounter.

"What I have to say to you will not be in the form of a discussion; it is a one-way exchange and you need to hear me loud and clear. Stay. Away. From. Him." Raj's unwavering stare was borderline menacing, as he advanced into her office.

"I'm afraid I don't know who you're talking about." She could feel her temperature rising as she struggled to rein in her temper before saying something too costly. Or before she got up and pounded his tiny ass into the floor.

"Stay away from Ramon. This is not a request."

"The last time I checked, Raj, I only answer to you during working hours. I'm free to see whomever I please afterwards. Or beforehand."

Cringing, and focused on what surely involved a mental picture of Carino waking up next to a sleepy-eyed Ramon, he continued with his barrage.

"Carino, I'm sure you can tell from the look of my face and the tone in my voice that this is a grave matter. You are strictly forbidden to see him."

"*Strictly forbidden?*" She nearly choked on her words, she was so taken aback. "I'm certain that's not what you just said. I'm a grown woman and you are completely out of line!"

Red flags were flying everywhere! But Carino was exerting so much control over herself that she couldn't even begin to scrutinize the situation logically.

As if suddenly realizing he was acting like an irrational idiot, Raj visibly softened his stance and wilted into the chair she'd previously offered. Taking a deep breath, he spoke in a calmer voice. "Carino, I know I'm not allowed to order you around. But you just don't know who Ramon is. He is trouble and his mere presence stains everyone around him. I'm trying to protect you!"

"Protect me from what?" Undoubtedly, he knew something about Ramon that he wasn't telling her. And if he knew about the nature of Ramon's involvement with Emerson, that meant he knew about Emerson too.

Is Raj one of Emerson's men as well? He can't be!

"Things you don't understand."

"So explain them to me."

Looking more defeated by the second, he shook his head and rubbed his palms into his eyes.

"While I appreciate your concern, Raj, it's misplaced. I'm a grown up and you have nothing to worry about. Now if you'll excuse me … " She hoped he would take the hint and leave since she was angry with him for interfering in her personal life, not to mention she was struggling to hide her shock and disappointment that he might actually be involved in the illegitimate side of Emerson's crooked world.

Without another word, Raj abruptly stood and left her office as quickly as he had entered. Carino sat back in her chair and pondered what had just happened. Raj was an enigma; always the gentleman, he'd never once made her feel inferior or irresponsible—until now. She also felt naïve for not recognizing sooner that he was somehow involved in furthering the dirty side of Emerson's business. Aside from that, she was infuriated that he'd taken it upon himself to have an opinion on who she saw and in what capacity, no matter who the person was. Had he cited office policy, she would've understood. But he didn't; he'd made it personal.

When she'd first begun her investigation into Emerson's illegal activities, she'd ruled Raj out as being a part of Emerson's group, since she'd found nothing in the records to indicate otherwise. In fact, this was the first time he'd ever even alluded to knowing there was a shady element to Emerson's business.

For all intents and purposes, Raj had been her boss for the past few years. For the most part she respected him, which was all the more reason she should be heeding his warning about Ramon. Was she really in danger from Ramon? And, if so, why wasn't she more worried?

In light of what had just happened, she would now have to officially add Raj to the investigation list. Even as she thought it, she knew it was ridiculous and irresponsible—not to mention career-damaging—to notify the director about Raj but not Ramon. And yet, she still chose to only mention Raj.

. . .

Concentrating on her work proved challenging, but Carino had put so much on the back burner while working on Emerson's latest transaction that she really needed to focus and catch up, before it became impossible. She had people counting on her ability to do a good job—both at Franklin Everly and at the Bureau.

She managed to return numerous emails and phone calls, and completed several time entries in the firm's billing system, hopefully escaping another nastygram from Payroll—and all before lunch! Raj didn't speak to her for the rest of the day, which was either because he regretted his outburst from the morning or was manic because he'd discovered she was going out again with Ramon. Either way, it didn't matter; her give-a-shit factor was currently at an all-time low where he was concerned.

Carino's rapidly-changing opinion of Raj had simmered just below the surface all day, and by mid-afternoon, she knew she needed to vent to someone about their earlier confrontation. Conveniently, Abby had a huge crush on one of the cashiers at the Starbucks across the street, so Carino knew she wouldn't turn down an invitation for an afternoon coffee break. Since Abby liked to gossip, Carino also wanted to probe her a little to find out if anyone had noticed her and Raj's heated exchange. Plus, Abby would most likely welcome the time together to make absolutely sure Carino wasn't still pissed about her little slip-up from earlier.

"You've gotta be shitting me!" Abby's exclamation drew several disapproving looks from the other patrons within earshot.

"Nope! He came in seconds after I'd sat down, and proceeded to *lay down the law*."

"Yeah, who does he think he is, your dad?" Her shoulders sagged as she realized what she'd said. "I'm sorry. I didn't even think … "

"Nah, it's ok. Plus, I already know Dad wouldn't approve, if he were here." Even though she was referring to her fake dad, she knew her real father wouldn't approve of Ramon either.

"So, are you still going to go out with Ramon tonight?"

"Definitely!" Even though there were countless reasons why she should say no, Carino replied without hesitation, unable to keep the smile from spreading across her face.

"What the hell was Raj thinking anyway? It's not like you need encouragement to go out with a seriously hot and sexy foreigner, but doesn't he know forbidden fruit tastes the best?" She used her best sultry voice, but the effect was diminished when she raised her eyebrows up and down suggestively.

Carino couldn't help but laugh out loud. "So true! But seriously, Raj was uber-angry. I've never seen him like that before. I can only imagine how unhinged he would become if he found out about tonight!"

"I wonder what his deal is anyway." Abby's contemplations were shut down because it was their turn to order, and all talk of Ramon and Raj was replaced with Abby's flirtatious giggles and Carino's gagging noises—which Abby later said she didn't think were very funny.

As the workday finally came to a close, Carino gathered her things, double-checked that her computer was off and all paperwork was secured, and headed off to the bathroom to change.

Abby winked at her as she walked past the reception area, and she could feel her face flame. She knew she was flirting with disaster where Ramon was concerned, but he was just so dang appetizing!

Carino kept repeating her mantra: she was only going out with him to help him pass the time while he was in town, and to gather information about what he was really doing in Denver—and maybe some intel she didn't already know about Emerson.

But she knew she was lying to herself. She'd been counting down the minutes until she saw him again, and her heart was racing like a thoroughbred at the prospect of what tonight might bring.

Chapter 10

The task reminder on Ramon's phone chimed, signifying he needed to call Emerson and provide an update on the progress he'd made toward finding the informant. He was currently sitting at a table in the back corner of the restaurant where he was meeting Carino, but since he'd gone early, unable to contain his nervous energy within his hotel room any longer, he knew he'd have time to make the call before she arrived.

He dialed Emerson's private line, anxious to get the conversation out of the way so he could enjoy his night, unfettered.

"Status?" Emerson rarely bothered himself with pleasantries, but sadly, Ramon had become so accustomed over the years to his mannerisms that his brusqueness didn't even faze him anymore.

"Still filtering through records." Ramon was cognizant of the fact that he was sitting in a public place and Emerson's was the only secure line; he kept his answer appropriately vague.

"What's causing the delay?"

"There's a lot of information to sort through, so it's taking more time than I had initially thought to firm up an identity."

"Are you focusing on anyone in particular yet?"

"Not really, just trying to get a feel for everyone at this point." Ramon didn't mention Abby's name, since it was still too early in the investigation.

"So, you don't think that sexy little broad you've been spending time with has anything to do with it taking you so long?"

Like a match to gasoline, Ramon's anger ignited. "No, I don't."

"When Raj called earlier to let me know he was concerned that your interest in one of his top paralegals was clouding your judgment, I must say it did seem a little out of character. In all the years I've known you, I don't recall you ever mixing business with pleasure."

Ramon shook his head in disbelief. Raj had contacted him that morning to say that he'd procured the personnel files and wanted to meet Ramon after work to deliver them. Ramon wasn't surprised, as Raj undoubtedly had ways of obtaining any information he needed within the firm. But Ramon had told Raj he would be busy with Carino—again—and would let him know when he had some time available. And it wouldn't be tonight, because it was going to be a late one.

The effect had been immediate. Raj had been furious, obviously more than he'd initially assumed, since he couldn't remember him ever snitching to Emerson about any of their other problems.

Since Emerson obviously knew about his interest in Carino, he didn't see any reason to deny it. "Yes, I'm seeing her, but simply because I need to get close to someone on the inside. You act as if I've never done this before."

"Fair enough." Emerson clearly detected the haughty tone in Ramon's voice. "I hope next time we speak you'll have something better to report."

And with that, the line went dead.

Ramon barely suppressed the urge to smash his phone on the floor, recognizing at the last second that it was his main line of connection to Carino. As he sipped his glass of wine, he moderated his breathing, trying to calm down before she got there.

Carino was the only good thing in his life right now and he didn't want to scare her off, yet every time he imagined her uncovering the wretched details of his past, he nearly choked from the pain in his chest. Would he be able to merely explain away the lives he'd permanently altered by his own hands? It seemed the more her presence seeped into his world, the brighter the spotlight shone on his dirty deeds.

Ramon had grown weary of living a double life and fighting the continuous battle between the man Emerson had twisted him into and the man he knew he truly was. If it was within his power, Carino would only ever see his decent side, but sooner or later he knew his laundry would be aired. He could only hope that when the time came she would find it within herself to forgive him, because the thought of never seeing her again caused his heart to palpitate.

Ramon checked the time on his phone again, anxious for 5:30 to roll around. Unaccustomed to feeling much of anything anymore, the anticipation he felt about seeing Carino was so strong that he was barely able to restrain himself from waiting for her by the front door. But above all, he wanted the evening to be perfect, which had made it easy to shell out $450 for what he hoped would be impressive seats at the Pepsi Center.

He'd been a victim of dragging time all day long, eventually burying himself in his investigation just so he could make it until his date with Carino. He'd focused on the review of a transaction Raj's team had worked on for the acquisition of some land in Chile a couple of years ago by one of Emerson's newly established joint ventures. It was one of the first files Carino had helped with and he'd felt like he was getting a private tour of her past by reviewing some of her handwritten notes and scribbles on various papers that had been scanned and saved in the electronic file. Ramon could tell she'd been trying to demonstrate her skills to Raj, since she'd appeared to have highlighted, underlined, or commented on nearly each and every document.

He hadn't remembered the deal because, apparently, Emerson hadn't needed his services. Based on his assessment of the documents in the file, Emerson had acquired a shabby block of land and then quit-claimed it to a brand new LLC that Raj had formed for him a few weeks prior to the purchase. At that point, the LLC entered into a contract with a real estate company in Chile to manage the property, including improvements and upkeep, leasing the houses, and collecting monthly rental payments.

Ramon had no doubt Emerson was a silent partner in the Chilean company as well, just as he was sure Raj had also helped broker Emerson's purchase of the land to begin with—off the books, of course. Assuredly, Emerson had scammed some chump out of the property for a miniscule purchase price, using the threat of bodily harm as his final bargaining chip.

Cross-referencing to online records, Ramon had come across an article with a corresponding picture in one of the local Chilean newspapers, which displayed Emerson shaking hands with a familiar face from his past. Grimacing, he'd immediately understood why Emerson hadn't asked for his services; he'd known Ramon wouldn't have accepted the job. He was resolute about not becoming involved with anyone from the cartel again.

Joaquin Morales, the other man in the photo, had looked older but still completely recognizable. It had amazed Ramon that Morales had never been proven to be involved in any actual crime, but Ramon supposed that was because he had people at all levels of law enforcement in his pocket.

The earliest article Ramon had found painted Emerson as an "*económico santo*", or economic saint, who took an almost philanthropic interest in the ramshackle area. Being the Good Samaritan, he was would set about restoring it, with the help of local businessman Morales.

He hadn't been sure if the author was just naive, or if he was simply another yes-man, compensated to portray the two men in a pleasant light. Ramon had wondered how public opinion would change if people discovered just how many of the residents were duped into becoming employees of the cartel in exchange for a so-called better life.

Upon reviewing one of the bank statements in Franklin Everly's file, he'd seen several large incoming wire transfers from the

Chilean company to the new LLC's checking account, each one around $20,000 USD, presumably reported as down payments and rental income. Someone had drawn a star beside each deposit, but Ramon hadn't been certain if they signified proper payment had been received or indicated a different connotation altogether.

He'd turned his attention back to the Internet search results, finding a more recent article showcasing the neighborhood as a thriving residential area—written by the same author, of course. An updated photo had shown that the properties were in slightly better condition than before, but still appeared run down. Only a few of the roads were paved, the paint on the houses was peeling badly, and there were saggy power lines draping down from slanted poles. There definitely hadn't been as much trash littering the yards and most of the junk cars had been removed which, Ramon had reluctantly admitted, were definite improvements.

But what had truly captured his attention was the solitary person pictured in the photo. He was young, but haggard well beyond his years, evident even though he wasn't looking at the camera. He had a large backpack slung over one shoulder, was wearing a dingy tank top that Ramon assumed had been white at some point, and had a bandana loosely tied around his neck. He had ripped jeans and some sort of sneakers on, and it looked like he could really use a sandwich.

Ramon had recognized him for what he was, since he was the mirror image of himself when he was Morales's employee, before he'd worked his way up through the ranks. Stashing away enough cash to buy his own warehouse had taken many years, but at least the rental income had ultimately gotten him off the streets.

There was no doubt that the young man's bag contained a jumble of drugs and money, and Ramon has been able to make out the bulge of a gun in his waistband. He was standing in the walkway leading up to one of the nicer houses, probably because Morales viewed him as one of his more valuable employees and had upgraded his living conditions accordingly. Ramon had bet he had already killed someone, or would in short order, and had definitely recruited numerous fresh suppliers that would expand Morales's web even farther.

The more he'd contemplated the scenario, he'd known full well he wasn't going to find anything particularly incriminating about the transaction; at first glance, everything was in place. But there had been no doubt in his mind that a deeper review of the LLC's bank accounts would surely reveal systematically increasing monthly deposits, which of course would continue to be identified as rental proceeds. The deposits would significantly grow over time, which would be falsely attributed to improved living conditions and, consequently, increased rents.

The properties would be reported as always being fully occupied, even if they weren't. The subsequent checks from Emerson's LLC to various companies in Chile, seemingly for the upkeep and improvement of the area, would be around twenty percent less than the "rental income"—which was really just Emerson's fee. Since all receivers would be part of the cartel, it was Emerson's money cleansing cycle at its finest.

As Ramon took another sip of his wine and checked the time once again, he thought back about what he'd found in Franklin Everly's file. To the average person, the whole thing would seem legitimate enough. Emerson's commendation for rejuvenating a derelict area of a Latin American country, while stimulating the local business economy, appeared accurate. Except Ramon knew it was really just another way Emerson was helping to increase the cartel's footprint in Chile, which was sure to result in massive kickbacks to him, and his ever-expanding network, for years to come.

Emerson's entire operation was a well-oiled, international machine that had been running efficiently for years, as no one had ever been foolish enough to risk turning him over to the Feds.

Only his most trusted inner circle ever got close enough to get any real dirt on him, and they would never bite the hand that fed them out of a diamond-encrusted bowl with a platinum spoon. Ramon assumed the Feds had been sniffing around for quite some time, but Emerson's extra-curricular activities had been no more than a topic of speculation; no one had ever been remotely close to obtaining any real proof of anything illegal ... until now. He just didn't know what exactly they had on Emerson.

Ramon couldn't remember ever feeling this disgusted about Emerson's conquests, or as disappointed with his part in their design. But this was also the first time he had a reason to want to be perceived as a good person. As someone who was worthy of redemption, not as a monster who fostered this predatory industry.

Somewhere deep inside, a thought began to take form: maybe he didn't want to find the informant after all.

Chapter 11

As soon as Carino stepped out of her office building, the cold air sliced through the opening of her jacket, prompting her to hurriedly zip it closed. The mixture of icy air and the slight wind that had picked up during the afternoon caused her eyes to immediately water, dashing the recent touch-up efforts to her mascara. Having decided earlier it would be too much trouble to find a downtown meter on game day, she'd left her car in the parking garage. Walking briskly to the intersection, she waited to catch the next shuttle bus down to Market Street, shortening the walk to the restaurant as much as possible.

Her heart was still thumping a furious rhythm in her chest at the thought of spending the evening with Ramon. She tried to tell herself it was only because she was excited about going to the game, but she would be lying—and poorly at that. Regardless of the cause of her anticipation, she had to get a grip before she saw him, or run the risk of acting like a complete idiot.

Loitering in the dark recesses of her mind was the reminder that she really shouldn't be seeing Ramon in a personal capacity, but if she used her time wisely by getting to know more of the ins and outs of Emerson's business practices, she could justify their time together … to a point. His intimate knowledge of the inner workings of Emerson's operation was a rarity and she shouldn't waste any opportunity to strengthen her case file. But the memory of Ramon's intense sex appeal quickly overrode her sensibility, and she was right back to acting like an anxious, horny teenager on prom night.

The tantalizing smell of fried rice wafted into her nostrils as soon as she stepped through the restaurant's front door. PF Chang's was popular at this time of day, but since it was the tail end of happy hour she noticed there were a few available tables.

Quickly checking the time on her iPhone, she saw that she had about ten minutes before she was due to meet Ramon, so she jetted off to the ladies' bathroom for a final inspection of her appearance. No sooner had she pushed the door open did her phone buzz in her palm, indicating a new text message.

I hope you didn't change your mind and leave.

Carino's heart skipped a beat.
He was watching for me!
All manner of witty comebacks echoed through her head, but all she managed to tap out in reply was, "LOL, no."

She tucked her phone into her jeans pocket, quickly restored the flyaway hairs that had escaped her ponytail and made sure she didn't have black rivulets of mascara running down her cheeks. Hastily, she checked her nostrils to make sure the coast was clear there too. Satisfied that she was looking her best, she headed back the way she came.

Carino spotted Ramon sitting against the far wall near the bar, so she bypassed the hostess and made her way toward the table. He was concentrating on his phone, but glanced up in her direction before she was even halfway there. Instantly, his gorgeous face broke into that wide grin she'd quickly grown to enjoy and he stood up to greet her.

She loved his style. His outfit, a dark gray cashmere sweater with a white collared shirt underneath, was simple yet absolutely sexy. White cuffs stuck out from the sweater sleeves and he had them pushed slightly up his well-defined forearms. She liked that he wasn't flashy, even though he totally could've been. In fact, the only adornment she could see was a sleek, silver watch that probably cost more than her car.

Carino floated toward him on a cloud, hypnotized by his lithe movements as he took a step closer and stretched out his hand.

His fingers curled around hers as she slid her right hand into his, her skin tingling on contact. She wasn't sure if it was because she was still cold and he was deliciously warm, or if it was because of the electricity that was suddenly crackling between them. Either way, it felt amazing and she didn't even mind when he pulled her in closer to plant a gentle peck on her blushing cheek, causing her left hand to land on his broad, well-defined chest.

Lingering after his kiss, he whispered into her ear. "You are breathtaking, *mi Cariño*, and as always the mere sight of you has captivated me."

His stubble felt enjoyably scratchy against her cheek and he smelled so manly that Carino unconsciously closed her eyes and breathed deeply. The softness of his sweater was a thoroughly enjoyable contradiction to his hard body, and she had to restrain herself from rubbing her hands all over him. To feel the sweater, of course.

Powerless otherwise, she let out a soft sigh. Her knees began to buckle and she needed to reach her chair for support before she fell at his feet like a star-struck groupie.

"I trust you are doing well today?" She felt his words rumble deep in his chest, reminding her of their intimate display.

Recovering her wits—somewhat—she nodded in answer to his question and hastily removed her hand. She managed to keep herself from face-planting as she sat down, removed her jacket, and placed her purse on the far edge of the table. Considering how off-kilter she was, those were actually major accomplishments.

Raj's words suddenly began playing over and over in her mind, like a bad song on repeat; she fought to ignore his unsolicited warning. "And how about you?"

His grin returned, causing slight crinkles to appear at the corners of his beautiful, brown eyes. "Much better now."

Clearing her throat and smiling from the compliment, Carino picked up the menu and tried to steer the conversation away from dangerously tempting territory. She desperately needed to fortify her internal boundaries and get control over her raging hormones, which of course shot into overdrive the moment she'd laid eyes on him. "I'm starving! Have you ever had their Chicken Lettuce Wraps? They're to die for."

Ramon signaled for the waitress, who rushed right over. "We would like an order of your Chicken Lettuce Wraps, please."

Completely fawning over Ramon while surreptitiously ignoring Carino, the waitress giggled some sort of affirmative reply and sashayed away before even asking for Carino's drink order.

Oh yeah, her tip just got a whole lot smaller.

Truthfully, she couldn't really fault the behavior because Ramon was dazzling, and his raw, animal magnetism seemed to neutralize all form of cohesive thought processes. In females anyway. Yet he hadn't even given her the time of day, which totally boosted Carino's self-confidence.

"So, have you gotten to do any sightseeing since you've been in town?" She needed to focus on something trivial. Anything. As long as it would keep her from fixating on his hotness.

"Not really, since I've been pretty busy doing some work for Emerson. But I'd like to, since I've never been here for longer than a day or so on previous trips."

It crossed Carino's mind again that she still didn't know what, exactly, Ramon did for Emerson. But she hated to admit that, right now, she didn't actually care. She knew that no matter what his reason was for being in Denver, it certainly couldn't be for anything good and she highly doubted he would tell her anyway. Not wanting to spoil the night before it even got started, she passed up what she knew was a prime opportunity to question him about his "work."

"That's unfortunate, since there really are a lot of things to see and do around here."

"I should have some free time coming up, and can think of no better way to tour the area than with a fantastic guide like you. Would you be interested in taking me for a spin?"

Carino stifled a laugh at the double entendre. "I think I'm available for a little while on Wednesday."

The waitress came back to the table with a tray containing three small, round dishes and proceeded to mix up a spicy concoction that was supposed to complement their food. Carino couldn't make out too much of the explanation since the waitress was facing Ramon the entire time. She was about to get upset when she looked at Ramon and realized he was gazing back at her across the table, completely ignoring everyone else. His look ignited her desire, and a smoldering fire began burning deep inside.

Flashing a mega-watt smile, he picked up his menu and opened it to the wine list. "What do you feel like drinking tonight?"

She'd already decided she was not about to risk losing her head from having too much alcohol. "I'll have a diet soda."

He peered over the menu and raised his eyebrows inquisitively. "Could I interest you in sharing a bottle of wine with me?"

"Okay."

So, I have no willpower. What of it?

At that moment, her phone vibrated in her pocket. She pulled it out, gaping at the caller ID before quickly clicking the power button to stop the incessant buzzing. As quickly as possible, she stowed it away in the front pocket of her purse, unwilling to allow anyone to intrude on her date with Ramon—most of all *Nathan!*

But the call had more than snapped her out of the spell Ramon had cast the moment she'd walked in the door. She was now engrossed with thoughts about why she'd gotten a call from him, out of the blue. When she'd reported his behavior after he'd nearly blown her cover before, he'd taken it so personally that she rarely ever dealt with him, even through official channels. And now, he'd broken protocol *again*. Of course, since she hadn't reported

Ramon as being one of Emerson's business associates, she was really freaked out that Nathan had figured things out for himself. If that was the case, she was royally screwed.

Carino felt dazed, viewing the room through a dream-like filter. Focusing her efforts on ignoring the cold sweat that had broken out across her body and trying to act normal, she centered her attention on the incredible man sitting across the table from her. But, truth be told, she was dumbfounded about why she was placing him in front of everything else of importance in her life. She'd only known him for a matter of days and already she was risking what mattered to her the most: her career.

Ramon fixed his gaze on her and she noticed his forehead was deeply furrowed, causing his thick eyebrows to draw downward into a point. Carino glanced at her water glass, surprised ice crystals hadn't formed on the surface from the abruptly frigid air that now surrounded them.

She knew there was no way Ramon could've known who was calling, but suddenly the atmosphere at their table had dramatically changed—and not in a good way.

Chapter 12

Carino's reaction to her phone call might've gone unnoticed by the average Joe, but Ramon knew panic when he saw it. And it most certainly had been panic that crossed Carino's face before she tucked her phone inside her purse.

"Is everything okay?" Ramon could see the whites of Carino's eyes all around the green middle, and her face had gone devoid of color. He wanted to flat-out ask who had called, but knew it wasn't any of his business.

"Um, yeah. I just, uh, I wasn't expecting to hear from that person again is all."

"Is there anything I can do?"

Carino pressed her lips together into a tight line before shaking her head. "Thanks, but no. He'll get the hint eventually, when I don't return his calls."

Irrationally, Ramon's mind suddenly filled with unsolicited, offensive images of her with another man. Just the thought of someone else touching her, bringing her to new heights of pleasure, infuriated him to the point of near collapse. It was unadulterated torture.

His body hummed with illogical and barely-contained jealousy, mixed with a smidgen of bloodlust. He clenched his hands so tightly against his menu that he left impressions of his fingers in the hard material. He knew he only had a split second to get himself back under control, or he was going to turn into a caveman, beating his chest and marking his territory.

Thankfully, the waitress chose that moment to arrive with their appetizer, effectively interrupting his tantrum. He managed to order the wine, but couldn't even think about his entrée, so he simply copied Carino when she ordered Crispy Honey Chicken.

"Would you excuse me for a moment?" Ramon stood so abruptly, he caused the legs of his chair to scrape across the floor.

"Of … of course." Her voice faltered, indicating that maybe he wasn't displaying as much control as he'd hoped.

Praying that his tone and demeanor didn't mirror the pure, undiluted rage coursing through his veins, he focused all his efforts on placing one foot in front of the other as he purposefully strode toward the restrooms. He could feel Carino's eyes boring into his back the entire time, but didn't dare turn around.

Powerless against the feelings of possessiveness that were assaulting him, he burst into the restroom, not caring if there were other occupants. The door banged against the wall so hard as it swung open, he'd be surprised if the handle hadn't left an imprint. He entered the nearest stall, locked the door behind him, and leaned against the wall. Clenching his fists, he closed his eyes and counted to ten. Twice. His breathing slowly began to return to normal as he started mentally talking himself down from the ledge.

Obviously, he was acting like a certifiable lunatic, and it wouldn't surprise him one bit to find the table empty when he returned. But for some reason, the mere thought of Carino and another man was more than he could handle.

She's mine, damn it!

Well, actually she wasn't. They'd known each other for all of four days and here he was acting like a jealous fanatic who had just discovered a cheating spouse.

"Way to turn on the charm." He was suddenly bursting with self-loathing as he left the stall.

Ramon had become well acquainted with his hot temper over the years, but was incredibly frustrated that he'd allowed it to penetrate their otherwise lovely evening. Who knows, Carino might have even volunteered information about who called, had he not envisioned the worst and bolted.

Stopping to wash his hands and splash water on his face, he scrutinized his reflection in the mirror. Thankfully, his hasty pep talk had sufficiently calmed him down; he no longer had crazy eyes and his heart rate was gradually returning to normal.

Upon exiting the restroom, Ramon made the decision to play off his hasty departure as merely a queasy stomach, and hoped she would buy it. Honestly, he'd much rather she thought he had intestinal issues over plotting the slow, painful death of another man, simply because he had her phone number.

Thankfully, Carino was still sitting at their table and was actually dishing up their appetizer. She appeared extremely cheerful as he reached the table, which he hoped wasn't her way of overcompensating for another emotion she was experiencing— like maybe terror?

"Please accept my apologies, but I fear I have not been feeling entirely well today."

Concern etched her features. "Oh no! Would you rather skip the game and go lay down?"

With you? Yes.

"No, I'm feeling much better now, thank you."

"Maybe you just need to eat something." She offered him a green rolled-up concoction he was instantly leery of.

"You're probably right." He took a tentative bite, but found that it was surprisingly good.

"So, where were you thinking of going sightseeing?" She began steering the conversation back to their previous topic, as she filled her own dish.

Once they began discussing future plans, the dreadful feeling that his mercurial temper had turned her off completely evaporated. And even though their "future" only consisted of the next two days, at least it was a start.

Chapter 13

Carino was grateful for the timely reprieve Ramon had unknow-ingly provided by leaving the table, since it had allowed her some time to regain control of her emotions. There would be plenty of time later to scrutinize the meaning of Nathan's call, while not being subject to Ramon's examination.

Funny, she hadn't even acknowledged that Ramon's unexpected presence in her life would cause his sudden reentry, but now it made perfect sense. In fact, if she were a gambling woman, she'd bet her life that Ramon was the reason for his call tonight. Which meant that he was still watching her like a hawk—even after all this time—which set her teeth on edge.

Ah, Ramon. Well, hadn't he just swooped in and turned her simple little life completely upside down? She felt like she was inside a blender that had unexpectedly been turned on high. There was absolutely no denying that he'd wriggled his way under her skin and her life was becoming more complicated by the minute.

Since Friday morning, Carino had allowed Ramon to take over her consciousness, which meant she was thinking less and less about her true purpose for being at Franklin Everly. She knew she was getting herself in too deep, but every time she was around him she couldn't, for the life of her, remember why she needed to resist.

So, of course it was the perfect time for Nathan to call. To remind her of his invisible presence.

Damn, couldn't he have waited until after the game so I could've enjoyed the rest of my night with Ramon without being all anxious and panicky?

Carino had tried to act normal, once Ramon had returned to the table, pasting on a smile to hide her inner mayhem. She eased back into their previous conversation, hoping to seamlessly return their date to its previous mood.

"I've always wanted to visit the Garden of the Gods while I'm here, but after looking at the map, it seems like a relatively long drive."

"True, but it is well worth the effort." Carino was unable to erase the sudden vision of the two of them walking along the winding path, hand-in-hand, reveling in amazement of the reddish-orange rock monstrosities jutting up out of the ground. "Another remarkable place is Red Rocks, and it's a whole lot closer."

"I've heard of it. It's where the amphitheater is, right?"

"Yes! You know, we should totally check their event calendar to see if there's going to be a concert coming up!" Carino suddenly realized she was being presumptuous. And ridiculous. There was no way she was going to be able to further whatever this was they had going on. Yet, even as she thought about never seeing Ramon again, she was filled with a dreadful sadness.

"That would actually be great. I'd love to." His face broke into a wide grin.

Carino cleared her throat, feigning nonchalance. "Well, anyway, I could ask to get off of work a little early on Wednesday to beat some of the traffic, if you'd like to go together." She could always cancel on him later, but right here, right now, looking at him across the table, it was the only thing she could say.

"That sounds very nice, Carino. And thank you."

"You're welcome. Wait, for what?"

"For everything." His smoldering gaze threatened to make her combust on the spot.

"Two Crispy Honey Chicken dinners," announced the waitress, aka Master of Interruption, who approached carrying two steaming dishes piled high with food.

After their meal was delivered, they made small talk until their plates were empty and the bottle of wine was drained. Carino was simply unable to escape how good it felt to be with Ramon. She'd even learned some basic stuff about him, like his favorite color was green, he liked jazz and rock music, and he loved sailing on the open water.

Well, at least our taste in music is similar. But maybe he could teach me how to sail?

He glanced at his watch. "I'm having a wonderful time, Carino, but if we don't leave for the stadium, I'm afraid we'll miss tip-off."

She'd gotten so caught up in their conversation that she'd spaced out the game completely. Grabbing her iPhone from her purse to check the time, her heart sunk when she saw that she had three more missed calls. All from Nathan.

Resisting the urge to start frantically looking around to see if he was lurking in the shadows nearby, Carino swallowed repeatedly to try and remove the sudden lump that had formed in her throat. Focusing all efforts on acting natural, she nodded in agreement as Ramon waved down the waitress to bring the check. Pulling out his wallet, he withdrew a stack of cash and paid the bill.

"Thanks so much for dinner." Carino realized he had bought her food twice now. She planned to buy him a beer at the game to even out the scales a bit.

"For you, anything." He walked over to pull out her chair.

When she stood, Carino was so close to him that she could feel the heat emanating off of his body. She ever so slightly leaned into his warm embrace as he removed her coat from the empty seat and wrapped it around her shoulders.

And for a brief moment, she forgot all about conflicts of interest and missed phone calls, and simply appreciated his nearness.

• • •

"There's no way these are our seats!"

She was so awestruck that she momentarily forgot all about the growing pit in her stomach and spun around, unabashedly throwing her arms around him. He'd gotten two seats in center loge and she couldn't even believe it; she'd never been lower than the balcony before.

"I take it you're pleased?" He chuckled, returning her hearty embrace.

Carino kept her arms locked firmly around Ramon's waist for another moment before realizing she should probably ease up so he could breathe. Feeling slightly embarrassed, she began to back away from him, only to feel him pull her in tighter.

"It makes me very happy to see you happy." His gaze was soft as he took one finger and placed it under her chin to lift her face toward his. "And I'm looking forward to a lot more happiness."

Carino's breath hitched at the sincerity she saw shining in his eyes, and all she could do was nod stupidly in return.

And then it happened.

Ramon looked down at her mouth as his tongue briefly flicked across his lips, an instant before he leaned down and slowly placed a soft kiss on hers. And it was quite possibly the best feeling she'd ever experienced.

Opening eyes that she hadn't remembered closing, Carino looked up at him and smiled. She registered every detail of the moment because she wanted to remember it forever. Her memories of Ramon would have to get her through the long and lonely nights she was surely going to be experiencing very soon.

Straightening to his full height, he released her from his grasp. "Shall we take our seats now?"

Suddenly becoming aware of the crowd around them, she quickly sat down, flustered by their blatant PDA. But she didn't have too much time to wallow in shame because the announcer's voice came over the loudspeaker.

"Good evening, ladies and gentlemen, and welcome to tonight's game between the Dallas Mavericks," cue the booing, "and your very own Denver Nuggets!"

The stadium erupted into cheers, and it felt like second nature to stand up and join in.

Once the game began, everything else melted away. It was fast-paced and entertaining, and their seats were totally out of this world. Even Ramon got caught up in the energy and began yelling at the refs when they made calls that even a blind man could tell were bogus. When the buzzer sounded at halftime, Carino was actually surprised. And disappointed. The night was clipping by way too fast for her taste.

"I need to use the restroom." She stood up, stretching deeply. "Would you like something from the concession stand? I could bring you back a beer."

"That actually sounds really good. Would you like some company?"

"Oh, it's totally fine. Thanks though. I'll be back before you have time to miss me." All teasing aside, she knew she could use some alone time so she could rebuild her crumbling resolve. She didn't think she could resist, if he made any further advances; she was enjoying his company way too much.

She walked the distance up to the area where the restrooms and concessions were located, grinning like an idiot the entire way. There was no denying that she was enamored, but kept reminding herself that she needed to slow down. This was going nowhere. The fact remained that he was part of Emerson's crew, which was obviously an issue. But the more time she spent getting to know him, the harder it was becoming to reconcile the warm and inviting man he was proving to be with the type of person that would be involved in anything illegal—no matter how naïve it was for her to do so.

Deep down, Carino knew she was seeing only what she wanted to see, but in her defense he had been extremely vague about what his actual work consisted of. So really, she could be making assumptions that were way off base.

Sure, I'll keep telling myself that.

No matter what though, Carino had to find a balance between her heart and her head. Her feelings for Ramon were developing more rapidly than she could even comprehend, but she hadn't gotten this far by making rash decisions. She was so engrossed in her thoughts that she didn't see him until it was too late.

"Carino," sounded a low voice directly behind her.

She must've jumped at least three feet into the air, clutching her chest in fright and startling those standing close by.

"Holy shit!" She whirled around to come face-to-face with her accoster.

He was slightly taller than her, and was wearing a white home jersey and a light blue and yellow Nuggets snapback. Combined with his dark jeans and sneakers, he looked like any other Denver fan in the stadium.

Carino noticed his dark hair curling out from under his hat to form tiny wings around his ears, indicating he was overdue for a much-needed haircut. She also detected a severe glint in his hazel eyes, which were visible behind thin, black-rimmed glasses.

As recognition sunk in, her heart skipped a beat. "Nathan."

He abruptly seized her left elbow and turned her back around. "Just keep walking. You're causing a scene." They were immediately swallowed up by the growing halftime crowd.

"What the hell are you doing here? You're going to blow my cover." She was surprised at how calm her voice sounded.

"Just shut up and move."

Carino allowed Nathan to direct her through the massive throng of people until it seemed they were halfway around the arena from where she and Ramon had been sitting. Pushing her up against the wall, Nathan firmly secured her in place by holding her upper arms. The concrete bit into her skin, and as he leaned in close she could sense the menace rolling off of him in waves.

"Just what do you think you're doing with him, Carino?" His eyes blazed with fury.

"It's none of your damn business."

"Really? That's what you think? That it's none of my business anymore—what you do and who you see?"

"Yeah, that's exactly what I think. Oh, and let me add one more thought: you're crazy. And your beard looks like shit. Yep, that pretty much sums up what I think." Anger was beginning to conjure up courage in the face of danger.

He tightened his grip slightly, causing her to wince. "Listen to me! You're being a complete idiot right now. I'm not supposed to come around you, but that doesn't mean I don't care about what happens to you."

Yeah, that's going to bruise.

"You should've just answered the phone, Carino, because we could've avoided all of this. I want you to stay away from him. He's not the man for you."

Apparently that was the warning of the day. She glared back at him, trying her hardest to convey more toughness than she was feeling at the moment. She wondered why he was bothered to the point that he'd risk getting caught violating his no-contact order. Maybe Raj had been right and Ramon was more dangerous than she thought. That's what she got for not formally investigating him, like she should have.

"You know, I could report you for this." Carino gritted her teeth.

"Yeah, but you won't because you know I'm right."

"You don't even know him! Or me anymore, for that matter."

"And neither do you! Oh, let me guess, you've told him all about yourself? What did you tell him, huh? Did he buy your backstory? Or is he stringing you along until he finds out who you really are? Do you really think he's not going to kill you? You have the power and the knowledge to take down his boss … and most likely him too. He'll never let that happen. Use your head!"

Deep down, Carino knew he was right, but refused to give in. "I'll tell him whatever I damn well please about my life. And FYI, you don't get to dictate anything to me anymore! Now get your hands off of me before I start screaming." She took a deep breath in preparation.

He immediately released his grip and backed up.

"Consider yourself warned." He turned and walked away, quickly blending into the mass.

Carino started to respond, but froze when the crowd abruptly parted off to her right, revealing a very anxious, very angry Ramon.

Oh shit.

Chapter 14

Surfacing from the crowd, Ramon saw Carino leaning up against the wall, ashen-faced.

He hadn't wanted to force himself on her when she said she was going to get drinks, but he felt uncomfortable leaving her alone in the huge crowd. He'd managed to squelch the urge to chase after her, reminding himself that she was an adult and had taken care of herself for this long without him. But less than five minutes later, after nearly vibrating out of his seat with pent-up energy, he bolted up the nearest stairs and took off in the general direction he figured Carino had headed.

When she turned and made eye contact with him, he couldn't immediately tell if she was relieved or worried that he'd appeared. He rushed to her side, frantically checking her over to make sure she wasn't harmed.

"Are you okay?" Concern deepened his voice.

"Yes."

"Did someone hurt you?"

"No."

"Carino, what's going on? Was someone bothering you? Was that the same man who called you earlier tonight?"

Up until that point, she had kept her face tilted toward the floor. She sighed deeply and nodded before looking up at him; he noticed her eyes were brimming with unshed tears.

"Thanks for coming for me." Her chin began to quiver slightly. "But I'm fine. Really."

Ramon wasn't reassured at all. Not even a tiny bit. Even though he'd only caught a fleeting glimpse, he'd gotten a good enough look at the man who had walked away from her to be able to recognize him later when he searched the stadium's camera footage.

"Did that man hurt you?"

"No, we were just talking." She tried—and failed miserably—to brush it off like it hadn't bothered her.

"Carino, if it's none of my business, just tell me. But generally when another man is harming a woman, especially *my* woman—well, that's not something I'm going to let go lightly."

Carino swallowed hard. "I had some trouble in the past, which I thought I'd handled, but apparently not. There isn't much more to say, really. He was ordered to leave me alone and he did—until you came along. You're the first man I've spent any time with in a very long while, and I guess he doesn't like it."

"So, when I asked if I should be watching over my shoulder for a boyfriend, didn't you think this qualified?" Ramon made an attempt to lighten the extremely tense situation.

Carino laughed a little, but her body language and the way she kept fidgeting and twisting her fingers gave away her true state.

"Well, you didn't clarify that your question included psycho exes also." She tried to joke, but it was half-hearted at best.

"Touché."

"I'm really sorry I spoiled our night." She suddenly choked up again and hugged her arms around her body.

"Baby, that's impossible." He quickly pulled her close. "So, are you ready to head over to the police station?"

She tilted her head back from where it was lightly resting on his chest and he could see the determination burning in her beautiful green eyes.

"Ramon, I know you probably won't understand this, but if you care about me at all, please just walk me back to the seats you spent what I'm sure was a small fortune on and help me forget about anything other than our lovely evening together. I don't want to think about any of this right now."

It took a heroic effort on his part to honor her request, but in the end, Ramon had respect for this lovely woman who had taken him by storm. He was also man enough to give her the space she needed to deal with this on her own, no matter how badly his entire body was twitching to chase after him.

"*Mi Cariño*, it's not my place to tell you how to handle your private affairs. Please just know that I'm here for you in any way you need me." Ramon placed his palms on each of her lovely, too pale cheeks and gingerly lowered his lips to hers.

Their kiss began slowly, but quickly became more heated. Pulling away before they made a scene, Ramon noticed that at least a flush had returned to her face.

To prove that he meant what he said, Ramon reached for her hand and began walking them back to their seats. He kept her close, all the while glancing around to see if he recognized any faces in the mob of noisy people, to no avail.

Whoever he was—and Ramon was certainly going to find out—he definitely hadn't stuck around.

Chapter 15

To say she was shaken up was an understatement. She'd never imagined Nathan would seek her out, and in an extremely public place no less. Ramon was unwavering in his support and thankfully didn't push the issue of her filing a police report either. He seemed willing to respect her privacy, for which Carino was grateful. There was only so far she could take the stalker ex story, and the police station was definitely off-limits. Later, once she was home, she'd have plenty of time to decide exactly how she wanted to handle this latest wrinkle—without Ramon's machismo clouding her mind.

As Carino allowed Ramon to masterfully thread them through the crowd, she thought back upon the day Abby had encountered her and Nathan together. Up until that point, she'd never thought she would have to explain who he was, so she had been completely unprepared for the situation.

Carino had stopped after work to pick up a few groceries at the King Soopers near her house, when he'd suddenly appeared next to her; she hadn't even noticed him lurking behind the bakery counter. It had taken her a minute to even realize it was him, since she hadn't seen him in over a year. His hair was different, a little shorter, and it looked as if he was attempting to grow a beard, but it was still pretty sparse.

She was pissed. She couldn't even believe he was there, especially since her operation was intensely clandestine. Any crack in her cover would likely result in her untimely death, as Emerson was ruthless and would have her eliminated without hesitation. And, as if the situation wasn't surreal enough, Abby happened to show up at the exact moment he was trying to coax her, albeit a little too forcefully, to follow him back into the bakery so they could talk.

Even though Nathan had tried to play it off as if they were getting ready to give each other a hug, Carino's facial expression obviously gave away the fact that she wasn't exactly enjoying herself.

"Carino? Fancy meeting you here!" Abby had broken the silence that had quickly grown uncomfortable. Looking back and forth between Carino's horrified face and Nathan's, Abby had finally extended her hand toward him. "Hi, I'm Abby."

"I'm sorry, Abby, this is my … " Carino had stopped abruptly, trying to decide how she should introduce him.

He'd moved his left arm around her shoulders, securing her in place, and extended his right arm toward Abby.

Nathan had shaken her hand. "I'm Nathan, an old friend of Carino's."

"Funny, she's never mentioned you before."

Carino had wanted to bring an end to the horribly awkward situation. "Yeah, I know. I just hadn't gotten around to telling you about him yet. This is Nathan and we used to, um, go out. I just haven't seen him in a while, is all."

Realization as to why Carino was acting weird had crossed Abby's face. She knew, as well as anyone, how difficult impromptu run-ins with ex-boyfriends could be.

"Ah, I see. Well, nice to meet you, Nathan. Sorry, but I've gotta run. I'm already late for a dinner party. Luckily I'm bringing the dessert!"

"It's nice to have met you too. Take care now."

Abby had paused to look at Carino questioningly. She'd nodded slightly, signaling to Abby that she was okay. Abby had taken one last glance at Nathan, clearly unsure about the whole situation, but then she'd shrugged, grabbed a nearby plastic container of brownies, and headed off toward the cashiers at the front of the store.

As soon as Abby left, Carino had jerked free from Nathan's one-armed embrace.

"What the hell? Are you following me now? You can't just pop up unannounced like this! If you have anything to say to me, you can call. Or email me. This is not okay. And it's uncomfortable having to introduce you to my friends."

"Maybe *she's* the one following you." His face had twisted into a smirk.

"Unlikely."

"Well, how was I supposed to know she was just going to walk up on us like that?" He was immediately defensive.

"I don't know! You're the *stalker*, not me! Shouldn't your super-stalking senses have already alerted you she was here?"

"Don't push it, Carino. I only came here to remind you that I don't like it when you let people into your inner circle. It's dangerous. You don't know who you can trust and who you can't. That Abby, she likes to talk. You should really be careful about who you choose to have close to you."

"Yeah, aren't you the perfect example of that!" She was shouting, but couldn't seem to stop. "And FYI, you don't get to dictate who I associate with! And now, you'd better leave me alone so you can figure out how you're going to deal with the consequences of your actions, since I plan on reporting your crazy ass!" Carino stuck her chin out in defiance.

"I always did think you looked cute when you tried to act tough."

"Screw you!"

"Tsk, tsk, such hostility. It doesn't suit you, Carino." He'd gotten the last word before quickly disappearing behind a nearby set of double doors.

Once Nathan was out of sight, Carino had slumped down onto the handle of her shopping cart. She knew she would need to report the encounter to the authorities, but didn't relish the thought of being dragged through an investigation. But how else was Nathan supposed to get the message to leave her alone? She could take care of herself! He just needed to realize that and stop micromanaging her.

"Carino? Are you sure you're doing okay?" Ramon's question jogged her back to the present.

"Oh wow, I'm so sorry. I guess I kinda zoned out there for a bit." Carino couldn't believe they were already at the aisle where their seats were located.

Even though it felt as if a lifetime had passed since she'd gone on the ill-fated beer run, the clock on the scoreboard indicated there were still nearly three minutes left until the start of the third quarter.

Thankfully, the game provided a significant distraction from her inner turmoil. Not only did she have the Nathan fiasco to deal with, but there was also no possible way to ignore the pivotal change in her relationship with Ramon. The light and flirty mood from earlier in the evening had been shattered, but in its place was something deeper and more significant. Whatever was happening between them had suddenly morphed into what could easily become a meaningful relationship with a man who genuinely cared for and respected her.

Stealing a glance in his direction, Carino was once again blown away by Ramon's amazingly good looks. When mixed with his unexpected compassion and winning personality—well, he was a triple threat.

As if sensing her appraising stare, Ramon turned and looked right back at her, reaching out to stroke her cheek.

"I think the same thing when I look at you." He spoke softly, correctly reading her mind.

Mortified that she might've accidentally commented aloud, Carino blushed from the top of her head to the tips of her toes, but still managed to infuse some much-needed humor into the otherwise serious mood. "Wow, so you think I'm in need of a shave too?"

Ramon threw his head back and laughed heartily. "Yes! Frankly, I've been meaning to mention it all night, because it chafes a little bit when I do this."

And with that, he pulled her in for a playful kiss before rubbing his cheek back and forth against hers.

Laughing, Carino realized how ironic it was that the very warning designed to keep them apart had done nothing more than bring them closer together.

Chapter 16

Maybe he was just projecting, but Ramon swore Carino was looking at him differently now. Deep down, he hoped it was because she was developing feelings for him, as he was definitely not a supporter of unrequited love. Lust. Whatever this was that he was feeling toward her.

Ramon's gut reaction earlier had been to go completely ballistic, track the asshole down, and proceed to beat him within an inch of his miserable life, or at least until he explained why he was bothering—no, stalking—*his* woman. But that was exactly the kind of behavior Carino didn't need from him. So instead, he was pretending everything was okay and that he wasn't being consumed by the inferno that was blazing inside of him.

Thankfully, Carino hadn't started crying. That would've been his complete undoing. Another man had caused her pain and he wasn't currently using the scumbag's face as a punching bag. So, no matter how much feigned calmness he displayed, as soon as she was safely home, he was going to launch a full-blown investigation on the unidentified man. And once he found out who he was, he planned on paying the guy a friendly little visit. The asshole had crossed the line where Carino was concerned, and apparently needed a refresher so he didn't ever cross it again.

The rest of the game seemed to have vanished into thin air because before he knew it, the final buzzer went off. The Mavs had beaten the Nuggets by eight points, causing the earlier euphoria in the stadium to quickly simmer down. Unfortunately, the jubilation was replaced by hordes of disappointed fans whose emotions were amplified by the amount of beer they had consumed during the game. Of course, these same people were now piling into their cars to endanger everyone else on their respective drives home.

Ramon was wholly uncomfortable with Carino being on the road at the same time as this pack of drunken idiots, because if something happened to her, he knew he would be a broken man. Sure, he'd only known her for four days, but when something was right, time became irrelevant. Regardless of his reasons, it was late on a weeknight and he knew they both had busy days on the horizon, so she would just have to drive carefully.

An unfamiliar ache was suddenly developing deep in his chest at the thought of being away from her, and he wished they were simply heading back to his hotel together after a typical evening out. Ramon knew they weren't a couple or anything—yet—but judging from earlier events, he knew he had staked his claim. Carino was his, which she would come to realize, and hopefully sooner rather than later.

While they exited the stadium, Ramon kept his arm wrapped around Carino as he hustled them over to the line of eagerly waiting taxi cabs. All the while, he was trying to figure out whether or not tonight was a good time to start expressing some of his growing feelings for her. He started to say something, but quickly closed his mouth when she looked at him expectantly. Instead, he just smiled at her and swallowed back the words he'd foolishly been about to say.

It was too soon to push Carino for something more, especially when he was sure she was much more sensible than he was when it came to relationships; he was pretty much hot-headed about everything in his life. She had also been through too much in the past few hours for him to start piling more on her emotional plate, and he stood a much better chance of having something long-term with her if he played it cool.

Silently pining for time to somehow slow down, Ramon grudgingly settled for enjoying the remainder of their night together. Thankfully, the air had grown even colder as the night had progressed, so he knew he could prolong their date by sitting together in her car while it warmed up. At this point, he would take anything he could get.

Flagging the nearest empty cab, Ramon opened the door and helped her in. He followed and quickly slammed the door behind him in an attempt to retain more of the glorious heat.

"Good evening, folks. Where to?"

"The Brown Palace, please," Carino interjected before Ramon could respond. She scooted closer to him and leaned her head on his shoulder.

He was stunned into silence. But instead of making a big deal about it and running the risk of spooking her, Ramon chose to hug Carino closer, and laid his cheek on top of her head.

"I'm just not ready to be alone yet, so I hope you don't mind my company for a little while longer." Her voice somehow caressed him; he felt tingly from head to toe.

"Please, you can stay as long as you want."

Forever would actually be a good start.

If she was worried that he didn't want her around, he definitely needed to step up his game. Here he was being so cautious about not appearing too forward that he was apparently sending her mixed messages. He'd be changing that straightaway.

As the driver expertly navigated the increasing traffic jam, Ramon could feel Carino's body start to relax against him, and figured now was as good a time as any to say what he'd wanted to say earlier.

"Carino?"

"Hmmm?"

"My suite has a separate bedroom, and I really don't like the idea of you being alone tonight. I would really appreciate it if you would consider staying with me. I promise I'll give you all the privacy you want."

Such a long stretch of silence ensued that, for a moment, he thought she'd fallen asleep.

"I would actually like that, Ramon. But I do have to work tomorrow, so I'll need to get my stuff from my car. The Walk of Shame will be much easier if I can actually put on some mascara and lip gloss."

Ramon was not going to allow a single second to go by for her to change her mind. "Driver, please take us to the Plaza Garage on 18th and California." In his haste, he realized he'd just revealed a detail about her that she herself hadn't told him.

Maybe she won't notice?

Immediately, he felt her tense up.

Ramon cleared his throat uncomfortably. "I, uh, I asked Raj where all the employees parked, because it seemed like there are never any open spaces near your building."

Of course he was full of shit. He'd checked her out and she knew it. And he knew she knew it, from the look on her face as she lifted her head from his shoulder to look him in the eye.

Ramon held his breath as he furiously tried to come up with something else to say that would make him seem less creepy. Carino only needed one stalker in her life at a time.

"Been checking up on me, have you?" Her face broke into a grin and she lightly prodded him in the ribs.

Ramon blew out his breath in relief. "You caught me!"

"It's okay, I totally understand. I'm irresistible, so I would've been upset if you hadn't," she joked.

"Oh really, irresistible, huh?" He fully turned in the seat, grabbed her above her knees and began squeezing.

Bursting into laughter, she began furiously shoving at his hands. "No, please, I'm super ticklish!"

Stopping his torture, Ramon joined in laughing with her and leaned in for a kiss. She returned it heartily before becoming embarrassed about providing the cab driver with a rearview mirror show. She turned away from him, but not before he noticed the beautiful flush that covered her cheeks.

Chapter 17

Normally, Carino would never dream of going to the hotel room of a man whom she'd only known for a few days. But the thought of spending the rest of the night alone, worrying about Nathan and when he would pop up next, held less and less of an appeal the more time she spent with Ramon. Plus, she figured this was the beginning of the end and she wasn't ready to say goodbye quite yet.

After retrieving her bag from her car, with Ramon standing guard of course, they continued the short journey to his hotel. He paid the driver and tipped him generously, and despite her protests, took Carino's bag from her shoulder as they entered the building.

As soon as they walked in, she was enveloped by the warm colors and the ornate designs that exuded Old World luxury. "I've never been in here before." She took in the sights as they walked to the elevator. "It's quite nice."

"Yes, the view is amazing."

She realized Ramon was looking at her. Immediately, she focused on her shoes and tried her best to tamp down the butterflies fluttering in her belly.

The elevator arrived and Ramon held his hand out to her. His touch instantly sent electric currents throughout her body and she wondered if he could feel it too.

Oh boy, maybe this wasn't such a good idea after all.

During the entire ride up to the seventh floor, Ramon held her hand. She knew she was completely overthinking it, but in her opinion, holding hands was a sign of being comfortable with each other—and she was anything but. In fact, those butterflies were beginning to really churn in her stomach. One wrong move and she'd probably toss her dinner onto the floor. She could feel her breathing pick up and her heart was beginning to palpitate. Maybe she should pull her hand out of his, but he was being so sweet and she really didn't want to hurt his feelings. So, yeah, maybe she should just keep holding his hand then.

When the doors opened, she glanced in his direction to find him watching her with a lazy smile across his face. Carino drew in a sharp breath. He was just so sexy. And intimidating as hell.

Holy crap, am I really doing this?

Her confidence from earlier in the cab was nowhere to be found and her knees were starting to feel wobbly. A cold sweat broke out along her spine.

"Shall we?" He still had a hold of her hand, so Carino allowed Ramon to lead her down a private hallway, which, presumably, ended at his hotel room. His hotel room that had a bedroom. A private bedroom with a bed. Where they would be alone with only a door separating them, in the dark, for the whole entire night.

Suddenly, she felt tawdry, even though she wasn't spending the night with him. She was staying over, but not like that. Although he was really mind-bogglingly sexy and she could definitely do a whole lot worse.

Oh no, what if he thinks that's why I'm here? I did kiss him twice—and okay, those were really amazing kisses—but still!

Her mind immediately flew to what Raj—or Nathan—would do if either of them found out she'd slept with him. Well, not slept with him, but slept over.

Oh yeah, that sounds so much better!

She had been a total smart ass with Raj earlier, only now it wasn't so funny. What if she lost her job at Franklin Everly over this? She'd be ruined, as would her part in the investigation.

Shit, shit, shit, this could really turn into a big deal, and that would ruin everything. Everything I've been working so hard for these past few years.

Carino was so caught up in her own head that she didn't hear Ramon ask her a question. He stopped short, causing her to bump into him.

"Carino?" A look of alarm crossed his face as he steadied her. "You look terrified and you're as white as a sheet. Is everything okay?"

"Y-yes. I'm good. Fine. Just fine."

He released her hand, which all at once had become cold and clammy, to cup her chin and tilt her gaze to meet his.

"No, you're clearly not fine. What's going on?" Concern laced his gorgeous features, causing his dark eyebrows to draw together.

Carino looked over his shoulder and could see the door to his room, which did nothing more than cause her stomach to lurch and her head to swim. She swallowed deeply.

One would think, at age twenty-five, she wouldn't be terrified of being alone in a room with a man. But it wasn't just any man, it was *this* man. This wonderfully attractive, compassionate, fierce man she was falling for but knew virtually nothing about. This man, who had the potential to bring her carefully constructed life crashing to the ground. So, obviously she was terrified, for countless reasons.

Finally meeting his eyes, Carino blinked back sudden, outrageous tears. "I'm sorry, Ramon. I never should have come here. I feel like an idiot and I wasted so much of your time. And cab fare. I'll pay you back! But I need to go home."

She abruptly turned to head back to the elevator, only to feel his strong hand seize her around the wrist. His hand, which only moments ago had caused the most pleasant of sensations, was now an improvised prison, preventing her from escaping this maddening situation.

"Carino, please." His tone was imploring, as he released the gentle pressure around her wrist, once she turned back to face him. "I don't want you to go. Not like this. I don't know what's frightened you, but I can assure you I won't hurt you. Ever. This I swear."

"I trust you." Surprisingly, she realized she actually did. "I just—I need to go."

Ramon's eyes were pleading and she could tell he was completely sincere, yet totally confused. But still, she knew she was making the right decision.

Carino knew he could tell that her mind was made up, so he didn't try again to dissuade her. Yet another plus in his favor.

"At least let me see you safely to your car. I could never live with myself if anything happened to you."

"Okay, thank you. I would appreciate that." Her voice was small, but very much determined nonetheless.

Chapter 18

Ramon sensed a shift in the air the moment Carino changed her mind. He hadn't been totally sure if she would actually stay the night with him—although he'd really hoped she would—but knew, in reality, she was probably just trading one difficult situation for another.

She had already expressed concern about people at her firm thinking she was dating a client, so the "walk of shame," as she'd put it, was sure to be disturbing. Plus, Ramon could tell they had an energy ramping up between them, and truthfully wasn't sure he could've been a total gentleman knowing she was sleeping in his room with nothing but a flimsy set of French doors separating them.

But what he hadn't been prepared for was the look of terror on her face. It was as if she'd gotten spooked, but by what, he didn't know—and she wasn't volunteering the information either. Quite frankly, he was surprised she was going to let him go with her to her car, since she seemed to suddenly want nothing more than to get away from him as fast as possible.

During the elevator ride back to the lobby, Ramon replayed his actions in his head, reassuring himself that he hadn't done anything wrong. The last thing he wanted was for things to become uncomfortable between them; he knew they didn't have much yet, but they had *something*. And it was strong enough that he wasn't about to just let her walk away and out of his life. Not when she had just arrived.

He walked swiftly to the concierge and requested a cab, after deciding it would take too long to have his car brought around by the valet. True to form, the man began barking orders into a headset. Ramon turned to find Carino standing a few feet behind him, arms protectively folded around her chest.

Her eyes were sad, but she smiled slightly back at him, so he felt confident that he hadn't completely lost her.

Not yet, but you will.

"The cab will be here in five minutes, sir."

Ramon nodded a quick thank you and approached Carino.

"Would you like to sit down with me while we wait?" He motioned toward one of the nearby lobby seating areas.

"Yes, thank you." All manner of flirtation and humor were completely absent from her voice.

He sat directly across from her and assumed a relaxed pose, hoping to put her mind at ease that he wasn't upset about her leaving, if she was at all worried about that.

"I had a lovely time with you this evening, *mi Cariño*. I'm really looking forward to Wednesday afternoon, and sure hope the weather holds for us." Unsure if she was going to back out of their sightseeing trip, Ramon held his breath in anticipation.

"I had a great time too. Thank you so much for everything. I really mean that. For the wonderful dinner and the amazing seats at the game and for being there for me when—well, when all hell broke loose." Carino laughed, but the humor didn't reach her eyes. After a long pause, in which it seemed Ramon's heart didn't beat once, she finally said, "And I'm looking forward to Wednesday too."

He exhaled in relief that whatever had her freaked tonight wasn't stopping her from wanting to spend more time together.

Maybe that's all it was; they just needed more time. More time for Carino to see that he wasn't one of the bad guys—well, at least he wasn't going to be anymore. More time for him to spoil her, to show her how his woman should be treated. More time for her to realize that she wanted to be with him as much as he wanted to be with her. And maybe, after more time, it wouldn't seem so crazy to already be falling this hard for her.

"I want you to know that I meant what I said tonight. I won't let anyone hurt you. If you wake up tonight and feel scared, call me and I'll come get you. I don't care if it's three a.m. You can stay with me any time you want and for as many nights as you want. And I will never violate your trust. Ever." Ramon felt a slight pang as he pledged his vow, knowing his investigation would require him to dig deeper into her personal life.

For a few moments she didn't answer, and he began to worry that his intensity had finally pushed her over the edge. But then, slowly, Carino rose from her seat and squatted down directly in front of him. She took his face between her cold hands and placed a lingering soft kiss on his lips. Ramon's eyes closed of their own volition and he had to tuck his hands under his legs to keep from dragging her into his lap and ravishing her on the spot.

She pulled back, but kept her hands in place. Ramon opened his eyes and was once again stunned by her beauty, and the feel of her skin on his face was nearly his ruin.

"I believe you. And I need you to know how sorry I am to be running away right now, but I have too much going on inside my head to think straight." Her jaw was set and her look was intense.

"You can talk to me, Carino. You're not alone. Let me help you."

She let her hands fall as she rose up and slowly returned to her seat. She shook her head. "These are things I can't talk to anyone about. I just need more time to sort them out on my own."

See, she even knows that more time is what we need!

A yellow flash caught his eye over her shoulder. The cab had arrived.

"Our ride is here." He felt the frigid tendrils of loss snaking their way around his heart at the thought of letting her go. Ramon couldn't ever remember being around someone who could cause him to feel so full of life and endless possibilities, but was also capable of inflicting such emptiness at the same time.

Carino pressed her lips together in a tight line and grabbed her belongings from the seat next to her, determination causing her features to go rigid. He followed her out the door and into the cab, contrasting the coldness of this trip with their previous one of the evening.

Simultaneously, they both tried to fill the gaping void with their words.

"Ramon, I—"

"Could you please—"

"Sorry, you first." She chuckled, which brought some of the warmth back into the awkward situation.

"I was just going to ask if you would please send me a text message when you get home so I'll know that you made it safely."

Truthfully, he would already know she was safe, but he was grasping at straws to prolong their contact.

She smiled genuinely. "Of course. I was just going to reassure you that I would go straight home and would be fine. Scout's honor." She pledged her honesty, drawing a cross over her heart with her finger.

"You obviously were never a scout, because that's not how they make a pledge." Ramon laughed, demonstrating the proper way by holding up the three middle fingers on his right hand.

"Oh and you were?" She grabbed his hand and squeezed, giggling a little.

"Of course I was! Scout's honor."

At that point, they both busted up laughing. Ramon wasn't sure if it was because of the late hour, the absurdity of their conversation, or from pure hysteria. But no matter the reason, he felt much better now about letting her go home alone.

Chapter 19

With each second that ticked by her determination slipped away, and it wouldn't have taken much longer before she would've forgotten why it was so important to go home. Which was why she had been both relieved and devastated that the cab had arrived on time. Joking around with Ramon during the ride to the garage helped her to feel more like herself again, so when they pulled up to her car—for the second time of the evening—she wasn't wound quite as tight.

Earlier, as she'd sat in the hotel lobby listening to Ramon pour his heart out, she had been overcome with remorse. He was so fiercely genuine that she'd nearly changed her mind and stayed, but she couldn't be fully honest with him about her feelings, and things were happening really fast between them. She'd been on a career path for the last few years and knew she had no choice but to follow it. She had to get her life back into alignment and figure out where Ramon fit in.

If *he fit in.*

As she'd squatted down before him, reveling in the sensation of his scratchy stubble on her palms, Carino knew she would miss this feeling if she never felt it again. As she'd kissed him, she'd savored the perfect texture of his lips and his minty breath, hot and moist against her face. She'd known in that moment that he'd successfully sunk his claws into her. Sure, she would still manage to heal if they were ripped out, but knew they'd leave a permanent, jagged scar. But right then, as she'd been holding his handsome face in her hands and watching his hooded eyes gaze at her with obvious desire, Carino had wanted nothing more than to succumb to his grasp.

And that had scared her to death.

She gathered her belongings, prolonging their goodbye for a few more seconds. So many things she wanted to say were hanging on the tip of her tongue, but she settled for short and sweet. "Thanks again for such an unforgettable evening."

"It's the first of many, I hope." He opened the door so they could step out. "Driver, can you give us a few minutes please?"

The cabbie nodded, and pointedly double-checked that his meter was running.

Carino started her car and turned the heat on high, set her bag and purse down on the passenger seat, and got back out to bid Ramon a proper goodnight. He reached for each side of her open jacket and proceeded to zip it closed up to her chin, before grabbing both of her hands and rubbing them vigorously.

It was wonderful, having someone take care of her—especially a man like him. He was rich, powerful, and lethal—although she chose to ignore that last attribute—and here he was, warming her hands up like she was the most precious treasure on all of God's green earth.

"You won't forget to text me the minute you get your deadbolt locked, right?"

"I promise, I won't forget."

"And you are still going to ask to leave early on Wednesday, right?"

Smiling, Carino nodded. "Yes, I'm going to ask first thing tomorrow." And she was actually considering following through with her request, as crazy as it seemed.

"Will you let me know what time you're able to leave so I can be ready too?"

"If you're asking me if I'll call you tomorrow, the answer is yes." She couldn't contain her smile.

Abruptly, Ramon held up both hands in defense. "Wow, Carino, you're coming on pretty strong here."

They were both laughing again, and it felt great.

"Well, then I hope you like your women aggressive!"

"One woman. I only like one woman aggressive." Instantly, the mirth in his eyes turned to white hot desire.

They reached for each other at the same time, feverishly kissing away the anxiety of the last hour. Ramon advanced, and Carino felt the cold metal of her car against her back as Ramon continued his glorious assault, caging her in with his powerful arms. When he finally pulled away, the smile on his face mirrored her own and her lips felt wonderfully bruised. Their rapid breathing caused puffs of white smoke to mingle in the cold night air.

"What have you done to me?" Ramon closed his eyes and rested his forehead against hers.

"I might ask you the same question." She willed her racing heart to slow down before she had a stroke.

"If you don't leave right now, I'm not going to let you."

Carino leaned back to look at his face, and his expression told her that he was a man of his word.

"Okay." She was less committed to her decision than ever before.

Something resembling a growl escaped his lips and he used her car as leverage to push himself backwards before opening her driver's door. "I'll be waiting for your text in, what, about thirty minutes?"

"Yeah, or sooner. There's not much traffic at midnight on a Monday."

"Just be safe, baby. I'll go crazy if I don't see you again."

In spite of the cold, Carino felt warm all over. Nodding, she wobbled into her car on legs of jelly.

"G'night, Ramon."

"*Mi Cariño.*"

The last thing she saw as she pulled away were his dark, gorgeous eyes watching her leave.

Chapter 20

Ramon saw her across the room and gave a little wave, not wanting to tip off anyone at her office party to their budding relationship. Carino returned his gesture with a deceptively innocent
smile, adding a sexy wink to really get his blood pumping, before
resuming her conversation with a tall blonde woman.

The explosion happened so unexpectedly that he didn't even
have time to react. Everyone hit the floor. Glass and other debris
were flying everywhere. The fire alarm rang with a vengeance,
adding to the cacophony of terrified screams.

In slow motion, Ramon saw Carino collapse under a bookshelf
that had been displaced from the force of the blast. Both of her
legs became trapped and she furiously thrashed around, struggling
to break free. As if plodding through wet cement, Ramon's
movements were thick and sluggish as he strained to reach her.
He looked to her left and saw several masked men rushing the
place, all brandishing various calibers of weaponry. Someone was
chanting her name loud enough for him to hear over the din of
the alarm.

Ramon flailed his hands in a futile effort to make purchase
with anything that would help him get to Carino. If they reached
her first he knew, in the depths of his soul, they would surely kill
her. Because those were the types of men that populated his world.
The types of men he'd now subjected her to by their involvement.

All at once, one of the men recognized her and waved the
others over. She was still trapped when the apparent gang leader
approached her and put his gun to her head. Ramon didn't need
him to take off his mask to know it was Raj, and neither did she.

Terrified, Carino reached up and grabbed the gun's muzzle.

"No, Raj, noooo!" Her desperate cry was deafening.

Ramon screamed and Raj looked his way, his eyes glinting with cold, putrid rage. "She's. Not. Yours." He squeezed the trigger.

Ramon shot out of bed, sweat pouring down his body, still shouting her name. His heart was jackhammering inside his heaving chest and the sheet was balled up tight within his iron fists. It took him a minute to realize he wasn't still hearing the fire alarm, but instead the GPS tracking alert on his phone.

He snatched the device off the nightstand and looked at the time: 7:40 a.m. No wonder the alarm was going off, as Carino seemed to have deviated from her programmed itinerary. She must've overslept, as the alert showed she was just now leaving her house.

He blinked away the moisture that had collected in his eyes so he could see enough to silence the alarm. He sat still for several minutes more, focusing on a spot on the far wall and breathing slowly in an attempt to regain his shattered composure.

"It was only a dream." He tried to reassure himself, but the images wouldn't seem to dissipate.

Ramon whipped his head toward the door, as a series of sharp raps rang out. Instinctively reaching for the 10mm Glock tucked under his pillow, his senses were instantly hyper-focused. Sliding into the robe he'd draped over the chair next to the bed, Ramon eased into the sitting room and silently padded his way closer to the door, gun in hand and back to the wall.

Knocking ensued again, harder and longer this time, and he quickly moved to the door under cover of the noise. Slowly easing onto his toes, Ramon peered through the peephole to get a better look.

Riddled with confusion, he quickly stowed his pistol in the rear waistband of his underwear, disengaged the bar latch, and yanked the door wide open.

"Holy geez, you startled me!" Carino screeched, jumping back at least a foot.

"What are you doing here?" She visibly flinched at his sharp tone.

"I, um, I thought I would stop on my way to work and surprise you with a coffee." Her eyes darted back and forth between him and the hallway. "You know, as an apology for falling asleep on the phone last night while we were talking." Last night, Carino had called when she got home, instead of texting, and they'd ended up talking for nearly two hours before Ramon heard soft snores drifting over the line.

He registered the white cup in her hand with the unmistakable green Starbucks logo. "Maybe I should just go." She began to turn away.

"No! Stay! I mean—shit!" Ramon ran his hands through his hair in exasperation. "I'm sorry, I was just surprised. I didn't expect you to be standing here because I thought you were running late and I had a dream and … " He sounded like a complete idiot.

"Running late? No, in fact I actually left my house early this morning. I had to come and personally tell you I was sorry for leaving you hanging." Her smile was tentative, but she stayed put.

"Did you drive your car?" Ramon was having trouble regaining his bearings.

She wrinkled her brow and cocked her head to the side. "Of course, silly! How else do you think I got here?"

"It's just that I thought … okay, wow. I'm still trying to shake off the sleep. And I'm really sorry about my behavior. Where are my manners? Come in, please." He moved to the side so she could enter. "And thank you for being so thoughtful as to bring me coffee. Apology accepted."

As she sidled past him, she paused to stand on her toes and plant a peck on his cheek. It took all of his restraint to stifle the sudden urge to scoop her into his arms and drag her—caveman style—to his bedroom and never let her leave.

"I took you to be an early riser. Maybe a runner or swimmer." She placed his cup on the coffee table and looked around the room, but she didn't sit down or remove her coat.

Ramon was riveted to the floor. Every time he saw her, she looked even more beautiful. Even this morning, in spite of the small amount of sleep she'd surely gotten last night. His nostrils flared as he inhaled her fresh scent. Her hair was artfully messy and his fingers twitched from the need to bury themselves in it. He yearned to have her toned legs wrapped around his waist as he—

"Ahem." She smiled and cleared her throat, snapping him to attention. "You were saying?"

"Uh, yeah, sorry." She'd totally caught him devouring her with his eyes. He surreptitiously made sure the front of his robe was properly closed, hiding the proof of his excitement. "Normally I try to work in a morning run, but this amazing woman kept me up too late last night and I couldn't seem to drag myself out of bed."

"Sounds like you're a lucky man to me."

"No complaints here." His grin stretched from ear-to-ear. "Would you please stay a while? I could order us some room service for breakfast."

"It sounds very tempting, but I definitely can't play hooky today. Your boss keeps me very busy. And Raj would shoot me if I wasn't there to help him!" She rolled her eyes dramatically.

Ramon's stomach instantly clenched and his head swam. He leaned against the wall for support as the room tilted slightly. She had no idea of the images she'd invoked by her seemingly harmless joke.

"Well then I'd just have to kill him if he did that, now wouldn't I?"

She smiled at him, then walked over and placed her hands against his chest. "Yes. I believe you would." For a brief moment,

Ramon thought she was going to kiss him again, but instead she stepped back and pulled out her phone. "Oh crap, I've gotta go or I'm going to be late. And then Raj definitely won't let me leave early tomorrow!"

She turned and began walking quickly toward the door, but paused as he spoke. "You know, a guy could get used to seeing your beautiful face first thing in the morning. And all day afterwards too."

Smiling, Carino turned around and blew him a kiss. And then she was gone.

He allowed himself exactly five seconds to bask in the lingering smell of her perfume and the pleasure that engulfed him at experiencing, first hand, this new level of comfort they'd managed to somehow reach after last night.

And then he refocused.

He had other shit to figure out, like why the hell the GPS was showing that Carino's car was still east of Denver when she was actually parked downtown.

There was absolutely no way the tracker could've fallen off, which meant someone had physically removed it. It obviously hadn't been Carino, so who was it? He'd used a high-grade, military-issue model, so who would've known that it was even a tracker to begin with? Much less, to even check for something like that on her car?

Ramon sat down on the couch and took a swig of his coffee. Damn, it was good. And she'd gotten it exactly how he liked it too: extra hot, no cream, two sugars.

He rubbed his hands over his face as he closed his eyes, trying to concentrate so he could sort out what he didn't know about this situation. He blocked out all mental images of Carino and his disturbing dream, Carino standing there in his hotel room with her tight little body and gorgeous green eyes, Carino and …

Okay, this clearly isn't working.

He strode into the bedroom hoping for a reprieve, as it was the only place she hadn't physically been—yet—and picked up his phone to review the GPS trace program. The blip was now completely gone.

Someone had killed the tracker.

Chapter 21

Carino wasn't sure how she was going to make a relationship with Ramon work, but after they'd stayed up late talking on the phone, she knew she had to give it a shot. He was just too perfect for her to pass up. They'd talked about nothing, but somehow it had changed everything. Instead of being distracted, for once, by his sultry charisma, Carino was getting to know his squishy insides. Which, of course, were turning out to be just as amazing as the rest of him.

They'd exchanged their likes and dislikes—from favorite books to what types of food their moms used to force them to eat to how many times they'd watched the movie *Scarface*. Which it turns out she'd seen more than he had.

Best. Movie. Ever.

When he'd invited her to stay this morning, it physically hurt to say no. Now that she'd been in his room, it didn't seem as scary as it had the prior evening. But even though she'd managed to momentarily suppress the memories of everything that had transpired last night, she knew she'd made the right decision by going home, and she knew it was also the right decision to get her butt to work, no matter how badly she wanted to stay.

Carino knew this thing they had between them had the potential to be all-consuming, considering the short amount of time she'd known Ramon and how deep her feelings already were for him. She hadn't even begun to think through all the implications. He didn't live in the same country, for crying out loud! Not to mention the type of work he did and the person he worked for. So far, the only person at the Bureau that knew about their burgeoning relationship was Nathan, and she hoped his desire for self-preservation would keep him from mentioning

Ramon to the director. If he did, he'd have to fess up that he'd broken protocol by contacting her … again.

Abby wasn't at her desk when Carino got to the office, which was a welcome relief. She knew Abby was poised to conduct the Grand Inquisition about her date with Ramon and she just wasn't ready to let anyone else into her happy bubble.

No sooner had she stepped foot in her office did her cell phone vibrate in her pocket. She furiously dug for it, silently willing it to be Ramon. Her stomach flip-flopped when she saw who was calling. It was the director. And he *never* called.

She composed herself as best as she could and pushed her door closed to protect against prying ears. "Hello, Carino speaking."

"We need to talk." His voice was nearly a growl.

"Y-yes, sir. Would you like me to come in?"

"No. I'm not going to waste any more time than necessary on this."

Carino gulped down the bile that was suddenly rising in her throat as she finally arrived at her office. "Okay, sir, I definitely don't want to waste your time."

"Is that what you've been doing the whole time you've been at Franklin Everly? Wasting my time? We took a chance on you—putting you on as big of a player as Emerson—and now I'm wondering if that was such a good decision. Maybe you weren't cut out for the job after all."

She could feel her blood pressure spike. "I know you took a chance on me, and I've done nothing but work hard these past few years. Of course I'm cut out for it and I know how important Mr. Emerson is." Carino was struggling to keep an even tone. "Hopefully, the work I've completed demonstrates that I'm doing everything I was hired to do."

"It's been brought to my attention that your recent actions may indicate otherwise."

Well, isn't this a shit sandwich first thing in the morning.

"I haven't forgotten about the importance of my job, sir, and I'm using all of my resources to help me do it better."

"Is that what *he* is? A resource?" His tone left no doubt in her mind that the "he" being referred to was Ramon.

"Of course, sir." Her reply was harsh. "I'm spending some extra time, outside of the office, with one of Mr. Emerson's close colleagues so I can learn more about his business, and hopefully some of his associates as well. I thought any information I could gather would be helpful to us in our dealings with Mr. Emerson."

"Keep in mind that you could be jeopardizing our connection to Emerson. But if you're confident you can manage yourself, then you should use your time with him very wisely. The way you handle Emerson will make or break your career."

"Yes, I understand that." She was seething inside. "In fact, I just wrapped up a transaction this week and all of the corresponding paperwork I've prepared is in the file."

Only one person could've ratted her out to the boss.

What a filthy, backstabbing jerk! And I'm sure he didn't tell the director about his little visit to the Pepsi Center when he was tattling on me.

Her blood was boiling and she knew if she laid eyes on him today, there was no way she'd be able to maintain control.

"I hope you aren't losing sight of what's really important here." His warning was clear.

Carino swallowed deeply, trying not to lose her shit. "I'm not, sir."

"Don't make me regret taking a chance on you, young lady."

The condescending asshat didn't even give her the opportunity to say anything more before he hung up on her.

Carino slammed the phone down on her desk and fisted her hands so tightly she was sure she was going to draw blood. She threw her head back, shut her eyes, and let out a silent scream.

"Carino? Is now a bad time?" asked a timid voice.

One of the freshman interns was holding a stack of files in his arms and hovering in the doorway like a skittish kitten. She'd been so caught up in her rage that she hadn't heard him knock or open the door. Realizing she probably looked like a lunatic just now, she couldn't really blame him for being wary.

"Yes, Eric?" She forced her tone to not match her mood.

"I, um, I h-have the files you asked me to get for you." He took a tentative step inside the room.

In all the hubbub of the past several days, Carino had completely forgotten that she'd asked him to pull a few of Emerson's older files from the archives in the basement. Truth be told, she didn't even need the files anymore because she'd already found everything she'd been looking for. She'd needed information about some land Emerson had acquired in Columbia a few years back, but had come across it in one of her notes files. The former land owner had suffered similar injuries to the man in Costa Rica and she'd wanted to compare and contrast the other aspects of the acquisitions to make sure she'd covered all of her bases.

She waved him in. "Oh right. Thanks. Please just put them down on my desk for now."

Eric did as she asked and turned to leave. Stopping a few feet from the door, he spun around. "Um, Carino? When I was down in Archives first thing this morning, I startled Abby as she was pulling a file from the shelf. She got really upset and kind of yelled at me, wanting to know what I was doing in there. She pushed the file back really fast, and then she turned and rushed out of the room. I was so shocked I didn't even say anything. When I got to the shelf to pull out the files you asked for, I noticed one of them was the one she'd been about to take. I don't want to get in trouble or anything, but I just wanted you to know, in case she thinks I was doing something I wasn't supposed to be doing."

Carino was stunned by his recount. Had Abby lost her ever-loving mind?

"Do you remember which file she was looking at?"

"Yeah, it was the one on top." He pointed to the file with the label that said "Emerson, Sebastian—Belize Townhouse Complex (2010)," along with the firm's internal file number.

"Thanks, Eric. You did the right thing telling me about what happened. I'll handle it if anything comes of this, okay? You've got absolutely nothing to worry about."

He immediately looked relieved and smiled goofily. "Okay, whew. Thanks, Carino!"

As soon as he left her office, Carino snatched up the file and began to thumb through the documents to see if she could figure out what Abby could've been looking for. She found everything in order, complete with the contacts sheet on top, just as it should be.

Fury was still coursing through her veins from her phone call moments ago, inciting courage she didn't generally possess, so she decided to quit tap-dancing around the issue and just confront Abby about it.

Stomping around her desk with the Belize file under her arm, Carino headed in the direction of Reception. Abby was going to come clean right now about all this, whether she wanted to or not.

No sooner had she stepped into the hallway did Carino hear a faint conversation coming from the file room next to her office. She paused to listen, immediately recognizing Abby's hushed voice ... and hers alone.

"No, I didn't have time to look through the file! I'll have to figure out another way to get you the information. Look, I'm doing the best I can here, okay? Other people have access to the same files." Abby was whisper yelling.

Holy shit, she's on the phone! But who in the hell is she talking to?

Carino inched closer to the door and peeked into the room. The phone base was on the small worktable, but the cord was stretched to capacity behind one of the file shelves.

"I said I would try, but I need a few more days." She was clearly getting angrier by the second. "Good. Bye!"

Abby marched back to the table and slammed the receiver down, muttering several expletives under her breath. Carino high-tailed it back into her office before Abby could catch her eavesdropping. She didn't know what Abby was doing, but whatever it was, she knew Abby was in way over her head. She couldn't possibly know everything about the way Emerson operated. He would kill her if he even suspected she was snitching on him!

No, he *won't kill her. That's what Ramon is here for, dumbass.*

Carino sank down in her chair and tossed the file she'd been carrying on top of the rest, causing the entire stack to topple over and slide haphazardly across her desk, knocking over her glass of water. She was too boneless to even care. Groaning, she rested her elbows on her knees, cradled her head in her hands, and closed her eyes. Light flashed behind her lids, which could mean a migraine was coming on.

Everything had suddenly become too much for her to handle and her emotions were staging a mutiny. She needed a break so she could comprehend what was going on around her, since she felt like things were suddenly spiraling out of control. It was time to get real.

Ever since Raj's outburst the other day, she'd been looking at him in a different light. He'd always been so professional with her and with anything Emerson-related, but his intense feelings toward Ramon signified there was more simmering below his serene facade. Carino had been so focused on becoming—and remaining—one of his key workers that she'd foolishly overlooked how vital he truly was to Emerson's empire. Her blatant naïveté was difficult to swallow.

Carino had quickly determined Ramon was struggling with an internal battle between good and evil, but she hadn't yet figured out which side was winning the war. Funny, she didn't think he knew either. He'd somewhat sugarcoated his role in Emerson's world, but obviously he wasn't here for a kindly visit; Emerson most likely only hired him when the situation warranted his brand of interference. Was it because of Abby that Emerson had called in the cavalry? If so, that meant Emerson already suspected her of funneling information to someone outside the firm; that, very simply put, was a death warrant.

Can I realistically pursue a relationship with Ramon if this is how he conducts his life?

Nathan already had Carino looking over her shoulder more than she cared to admit. She knew this was merely the tip of the iceberg—she just had to figure out his next move before he crossed the line and did something they might both regret.

The director was questioning her ability to do her job, and her involvement with Ramon. Of course he saw through her flimsy excuses, so she'd be lying if she said she wasn't a wee bit worried about what that meant for her future career.

And finally Abby, who'd been the closest friend she'd had in a while, had succumbed to temptation. Carino wondered who had convinced Abby to blatantly break the rules, and what exactly had tipped the scales, because the risk she was taking was enormous. It could've easily been anyone walking by the file room this morning. Abby was unbelievably fortunate it had only been her.

Chapter 22

Someone knew he was tracking Carino. But who? And why only destroy *her* tracking device? Why not all the other ones he'd installed, which he hurriedly verified were still functional and accurate.

Is someone trying to make me suspicious of Carino?

Ramon marched back into the sitting room and flopped down on the modest couch. He needed to clear his head so he could formulate a plan to deal with this latest event—and his odd reaction to it. Sooner, rather than later, he had to come to terms with the fact that if anyone else's tracker had been permanently disabled, he would've been all over them like stink on shit. But here he was, pussyfooting around whether or not someone was trying to incite suspicion, instead of admitting to himself that he very well *should* be suspicious of Carino.

Ramon clenched and unclenched his fists repeatedly, unsuccessfully tamping down his heightening anger. The truth was, he should be mad at himself. He knew what working for Emerson entailed, as he'd been on retainer for many years. He knew Raj was a snake who would strike when cornered. He knew Abby perfectly fit the mold of a snitch. And lastly, he knew Carino was an unnecessary distraction.

Frankly, Ramon didn't know much about Carino at all. No more, really, than he knew about anyone else at Franklin Everly. Sure, they'd spent enough time together for him to know that his attraction to her was intense and most likely permanent, but it wasn't like she'd bared her soul during any of their conversations. Last night, they'd mostly kept to simple topics, neither of them willing to show all of their cards just yet.

In a moment of brutal honesty, Ramon reluctantly conceded that he'd taken his eyes off the prize. He had allowed his intense feelings for Carino to swarm his every thought like a poisonous weed. As a result, he was basically useless in this investigation. At this point, if he hadn't been operating with his head squarely up his own ass, he would've long since had surveillance in place at Franklin Everly, as well as at all of Raj's team members' personal residences. Sure, he had trackers on all their vehicles, was monitoring routines, and had warning indicators for various locales—but still, he was long past making excuses for his shoddy work.

If he had been following his own S.O.P., there'd be no question as to who had snuffed Carino's tracker. Or why. Instead, he was a chump sitting in an overpriced hotel room in a bathrobe, drowning in a pool of unanswered questions, wondering when he would see Carino again.

He felt utterly pathetic.

Ramon snatched the coffee cup off the table, frustrated that he felt a flutter of excitement in his stomach at the thought that Carino had remembered how he liked it. Suddenly, his gut clenched at the thought that she probably used to bring *him* coffee too.

Case in point: when had he had become the girl in this relationship?

Instead of drinking the rest of it, like a sane person would've done, Ramon stalked over to the wet bar and dumped every last drop down the drain, throwing the cup into the sink with all the disdain he could muster.

Yeah, that'll show 'em.

Here was yet another example of how he'd recently gone soft. He should've had that asshole hog-tied and bloody by now. Instead, he was tending to his hurt feelings about Carino's sketchy past with the mystery stalker.

As Ramon concentrated on his memories of when Carino was accosted at the game, he felt the familiar surge of adrenaline rush through his veins at the idea of tracking the man down—and all the fun they would surely have while getting to know one another.

That's more like it. I need to stick to what I know and do best.

Booting up his laptop, Ramon began hunting. Using the images he was able to hack from camera footage taken at the basketball game, he used facial recognition software to begin methodically sifting through information gleaned from various database searches—both private and public. About an hour later, he came across the man's picture on an ID badge that displayed the name "Nathan Jones, A+ Cleaning Services." Not very helpful, since his next search returned 637 other Nathan or N. Jones in the Denver Metro Area.

Records for the business indicated it was a defunct janitorial company, which voluntarily dissolved about three years ago. Nathan wasn't registered as an owner, but Ramon found one A+ Cleaning employment record for a Nathan Jones, which listed a social security number that turned out to belong to a woman who had been dead since 1941, and a P.O. Box with an invalid Denver zip code.

At every turn, Ramon hit a brick wall. He couldn't even seem to come up with a freaking middle initial! Essentially, this guy was a ghost. Whoever Nathan Jones really was, he obviously didn't want to be found. And that fact alone made his connection to Carino much more problematic.

Ramon considered his options. Maybe he was going about this all wrong. Nathan Jones might very well be invisible, but Carino wasn't.

He didn't remember seeing anything about a Nathan Jones when he did Carino's initial background check, and she hadn't elaborated on their dating history, so he had no clue as to when their paths had first overlapped. Had Nathan followed Carino here from Wyoming? There was certainly no connection Ramon was able to find through social media, which he would've found, even if she had deleted it later. Nothing was ever *truly* deleted once made public, and the shit people posted online never ceased to amaze him.

After gaining access to Carino's mobile phone account, Ramon searched her logs until he found Nathan's first call during their dinner. He noticed Nathan had left her a five second voice mail, and immediately clicked the play button, thankful for the convenience of online account management. It made his job so much easier.

"We need to talk," was all Nathan said.

He tried tracing the phone number but the location of the caller kept shifting between random places such as Sydney, Australia to Bangor, Maine to Cape Town, South Africa. Clearly, the number was being blocked by someone who didn't want to be found. Ramon didn't see any outgoing calls to his number, so Carino either didn't contact him or she did it by a different means than a telephone. Quickly remote-accessing her work computer, Ramon searched every nook and cranny for evidence of a personal email account, but to no avail. So maybe she just didn't contact him at all.

Or maybe she's more secretive than I thought.

Pushing unwanted thoughts to the side, Ramon focused on the task at hand: he had to find out if Carino had sent Nathan an email. And if so, he absolutely had to read it, for a couple of reasons. One, he wanted to know what they needed to talk about so urgently; two, he needed Nathan's MAC address. At this point, it seemed like it would be the easiest way to figure out where this guy was located.

Satisfied that it was only a matter of time before he would track down the location of Nathan's computer, which Ramon hoped Nathan would be sitting in front of when he found it, he jumped in the shower. Realization quickly dawned that he'd spent more time determining who Carino's ex was than trying to solve Emerson's problem. Ramon knew he needed to set his priorities straight, but at this moment he wasn't entirely convinced he had them out of order.

Redirecting his thoughts to Abby, who was his only semi-lead in this whole ridiculous snarl of Emerson bullshit, he decided to review last night's surveillance footage from her place while eating breakfast. Afterwards, he would head out to Carino's house to put up at least one camera. Maybe then he wouldn't feel quite so useless and could put some effort into planning his unannounced visit to Franklin Everly later this afternoon.

The footage, just like every other night, was horribly boring. At some point soon, Ramon would be forced to admit that he was looking in the wrong place; Abby wasn't the mole. But right now, he was still clinging to circumstantial clues, and a gut instinct that told him she was into something she shouldn't be.

So far, his intelligence had ascertained that she had a common weeknight routine of changing out of her work clothes into sweats and a tee shirt, ordering some sort of take-out, and watching TV for several hours. Not exactly state secrets.

A flurry of activity suddenly broke out as he was fast-forwarding through the recording, breaking the monotony of his review. Backing up, Ramon watched her answer her cell phone and abruptly begin pacing around her living room. Unfortunately, she ended up having the majority of her brief conversation in the one area of her small house that didn't seem to transfer sound very well. Even with his speaker volume maxed out he couldn't decipher much of what she said, which thankfully wasn't necessary, since her body language spoke volumes; she was instantly stressed and upset, and immediately began rifling through paperwork in the drawer of her small desk after ending the call.

Switching to the second camera view, Ramon paused the video feed as soon as she laid several file folders on her desk. Zooming in on a solitary yellow sticky note, he read the initials "S.E." Resuming playback, Ramon watched Abby quickly flip through several papers from inside the file. Even though he could only make out the bottom portion of the first document, it was all that was necessary to conclude that S.E. stood for Sebastian Emerson.

Damn it, now he was going to have to deal with her, and that just didn't sit too well with his conscience.

...

Even though Ramon had a bead on Abby's treacherous activities, he couldn't shake the feeling that he still needed to go through with installing surveillance in Carino's house. During the drive out to her place, his mind kept reverting to the fact that he'd actually found proof that Abby was compiling a dossier on Emerson, yet here he was, still wasting time on this ridiculous Nathan obsession he'd quickly developed. There was just a much too conspicuous lack of information on what Ramon now knew was Nathan's fake identity, which had really ramped up his burgeoning suspicions.

He also couldn't shake the feeling that something about this whole situation was *off*; that there was more to the Carino/Nathan story. He needed to look beyond the obvious, which was how he convinced himself that invading Carino's private space wasn't that big of a deal. Well, unless she found out about it, that is. And surely that wouldn't bode well for their long-term viability, especially since he'd vowed never to violate her trust. But he had to take the risk.

Like a bloodhound on a fresh trail, Ramon knew he wasn't going to be able to let this go until he figured out what was really happening between Nathan and Carino; her explanation was becoming increasingly difficult for him to accept. Ramon assumed Nathan had been the one that disabled the tracking device he'd placed on her car, since he'd probably seen Ramon install it; Nathan was obviously not a run-of-the-mill, disgruntled ex-lover turned stalker, as Carino would have him believe.

More than once that day, Ramon wondered if Nathan was blackmailing Carino and, if so, why? What did she possess with that kind of value? The only answers he could come up with were knowledge and connections. But to who? Emerson?

Once Ramon reached Carino's neighborhood, he moved between several different areas and surveyed the surrounding area for about an hour to see if he could spot Nathan anywhere nearby. It sure would make his job simpler to roll up on him, unannounced, and get down to business.

But Ramon didn't see Nathan, and truth-be-told, he hadn't really expected to. Someone of Nathan's caliber wouldn't be sitting there, day-in and day-out, staking out the place; he would have his own surveillance equipment tucked away on the premises. Ramon wasn't worried Nathan would mention his covert visit to Carino either, since doing so would cause him to have to admit his own surveillance. If Ramon saw one of Nathan's cameras, he'd make sure to flip him off. Maybe it would give him a chuckle while reviewing footage.

Ramon was able to access Carino's house very quickly, thanks to years of practice disabling all manner of home security systems, most of which were considerably more sophisticated than hers. He didn't know whether to be more relieved or upset that forced entry was so easy; it made him that much more worried about her safety.

But only a man like me could get in here this easily.

He installed wireless microscopic cameras with audio and video capabilities in the hallway between the bedroom and bathroom, as well as in the living room and kitchen, which would allow him to see and hear virtually everything that went on.

His entire visit took less than fifteen minutes, so he still had a few hours left before he was scheduled to meet Raj and Emerson downtown at 3:30 p.m. To kill some more time, and to help him feel less guilty about bugging Carino's house, he headed over to two other employees' homes and repeated his performance. That way, if Carino found out what he'd done, he could at least say it wasn't personal; he'd broken into *everyone's* house and installed secret cameras.

Yeah, that definitely sounds better.

As he pondered how his meeting with Raj and Emerson would go, he knew he wasn't going to share any information he'd learned about Nathan or Carino, but was struggling with whether or not to divulge his recent discovery about Abby. The problem was, he knew that Emerson would want any threat—perceived or actual—eliminated, so if he made Abby's involvement known, Emerson would expect him to handle it. Ramon figured Raj wouldn't care either way, as long as there was no implication in his direction.

But Ramon also knew Emerson would expect him to have some pertinent evidence at this point. He'd already been here for nearly a week, and by this time in the past, he'd generally "resolved" whatever issue was going on.

It certainly wasn't helping matters that instead of figuring out his game plan with Emerson, Ramon kept mentally regurgitating the information he'd found on Nathan this morning—specifically his picture. There wasn't much about him that was memorable, but the more his subconscious pondered the image, the more one feature began to stand out: his eyebrows.

Nathan's hair had been dark and so had his goatee, but his eyebrows weren't. They had been noticeably lighter, almost reddish-blonde, which meant his hair had been dyed much darker than his natural color. Ramon wondered what other features Nathan had altered to mask his true identity.

Myriad questions were swirling in Ramon's head, but he kept coming back to two main ones: 1) what the hell was this guy into, and 2) how much of it was Carino involved in?

• • •

"Rumor has it they made contact just this morning." Anger emanated off of Emerson in waves. "What's the damned holdup, Ramon? Are you waiting until they bring my whole operation down?"

"Of course not." Ramon's response was nearly inaudible through his gritted teeth. "I'm following through on a very promising lead as we speak, but I won't accuse someone without having more concrete proof. I should have a more definitive answer by this time tomorrow."

"How's that?"

"I've got surveillance cameras in the homes of all Raj's team members, so I just need to review a little more of the footage to be sure."

Emerson nodded, then tossed back the rest of his drink and signaled for the waiter, who rushed right over. "Jameson. Neat."

"Of course, sir." The waiter scurried off to the bar to fill the whiskey order.

Ramon continued to sip his scotch and soda while Raj sat back in his chair with his hands folded in his lap, glaring over the top of his lemon water; he was a little bitch who couldn't hold his liquor if he drank too early in the day.

"Spit it out, Raj. You've been shooting daggers at me ever since I sat down. Might as well get it out in the open." Ramon's command was rather forceful.

"What do you want me to say? That all of this is simply no problem? That it's just fine for someone on the inside—someone close to me—to have daily contact with the Feds and you don't have a damned clue as to who it is? That I have confidence in your ability to fix this shit? Well I won't. And I don't. You are jeopardizing a life I've spent years building; a career I've spent countless hours honing to perfection. And for what? A piece of ass?" Raj's face twisted into a sneer. "Let me assure you, Ramon, she's good—but not that good."

Ramon peeled his lips back from his teeth in a feral snarl, which caused Raj to scoot slightly farther away, but he managed to rein in his temper before he launched himself across the table. "First of all, someone *you* might have hired is doing this right under your nose and you didn't even have a clue. And if you're speaking of Carino, I couldn't care less whether or not she was the best lay of your miserable, wretched life. She means nothing to me at all. She's a pawn in a game she doesn't even know she's playing." Ramon paused to take a deep breath. "Here's a little reminder: I don't work for you, Raj, and I don't give a damn if you spend the rest of your life in prison getting passed around like a well-used blow up doll. I work for Emerson. And if I choose to use Carino to bring this charade to an end, so be it. Just stay the hell out of my way."

"Ok, let's take it down a few notches, gentlemen." Emerson placed a cautionary hand on each of their shoulders as he glanced around the room. "We're beginning to generate interest with several of the other customers."

Ramon clenched his jaw and straightened his jacket. "Yes, sir."

Raj simply cleared his throat, sipped some of his drink, and excused himself to the men's bathroom.

He's probably got to go make sure he didn't shit himself.

Once Raj was gone, Emerson leaned in close. His breath reeked of whiskey and wickedness. "Whatever the gripe is between the two of you, get over it. No matter how you feel about Raj, his words carry some truth. This informant has the potential to bring us down, Ramon. And I mean *all* of us. If this broad has got you twisted up, cut her loose. Remember where your loyalties lie, and they aren't with some girl you've been screwing for less than a week."

Ramon swallowed hard and stood up from the table. He looked Emerson square in the eye. "Yes, sir."

As he turned to walk away, Emerson reached out and grabbed Ramon's forearm. "Don't fuck with me, Ramon. You, of all people, should know that I bite back."

Ramon snatched his arm out of Emerson's grasp and strode out the front door before he suffocated from the tension in the air. He knew Raj was just trying to rile him up, since he knew there was absolutely no way Carino would sleep with someone as slimy as Raj. Of course, he hadn't meant a thing he'd said about her either, but that was no business of theirs; Ramon just didn't want her to get dragged into the crooked side of his life.

And what Emerson didn't seem to realize was that Ramon's loyalties were quickly moving in the opposite direction of anyone he'd left sitting at the table.

Chapter 23

Shortly after 4:30 p.m. Carino's intercom buzzed, breaking her deep concentration. She had spent a large portion of her afternoon doing some land use enforcement research for another of the firm's attorneys, since one of their clients was embroiled in a fierce legal battle over a shared easement with their neighbor.

Riveting.

But at least I'll have some skills to fall back on when I lose my job with the Bureau.

"Hi, Carino, Mr. Ramon is here to see you," Abby said.

Her heart skipped a beat and her face instantly heated. "Okay, will you please send him back to my office?"

"Of course!" She poorly concealed the excitement in her voice.

Carino had definitely not been expecting to see Ramon again today! She immediately took out her compact and checked her appearance, reassuring herself there was no spinach lingering in her teeth after the salad she'd eaten earlier. Then she popped two breath mints, for good measure.

After Carino had devoted the morning to reassessing her overall situation, she'd settled on what she wanted to say to Abby after work ended today; she had to warn her that whatever it was she was doing had to stop immediately. She had also thought long and hard about Ramon, and felt more confident that she knew where she needed to draw the line in their relationship. Emerson was her priority, and doing her best work on his account was essential. If Ramon became too big of a distraction, she would simply have to stop seeing him.

Carino really liked Ramon—*really* liked him—but knew she had to be very careful. She couldn't allow herself to get completely derailed from her life. Sure, things were spectacular when they were together, but he had a life too, and Carino didn't think there was going to be room for someone like her in it. Plus, their interactions were on the radar now, so that meant people were watching—closely.

"Hello, beautiful." It literally only took two words for him to steal her breath and disintegrate all of her convictions.

Ramon brought his hands around from behind his back, revealing a carryout bag from the Cheesecake Factory.

"What have you done?" Carino slowly inched out from behind her desk, eyeing the bag as if it contained a ticking bomb.

"Well, I have a meeting this evening and I couldn't bear the thought of going through the rest of the day without seeing you again. I figured we could shut ourselves in your office for a bit," he grinned, "and enjoy something sweet."

Carino snatched the bag from his hands, provoking full-on laughter, and furiously dug around for the closest Styrofoam container full of decadence.

"I never, ever splurge on Cheesecake Factory dessert." Her voice was a whisper as she reverently opened the first container and inhaled the sugary-sweet smell of Godiva Chocolate Cheesecake, which caused her eyes to roll back in her head.

"I can't tell if you're upset or pleased." His tone was playful.

Carino opened her eyes and looked pointedly at him. "Well, that all depends on what the other kind is!" She reached into the bag again, withdrawing the second container and setting it gingerly on her desk. "This could be a game-changer, Ramon."

"I'm feeling pretty good about my chances." Carino flipped the lid open to reveal a slice of White Chocolate Raspberry Truffle Cheesecake. "So, how'd I do?"

"Absolutely perfect … except for one thing. It looks like only one of us gets to have any. There's only one spoon."

He laughed as she safeguarded the single plastic utensil. "I'm sure we can manage."

They dug into the delicious sweets and managed to finish both slices, sharing the flavors until they were bursting at the seams.

"That was fantastic!" Carino licked the last bit of cheesecake residue from her lips.

"I couldn't agree more. I only wish I didn't have to leave so soon."

Her iPhone was still sitting on top of the desk where she'd left it, after Ramon convinced her that he just *had* to take pictures of her enjoying the feast. He'd texted them to himself, but only after Carino had made him swear on his life that he wouldn't post them on Facebook. She clicked a button and revealed the time as 5:35 p.m., which would explain the empty feeling of the building. That also meant she'd missed Abby, so their unpleasant conversation was going to have to wait until another time.

"I'd like to walk out with you, if you have just a couple more minutes to wait while I use the restroom."

"Of course. I'll be right here when you get back."

Several minutes later, as she made her way back to her office, Carino found herself thinking about their road trip tomorrow. She'd not only decided she was going to take the time off after all, but she'd asked for the entire day off—and Raj had authorized it. She had simply told Raj that she needed a mental health day to reassess her recent decisions. He had agreed wholeheartedly, after taking another opportunity to remind her that Ramon was trouble. He would've had a heart attack if he'd known her real reason.

Entering her office, Carino noticed that Ramon had tidied up their mess and was waiting with her jacket in hand.

So chivalrous!

She grabbed her purse and phone and as they exited the building, he pulled her in for a soft, lingering kiss.

"Until tomorrow?" His gorgeous brown eyes were mere inches from hers and she could make out every single fleck of gold.

She simply nodded her head, since her coherent thoughts were clouded by a sugary Ramon haze. Carino watched him until he retreated around the corner, again struck by the magnitude of feelings she had developed for him in such a short time, in spite of her efforts not to.

• • •

She hadn't yet told Ramon she had the entire day off—she wanted to give herself ample time to talk herself out of the trip. But, again citing the excuse that it would be the perfect opportunity to extract useful details about Emerson, she knew she wasn't going to back out. Of course, she was conveniently avoiding the fact that she really just wanted him all to herself for a whole day. No matter how hard she tried to convince herself that her interest in Ramon was mostly business, the truth was that she simply just wanted to spend some quality time with him, outside of the chaos of their respective lives.

She dialed his cell number, feeling the familiar butterflies in her stomach at the mere thought of hearing his voice. When the call went to voice mail she was certainly disappointed, but reminded herself that he was not at her beck and call. And she wouldn't even let her mind drift to thoughts of what he could be busy doing; she just hoped it was legal. Infusing cheer and nonchalance into her voice, she left him a message, inviting him over for breakfast the next morning.

There's no going back now.

She imagined him subsisting night-after-night on meals prepared by nameless faces, and thought he would enjoy the mere fact that she'd taken the time to cook for him.

After looking through several recipes, Carino chose an asparagus quiche with a potato crust, and thankfully already had all the ingredients on hand. As she set about cooking, her thoughts unfortunately drifted to Nathan. Even though she didn't want him to sully her evening, she decided she should probably check to see if he'd tried to contact her again, since he would undoubtedly be borderline psycho by now; he didn't like to be kept waiting, and Carino knew his impatience bred more trouble.

Reluctantly, after she put the food in the oven and cleaned her mess, Carino grabbed her phone again and clicked into her email. She had three, all from him.

Seriously?

The first one was from earlier today, telling her she'd better talk to him—or else. The second one was from 7:15 p.m. and he was insinuating that she was running out of time to get in touch and he couldn't believe she hadn't responded to him yet. The last one was from about twenty minutes ago, and she didn't actually know what it said because she stopped reading when he called her a stupid fool.

"Leave me alone!" Her words echoed through the empty house as she plopped down onto the couch. "Please, Nathan, just give me some breathing room. I can't deal with you right now."

Carino closed her eyes and leaned back against the soft cushion. The more she thought about it, tomorrow really was going to be the perfect getaway. She hadn't been out of the confines of this town in so long that she'd forgotten the road extended past her freeway exit. Sometimes, the claustrophobia of her life was overwhelming and she just needed to escape. And that's exactly what she planned to do tomorrow. In fact, after Ramon picked her up, she was going to shut herself off from the outside world and exist only in the moment; her cell phone was going into the bottom of her purse and it would be switched off.

Several minutes passed as she sat in silence, letting the weight of her decisions settle over her. Soon, the timer called her attention back to the kitchen; the quiche was done. She took it out and left it to cool, then decided it was definitely time to take a relaxing bubble bath. She'd barely taken two steps when her text notification dinged. It was Ramon.

Carino smiled when she read his message telling her that he'd be there in the morning. And as she clicked out a reply and hit send, she knew she'd just turned the page of a new—and exciting—chapter in her life.

• • •

The ramifications of her actions began to rear their ugly heads as she lay in bed, staring at the ceiling. Carino had a sinking suspicion that several people weren't going to be pleased with her dropping completely off the radar tomorrow, considering they were right in the midst of Emerson's last acquisition.

She didn't know if Ramon would mention to Emerson that they were going out of town together, but figured there was a good chance he might. And it certainly wouldn't bode well for her if the director heard about their little sightseeing excursion from someone other than her—especially after his warning the other day. She couldn't even begin to consider Nathan's reaction.

After battling with her conscience for several heated minutes, Carino finally decided that she needed to send an email to a few interested parties to let them know she'd be somewhat "off the grid" tomorrow. She knew she'd have hell to pay when she returned, but in the end figured it was easier to ask for forgiveness than permission. And right now, at a little before midnight, she didn't figure anyone would still be awake for her to ask anyway.

Carino typed out a brief message on her phone and sent it as a separate email to all of the "bosses" in her life. She kept it simple by saying she was going to be working offline tomorrow with one of Emerson's close associates. Obviously those in the know would realize she was talking about Ramon, but for some reason including his name seemed like it would make things worse. She told them she'd be back to work on Thursday. She mentioned she would have limited cell phone coverage, so she probably wouldn't be immediately returning calls or emails.

Carino read and reread the short message, hovering her finger over the send button for way too long, but couldn't seem to bring herself to click it. She reminded herself that if she was going to go through with this, she needed to let them know; now that the director was aware of Ramon, she couldn't just take off with Emerson's right hand man and expect that no one would find out—or care. This was not brand new knowledge to her, but now that she'd finalized her plans with Ramon, things had quickly gotten real.

After finally convincing herself to send the damn email, she was finally free to think about their road trip. They would have an entire day to themselves, and by the time they got home tomorrow she hoped to have a better idea of why Ramon was here in the States and what his intentions were where she was concerned. She also intended to figure out if his being here would have an impact on anyone close to her—namely Abby, if word had gotten out that she might be sharing confidential information outside the firm.

Sure, I might find answers, but am I prepared for something I don't want to hear?

Chapter 24

Once Ramon made it back to his hotel room, he called room service and ordered the Baja Fish Tacos for dinner, along with two bottles of Tecate, and waited for his laptop to boot up. He was starting to feel pressure to tie up the loose ends at Franklin Everly—especially after his meeting with Emerson and Raj—but he still couldn't seem to free himself from Carino's stronghold; he absolutely had to get to the bottom of the Nathan thing.

Showing up earlier at her office with dessert had turned out to be a genius move, as was using her phone's camera to take pictures while she'd devoured the delicacy; she never suspected his ulterior motive, or she wouldn't have left it sitting unguarded on her desk. The ease with which he'd managed to gain her trust was almost like taking candy from a baby, and it took a laser-like focus to ignore the guilty feeling that was beginning to seep out of the tattered remnants of his conscience.

When Carino had excused herself to the bathroom, he'd seized those few precious, unaccompanied minutes. Thankfully, she hadn't yet upgraded to an iPhone with a fingerprint scanner, so when she had typed in her passcode earlier, he'd followed her movements closely; it only took him two tries to unlock the device.

When he'd accessed her email app, Ramon immediately saw an unopened message from Nathan Jones, which was actually the only one in her inbox. Anxiously watching the door, he'd opened the message, clicked "Forward" and entered his own email address. The wi-fi connection had been weak because it had taken an eternity for it to finish sending. He'd quickly deleted the forwarded message from her Sent folder and then permanently from the Trash, and marked the original email as "Unread."

Ramon pulled up his email, opened the message Nathan had sent to Carino, and read it aloud.

"You should know by now that I'm not just going to let this go. We need to talk. And I don't think you need me to remind you of what could happen if you don't listen to me."

What an asshole.

Ramon reminded himself that he needed to be realistic about his actual chances of finding this guy. This was definitely not the most ideal way to pinpoint Nathan's location, since he knew how dynamic IP addresses worked, but it was the best—and only— lead he had right now. While he might not be able to isolate the exact location from where Nathan sent her this message, Ramon hoped to at least get within a mile. The odds were slightly in his favor since Nathan had sent it late this afternoon, so the ISP might not have reassigned his IP address to another user just yet.

Ramon accessed the "Show Original" selection within his Gmail account and was immediately faced with multiple lines of XML code. He copied the entirety of it into a text file and searched for the term "Received From" in the line headers. He had to find the first occurrence in order to locate the originating computer's IP address.

After scrolling through several search hits, Ramon finally landed on the data he was looking for, but found two IP addresses listed on the same line. He pulled up an IP search website that would help him determine the location and plugged in the first number. He quickly discovered it was private and couldn't be traced.

It had been years since he'd searched for someone this way, so it took a few minutes for him to remember that the second number should correlate to the public gateway Nathan used to access the Internet—which *was* traceable.

A sharp rap on the door had him instinctively reaching for his pistol, which was sitting on the desktop near his computer. A female voice called out, "Room service."

Ramon peered through the peephole and could make out the hotel's uniform, as well as a rolling cart with silver dish covers. Tucking his piece into his waistband, he opened the door and was met with a pair of striking blue eyes, long blonde hair, and porcelain skin.

"Well, good evening." Her eyes roved over Ramon's body in frank appreciation. "Where would you like me to put your dinner?"

He stepped aside so she could roll the cart into the room and motioned toward the coffee table.

"Right there is just fine, thank you." He noticed the deliberate sway of her hips as she removed the serving tray from the cart and walked it over to the table.

She turned to face him. "Is there anything else you would like this evening, sir?" Her carnal invitation might as well have been spray-painted on the wall, it was so obvious.

Sure, she was a lovely young woman and even a week ago, Ramon might've been tempted to take her up on her offer. But it wasn't a week ago. And she was definitely no Carino.

"Thank you, but this will be all." He kept his rejection polite as he withdrew a twenty-dollar bill from his wallet, placing it into her hand.

She smiled and curled her fingers around his.

"Well, if you change your mind, I'll be here until midnight."

"I'll make note of that." He walked her to the door, anxious to return to his work.

After she was gone, Ramon moved his laptop to the coffee table so he could keep up his research while he ate.

He returned to the website and repeated his earlier search process with the second IP address. The site immediately produced results that indicated the originating computer was located in the city of Thornton, along with a map that pointed to a more precise location. Noting the latitude and longitude coordinates provided,

Ramon entered them into his phone's GPS app to triangulate the position of the marker. The address search came up with 701 E. 120th St, Thornton, CO.

"Bingo." He was pleasantly surprised the process had been so quick.

His happiness rapidly faded as another search revealed that the address belonged to a Barnes and Noble bookstore in the Thorncreek Shopping Center. Ramon knew that the chances of Nathan visiting the same public place twice were slim, especially if he was as smart and careful as Ramon was beginning to think he was.

He leaned back on the couch, clenching his jaw. His shoulders were at his ears and he felt a headache creeping up the back of his skull. He hadn't expected to reach a dead end so quickly. And he was seriously regretting his decision to spend time searching for Nathan before he finished Carino's security setup. Nathan could've called her, or even stopped by for a freaking seven-course meal by now, and he would've missed the entire thing. He literally had no leads on the guy and the one thing that actually could've produced something helpful was sitting on his computer, incomplete.

I'm getting sloppy.

Shutting down his subconscious, he quickly accessed his surveillance software and finished programming the various cameras he'd put up today. A quick glance at current images showed nothing conspicuous, but he was still kicking himself that he had no history on any of the new installs.

His eyes kept roving to Carino's video feed, and he could see she was sitting at her small dining table looking through a book of some sort. In fact, she had several books stacked around her and a couple more on the kitchen counter. Ramon zoomed in on the closest one and could tell from the title that it was a cookbook.

He longed to be with her, doing mundane, everyday things like browsing through cookbooks to determine the weeknight menu. He wanted to peruse the aisles of the local market with her, reading food labels and complaining about the rising prices. He wanted to put on some music and dance around the kitchen as they chopped and sautéed and just enjoyed each other's company.

Instead, she was alone and he was watching her through his secret peephole. And he felt like a total jerk. He couldn't bring himself to shut down the feed, no matter how major his privacy invasion was, but he muted the sound in a lame attempt to assuage his guilt.

Filled with self-loathing, he ignored the last half of his dinner, downed the remainder of his second beer and went to the minibar in search of something stronger. Pouring two small bottles of Jim Beam into a tumbler, Ramon opened the curtains and looked out at the city lights that stippled the darkening night sky. Taking a pull of bourbon, he once again mulled over his current situation.

Even though he knew Carino had her own drama to contend with, Ramon knew he could help her resolve the Nathan situation, if only she'd let him in on the full story. Sure, he was tired of violence for the sake of violence, but he was capable of virtually anything when it came to protecting his woman.

No matter, if he didn't get a handle on what was going on at Franklin Everly before the Feds swooped in, there was a strong chance he was going down, along with Emerson and Raj. In fact, it might even be too late to stop the inevitable. He supposed he deserved whatever justice he received, since he'd certainly played his part in Emerson's rise to the top.

But the more he thought about Abby and how she may very well be the key to solving this puzzle, he knew deep down the reason he kept putting off questioning her was because he wasn't going to be able to permanently take her out of the equation. Carino knew he was in town for a specific reason, and even though she didn't know exactly what it was, it wasn't going to take her long to put two-and-two together if something happened to

Abby; Carino would know it was at his hand. Ramon had no idea how this situation would ultimately play out, but he knew he had to determine the extent of Abby's treachery, if for no other reason but to protect himself.

Draining his glass, Ramon looked at his watch and was surprised to find it was already after ten p.m. Since he'd spent too much of his evening looking for Nathan, Abby would have to wait yet another day. He couldn't wait any longer to talk to her than tomorrow night, after he and Carino returned from Red Rocks.

Content with his resolution, Ramon chose to head to bed, as opposed to emptying the minibar and wallowing in self-pity for the rest of the evening. He retrieved his phone from the desk and realized he'd missed a call from Carino a while back; he should've taken it out of Do-Not-Disturb mode. Noticing she'd left a voicemail, he quickly played the message, instantly tormented by the thought that she might be cancelling their date tomorrow.

"Hi, Ramon. I was going to surprise you in the morning, but thought you might want some advanced notice that I actually have the whole day off tomorrow! I thought we could go down to Colorado Springs and to the Garden of the Gods after all. I totally understand if you already have plans, but if you're able and want to go, I was going to make you breakfast at my place to get us started. I was thinking nine a.m.? Anyway, let me know. Oh, and I hope you like quiche!"

Ramon barely suppressed the urge to pump his fists in the air, and his heart was beating like a marathon runner. They had the entire day together! He would've called her back, but chose to send a text instead. He didn't think he could play it cool with the level of excitement—and alcohol—he had running through his veins.

"I don't have plans tomorrow morning and would really enjoy spending the whole day with you. I'll be at your house on time, and yes, quiche sounds great. Rest easy, *mi Cariño*."

Unable to help himself, he raced to his laptop and maximized the video feed that showed her walking down the hallway, phone in hand. Ramon could tell the exact moment his text came in, and the smile that lit her face was enough to set him on fire.

"See you then. Enjoy your evening. XO."

And with that he headed off to bed, because tomorrow couldn't come soon enough.

Chapter 25

So far, Carino's morning was going smoothly, and she'd had plenty of time to get ready before putting the finishing touches on their breakfast. She put some blueberries in a bowl, added her prettiest serving spoon, and set it on the table. She went back and added some bananas, before refolding the napkins a little straighter. She contemplated slicing up some strawberries.

Are those spots on his fork?

She rushed over with a hand towel and shined the silverware.

Her quiche had set up very nicely overnight, and she was as prepared as she ever would be for her visitor, with time to spare for a cup of coffee.

Sitting at the breakfast bar, she allowed her mind to wander back to the last time she'd had coffee with her mom. They had been at her mom's kitchen table and the morning sun had been shining brightly through the open blinds. Freshly baked cinnamon rolls had been giving off a delectable aroma as they cooled on the counter. Her mom had been wearing her favorite soft, purple robe and her hair had been pinned up into a loose bun. Her eyes had been sad.

"Of course I'll miss you terribly, but I also understand this is something you need to do."

"I won't be that far away, Mom. And this really is a great opportunity for me." Carino tried to reassure her, but the look on her mom's face was difficult to handle.

"I know, baby, and I want you to know that Dad and I are very proud of you." She'd softly patted Carino's hand before taking a sip of coffee.

Carino had waited until her mom had placed her cup back down on the table before pulling her into a fierce hug. She'd known they weren't going to see each other for a while, but had she known then that she'd be on assignment for years instead of months, she didn't think she would've ever let her go.

Her doorbell rang. Carino glanced at the clock on the stove noting that Ramon was fifteen minutes early. Thankfully, due to years of practice, she could think of her mother without breaking down into hysterics; she quickly pushed her memories to the back recesses of her mind. She opened the door to find him standing on her porch, a gorgeous bouquet of flowers in one hand and a paper sack brandishing the Bruegger's Bagels logo in the other.

"I couldn't wait any longer." He flashed a toothy smile.

She didn't know if she was still sad from her short jaunt down memory lane, or if Ramon wielded some sort of magical power over her, but she found herself wrapping her arms around his waist and burying her face in his powerful chest.

"Good morning." Her words were muffled by the fabric of his sweater.

Ramon wrapped one arm tightly around her and kissed the top of her head.

"Yes, I would say it's a very good morning indeed." He chuckled.

His warmth seeped into her body and restored her balance, and after several moments Carino removed herself from his grasp, suddenly self-conscious about her dramatic display of affection.

"Please, come in." She cleared her throat and took the Bruegger's bag from him, before walking back to the kitchen. "Thanks for bringing bagels too. They're my favorite."

"These are for you. Do you have a vase?" He held out the bouquet and she inhaled their scent deeply, realizing she couldn't even remember the last time someone had bought her flowers.

Thanking him, she nodded and they easily fell into a comfortable partnership; in short order, everything was ready. As Ramon opened a cabinet and found two small plates for their bagels, Carino paused to let the atmosphere fully sink in. It had been so long since she'd had a man in her house, or in her life for that matter, and the warmth that washed through her body awakened her most dormant emotions.

Just then, Ramon turned around and caught her staring.

"What's wrong?" He stopped in mid-stride, concern apparent on his face.

Carino shook her head quickly and turned away before he could see the tears that had suddenly formed in her eyes. "Oh, nothing at all. I was just making sure you found the plates."

Ramon walked up behind her and wrapped his arms around her shoulders, clearly not buying her obvious lie.

"This meal you've made is amazing. Thank you for inviting me into your home and sharing your time with me. I don't think you realize how much this means to me, Carino."

She took a deep, shuddering breath as he turned her around to face him. When she looked up into his eyes, she could see the sincerity of his words. But she also saw something else, and it looked an awful lot like the sadness that had reflected in her own eyes too many times over the years.

"Geez, look at me being a sap this morning!" Carino felt the need to immediately lighten the oppressive mood; this was not how she wanted to start off their amazing day together. "You're welcome and we'd better eat because our food is getting cold."

And just like that the moment passed, buried deep under the cover of their practiced emotional surfaces.

• • •

After the small hiccup at the beginning, the remainder of their meal was fantastic. They enjoyed each other's company and their conversation flowed freely, as they discussed their plans for the day and what the weather might hold. He helped clear the dishes, and before long they were speeding down the interstate with Ramon behind the wheel.

The sun was shining, there was barely a cloud in the sky, and it looked like it was going to be a beautiful day. Traffic was fairly light too, which was probably because it was shortly before lunchtime on a weekday. Carino put on her sunglasses, leaned back in the cushy leather seat, and seized the opportunity to really take in the scenery. Always the driver, she'd forgotten how nice it was to be able to just sit back and relax.

"Mind if I put on some music?" Ramon broke the comfortable silence.

"Not at all." Carino was curious to hear what he'd been listening to.

He switched on the stereo and the crisp, classic sound of a Spanish guitar flooded the air. "What are you in the mood for?"

She cleared her throat, suppressing the sudden urge to reply with something completely inappropriate. "This sounds lovely, actually."

He smiled, evidently pleased that she enjoyed something so intrinsic to his culture.

"What's the name of this song?" She became instantly caught up in the beautiful, haunting melody.

"It's called 'Spanish Romance,' but no one knows who wrote the original. Why, do you like it?"

"It's amazing." She closed her eyes, allowing herself to become fully immersed in the sound.

Carino had loved the guitar ever since she was a young girl. Her dad used to play all the time, but only for her. He'd never thought he was good enough to play for anyone else—even her mom—but she thought he was terrific. It used to be part of their nightly routine. He'd wait until her mother had tucked her in, and then would sneak into her room and play several bars of whatever new song he was learning.

As he got older, he developed arthritis in his fingers and it became much too painful for him to play. His guitar sat in the closet gathering dust for years, until Carino decided that if he couldn't play for her, she would take lessons and learn how to play for him. Her mom helped find a teacher that would work with her after school three days a week, and after a few months she was finally ready.

The first time she played for him was on Father's Day when she was thirteen. She'd told her mom the plan, who had then fabricated an excuse so she and her brother could leave the house for a little while to afford father and daughter some private time. Carino had set up her chair and music stand in the living room while her dad had been working in the garage, and when he came back inside she already had his old guitar in her lap.

He'd immediately choked up when he saw what she had done, and sat down in his old recliner, eager to hear her tune.

"Tell me if you recognize this, Dad." She'd poised her fingers over the strings, just like she'd practiced so many times.

Carino had only glanced up at him once, mostly so she wouldn't cry but also because she'd needed to concentrate on her sheet music. But when she did, he began singing the words along with her melody.

" … that saved a wretch like me … "

He'd been so proud of her that day and said it was the best Father's Day gift he had ever received. That very same guitar was now sitting in her hallway closet, once again gathering dust.

"Amazing Grace" was the only song she'd ever fully learned to play, because as soon as she'd hit high school, guitar lessons were swapped for volleyball practice, and father/daughter quality time was replaced with arguments over what she was wearing and who her friends were. And now, so many years had passed that she doubted she could remember how to play a single note.

The artist on the radio picked and strummed at her heartstrings, and Carino was thankful that Ramon couldn't see the evidence of her memories once again welling up in her eyes. This was the second time this morning she'd been bombarded with thoughts of her past, which was exactly why she kept a tight lid on her memories; she was struggling more and more with keeping them at bay.

As the beautiful melody came to an end, another immediately began and she recognized the tune of "Stairway to Heaven."

"I've never heard this song played this way." She was glad the tone of her voice didn't betray her feelings.

Ramon clicked one of the many buttons on his dash and a large display lit up with the name of the artist and track. He glanced briefly at the screen. "Rodrigo Gabriela. I really enjoy the variety on this Pandora station."

Carino smiled, realizing that she'd been wrong about yet another thing; she'd thought Ramon had carefully orchestrated the music selection just to set a romantic mood. But now, she realized this was just who he was. Frankly, she wasn't even sure if he recognized the effect he had on women—and not just her.

As she admired the chiseled set of his jaw and the intense concentration he employed while driving them safely to their destination, she was immediately overcome with the premonition that this was going to end badly. She enjoyed his company entirely too much and they fit together entirely too easily. And when he was gone, she was going to be lonelier than she'd been in her entire life.

Chapter 26

This could be them, every single day. They meshed really well. Ramon had never really gotten close enough to a woman to learn what her likes and dislikes were, but Carino's lessons were proving to be thoroughly enjoyable. She seemed to really relax in the car, and it made him happy that they shared mutual musical interests. Given time, he imagined he'd find that they actually had a lot more in common.

Prior to heading out, Ramon had asked to use Carino's bathroom and took the opportunity to double-check Abby's whereabouts. Her car appeared to be parked downtown, as usual, and a quick call to Franklin Everly confirmed she was at work. Of course, he blocked his number prior to dialing and hung up as soon as she answered.

Ramon didn't think one more afternoon would make too much of a difference where she was concerned, since it seemed that she'd already provided the Feds with whatever information they'd obviously needed to launch a full-scale investigation into Emerson. He just needed to find out what exactly she'd divulged and when the Feds were planning to move against Emerson; frankly, he didn't think he could prevent anything from happening at this point.

So, he'd silenced his phone and tucked it into his pocket, eager to shut the door on his illegitimate responsibilities. Today was about him and Carino, and it was definitely the best chance he was ever going to get to prove that they had a good thing going. If possible, he might even be able to gain some pertinent information about Nathan, but he'd be careful to not come across too pushy.

They made good time to Colorado Springs, even though they stopped once along the way for coffee. Upon arriving at the Garden of the Gods, he immediately realized that the clear, sunny skies were deceiving; it certainly looked much warmer than it actually was. Thankfully, he'd brought his jacket, as that made it much easier to tuck away the essentials: cell phone, wallet, and knife.

Entering the visitor's center, Ramon was immediately stunned by the breathtaking photography of Rich Buzzelli, which really showcased the true beauty of the unique landscape. There were families everywhere engrossed in one activity or another, and the inviting aroma of the café beckoned. But what he loved the most was that it was just normal people doing normal things. Exactly what he wanted to be doing on a regular basis with Carino.

Like it's even possible for someone like me to be normal.

Shutting down his negative thoughts before they poisoned the day, he concentrated on browsing around the center, pausing to look at several of the exhibits. Even though Carino had been there before, she appeared to be just as captivated as he was. Eventually wandering through the gift shop, Ramon zeroed in on a bracelet that he knew was perfect for her. He hurriedly purchased it, tucking the bag into his coat pocket so he could surprise her with it later.

"Would you like anything to eat before we head out into the park?" He worried she might get too hungry while on their walk.

"I'm still a little full from breakfast actually, but thank you." She turned away from the exhibit she was looking at to flash a brilliant smile that stopped him dead in his tracks. "And I guess I'm just too excited to go exploring! I brought my camera and can't wait to take some pictures."

All it took was one look from her to light up his entire world. He, too, couldn't wait to explore the garden's majestic beauty, even though he knew it would pale in comparison to her.

They wasted no time locating the kiosk containing the variety of trail maps, and once again, Carino reminded him that she was unlike any other woman he'd ever known; he'd asked if she wanted to walk the Central Gardens Trail, but she suggested they take on a moderately difficult hike on the Ridge Trail instead. He would've happily gone anywhere with her, but secretly had wanted to hike that route so he could be right in the middle of the rock formations. Every once in a while, he'd found that it was important to be reminded of his insignificance in the face of Mother Nature.

Adopting a leisurely pace, Ramon became completely lost in his own head. Even though he was trying his hardest to keep his mind locked onto the present, thoughts of Emerson and Raj kept sneaking in through the side door. He didn't know if Raj had figured out he was gone—or that he and Carino were together—but if so, Emerson surely knew as well. It would be impossible for Raj to pass up an opportunity like this to knock him down even farther in Emerson's regard.

Normally, Emerson would exit the country when rumors of investigations started swirling around, and Ramon would be left tidying up the mess. Although they hadn't discussed the matter, he knew Emerson was cognizant that leaving wasn't an option right now; the heat was simply too high. If the Feds had him in their crosshairs, he would most certainly be detained at Customs. Feeling the breath of the government on his neck had probably driven his edginess to new levels, and it certainly didn't help matters that Ramon had let his call go to voice mail this morning.

He knew he was beginning to push the envelope with Emerson, which wasn't entirely smart; Ramon knew exactly how volatile Emerson truly was. His skills helped protect him from Emerson to a great degree—his lethal capabilities had been proven time and time again. But when dealing with someone as cold-blooded as Emerson, he never really knew what to expect.

He'd personally witnessed the level of Emerson's brutality toward those who finally crossed the line. It had been fairly early on in their working relationship and he'd asked Ramon to go with him to Colombia. Apparently, he'd caught wind that one of his lead men was keeping a few bricks of cocaine out of each shipment he was preparing to send to the States. Emerson's swift justice involved a public execution in front of the entire crew of the processing plant, followed by the immediate promotion of the second-in-command—all without batting an eye.

Later, Ramon had found out the man Emerson had killed had worked for him over ten years, and had actually been one of his original recruits. They had plenty of history, but none of that mattered to Emerson; betrayal equaled death, as far as he was concerned. Which definitely meant Abby was as good as gone, if Emerson had somehow gotten wind that she was involved in this whole thing. She was a perfect stranger to him, and therefore was completely and utterly expendable.

The more Ramon thought about the fiasco unfolding in Denver, the more he knew he was playing with fire. And leaving today, without notice, was like poking at the flames with a gas-soaked Roman candle. He would need to seriously watch his six when he got back into town; Emerson had sleepers planted all over the country. He'd never considered that Emerson might someday actually use one to retire him, but now he wasn't so sure.

" … don't you think?"

Ramon was embarrassed by his rudeness. "I'm truly sorry, *mi Cariño*, but I didn't hear what you were saying."

He needed to compartmentalize the worry that was beginning to trickle down his spine. There was nothing he could do about any of it now, except cut their trip short and head back—which he was not about to do. Carino was truly the first person he'd enjoyed being with in an extremely long time, so he would just deal with whatever Emerson had in store.

She chuckled. "Oh, it was nothing important—just my deepest, darkest secret."

Ramon grabbed her around the waist and pulled her close before lifting her slightly into the air.

"Oh *that* secret. You mean that I've finally swept you off of your feet?" He laughed, gently placing her back on the ground.

She blushed, adorably. "Ha, you wish!"

"Wow, Carino, this is just truly amazing!" Ramon was still holding her tight while he gazed up at the 300-foot tall sandstone rocks framed by the deep blue of the cloudless sky. "Thank you so much for bringing me here today. This is a trip I will certainly never forget."

He glanced down to find her gaze fixed on the scenery as well.

"You're very welcome. It's crazy—I'd forgotten how completely breathtaking the view is." She was clearly as awestruck as he was.

This was quickly turning out to be one of the best days of his life, and one thing was certain: he definitely needed more. He wanted to whisk Carino away from this place and keep her by his side forever. There were so many places he wanted to show her, and each day wouldn't be complete until he made her face light up, just like it was at this very minute. He knew he could spend every moment making her happy and it would never get old.

She must have sensed Ramon's stare because she turned and looked at him, and the smile on her face caused him to tingle from head to toe. Seizing the opportunity, Ramon moved in for a kiss and she answered his advance by wrapping her arms around his neck and pulling him closer. She felt so damned good in his arms, and he'd give anything for the freedom to kiss her like this any time he wanted.

Just then, a group of people rounded the corner and interrupted their rapidly intensifying display of affection.

"Oh my, we didn't realize … " said one of women in the small crowd, clearly just as embarrassed as they were.

Carino quickly straightened her jacket and Ramon smoothed her hair, before they turned around and briskly began walking farther down the trail.

As soon as they were around the next bend, they burst into laughter.

"Did we just get busted making out?" Carino was clutching her stomach and grinning from ear-to-ear.

"Yep, we sure did."

She covered her face with her hands, completely embarrassed, until he grabbed her arm and started dragging her farther down the trail. Soon, he could tell her mortification was outranked by the sheer beauty of their surroundings, and they began filling up her camera's memory card with pictures of the two of them, as well as others of just her against various natural backdrops.

But no matter how gorgeous the scenery was, she was hands-down the most beautiful aspect of each photo.

• • •

"That was really good." Carino wiped her mouth after finishing the last bite of her cheeseburger. "I'm completely stuffed!"

Ramon sat back in his chair, enjoying not only a full body, but also a full spirit. Spending the day with Carino had been therapeutic. She made him laugh, and not just a little chuckle, but deep belly laughs that made his muscles cramp. She was adventurous and silly and daring and thoughtful and romantic. Not to mention completely and utterly gorgeous.

"Yes, it was. I think I'm going to need a nap soon." He stretched deeply, stifling a yawn.

"Me too!" His mind was instantly flooded with images of their bodies entwined under a cozy blanket.

Quickly guzzling his water in an attempt to cool down his suddenly overheated libido, Ramon waved the waitress over for the check. After arguing over who was going to pay, he finally relented, only after getting her to agree that he could buy her dinner later. Truthfully, he just wanted to make sure he extended their time together as long as possible.

"I'm going to use the restroom really fast before we leave. Be right back." He watched her walk away, enjoying the view until she was out of sight.

Ramon wandered out onto the terrace, not ready to trade the quietude for the hustle and bustle of real life. His phone vibrated in his pocket, and he reluctantly took it out to see who was calling.

Raj.

There was no way Ramon was going to defile the tranquility of this place with Raj's venomous personality, so he sent the call to voice mail.

Moments later, he called back again.

Okay, that's unusual.

"What the hell do you want, Raj?"

He walked over to the railing, making sure he was out of earshot of the young kids nearby, since he wasn't sure he could control his language.

"Where are you?" Raj was yelling, but Ramon didn't give two shits.

"None of your business. Answer my question."

"You need to get over here, Ramon. Emerson is ballistic. His contact said something major is about to happen. He's tried calling you several times but said he keeps getting your voice mail."

The giant rocks must've blocked out the cell service, because Ramon hadn't noticed any missed calls or message notifications. "I'm busy right now. I'll call him later tonight." He gritted his teeth against the annoyance he felt at having to explain himself to Raj.

"There you are! I thought you'd gone out to the car." Carino was suddenly behind him. He hadn't even heard her approach.

Ramon immediately covered the mouthpiece of his phone when she spoke, but it was too late; Raj had heard. Upon noticing he was on the phone, Carino whispered a quick apology and stepped away to give him some privacy.

"Is that who I think it is?" Raj's tone was demanding.

"How would I know who you think it is?" Ramon closed his eyes and gripped the rail. He couldn't believe he'd been so careless as to allow Raj the opportunity to hear Carino's voice.

"Is. That. Carino?" Raj pressed, anger punctuating each word.

"Goodbye, Raj."

"You son of a—"

Ramon ended the call before he could finish.

He shouldn't have even answered the damn thing. Not only had Raj's call ratcheted up his anxiety again, but now he knew for certain that they were together. That surely wasn't going to sit well with her.

Ramon turned around, pasted on a flimsy smile, and walked over to where she stood snapping last minute pictures of the gorgeous scenery.

"I'm sorry about that."

"No, it was totally my fault! I just hope I didn't interrupt anything important." She'd have to be oblivious to not pick up that something was amiss, but thankfully didn't press him for more details.

"It's nothing that can't be dealt with later."

"Well, I thought—since it isn't too far away—that you might want to go check out Glen Eyrie Castle. But if you need to get back … " She gestured to the phone he was still holding in his hand.

Just then it vibrated again, indicating another incoming call. This time, the caller ID showed it was Emerson. Obviously, Raj had wasted no time contacting him.

He contemplated what would happen if he answered. Emerson would start yelling, threatening all manner of consequences if Ramon didn't get back immediately and handle the situation. On the contrary, if he didn't pick up, Emerson would just say the same things on his voice mail. Either way, Ramon simply wasn't going to trade this wonderful day with Carino for anything Emerson expected him to do.

He took a deep breath. "I'd love to go see the castle. In fact, there's no other place I'd rather be."

So, for the second time that day, Ramon deliberately sent Emerson's call to voice mail. And as he put his phone back in his pocket, he knew he'd completely sealed his fate.

Chapter 27

Carino felt terrible that she'd barged in on Ramon's cell phone conversation, since she knew he was a private person—just like she was. She even tried really hard not to overhear what he was talking about, but of course couldn't miss the tone of his voice, which was menacing to say the least. He'd tried to act nonchalant about the whole exchange, which further backed up her theory that he held his cards close to his chest. And judging from the hackles he was desperately trying to conceal, it wasn't even worth the effort trying to pry for more details.

She really hoped Ramon's phone call wouldn't ruin his mood, since she'd been having such a great time with him today. About ten minutes into their trek through the sandstone giants, he'd tested the waters by leaving his arm around her after taking a selfie of the two of them, and before she knew it, they were holding hands. In fact, the only time Ramon wasn't touching her in some way was when he was taking pictures of her, but as soon as they were back on the trail, they were once again locked together. And she hadn't minded at all.

When she was with him, there was no way Carino could convince herself that she was anywhere other than exactly where she belonged. With each laugh, touch, and kiss, Ramon reanimated her, whittling away at the last remaining shreds of her determination to keep him at arm's length. In fact, they were well into the afternoon and she hadn't brought up Emerson or anything remotely business-related at all.

She joked around. Acted silly. Spun in circles like a little girl with her head tilted back and her arms out to the side. Pulled Ramon down the trail to show him a squirrel running up a tall tree. Basically, she was her true self. And now that she'd experienced a small taste of what she'd been missing out on for so long, Carino wasn't sure she could turn back. What had seemed so important just a week ago was quickly becoming a burden she was eager to unload.

Carino had lived and breathed Emerson for years, filing status reports and working under the all-consuming pressure of becoming fully integrated into his account; her career had depended on it. But now, after the conclusion of this last transaction, she was seriously ready to absolve herself of all obligations where Emerson was concerned.

She'd worked her ass off over the last several years, answering to multiple people about what she was working on and always being pushed to do more—and do it faster; she was downright exhausted.

Looking back, Carino couldn't really pinpoint what the last straw had been; everything seemed to have happened so fast. But she was pretty sure it had been Raj's self-imposed regulation of her personal life. She'd given control over to others for as long as she could remember, and she was taking it back—starting with who she was going to spend time with romantically; Raj certainly didn't have any jurisdiction there. He'd been decent to work for and had definitely helped her advance within the firm, but he'd completely overstepped his bounds. In that moment she'd lost virtually all respect for him. Not to mention, she was now sure there was more to Raj than met the eye, even though he'd managed to keep his ugly parts hidden very well.

She'd submitted a status update last week, letting all interested parties know exactly where the Costa Rica transaction stood. Emerson was such a high priority that she'd spent hours poring over financial records specifically formatted to mystify auditors, long-winded agreements chocked full of legalese, and contact sheets containing seedy associates in various other countries. People were relying on her to make sure all the bases were covered, and the moving parts and pieces were in place. She'd more than done her part and was ready to move on to something bigger and better.

It was ironic, really, that Ramon had been her game-changer, especially considering that he was an integral part of the very thing Carino had always disliked about Emerson—the illegal side of his operation. If the rumors about Emerson were accurate, the truth about Ramon was probably much worse. He'd certainly shown her that he could be a gentle, caring man, but was it all just an act? Could someone with his background even be decent and honorable?

She'd only known him for several days, so it was virtually impossible to identify his true character. Or how deep his loyalty to Emerson went and what he would be willing to do as a result. She really wanted to find out, but was afraid to expose herself to him, since she wasn't sure if she could trust him with her heart. Or her secrets.

Even though Franklin Everly's dealings with Emerson were always legit, the last several weeks had really opened Carino's eyes to the amount of meticulous planning it took to keep it that way. She'd been so caught up with her own purpose that she hadn't allocated the proper amount of focus on all the cogs in Emerson's wheel—specifically Raj. Obviously she knew he worked closely with Emerson, but since she'd never been able to tie him to anything questionable, she had just assumed he was operating within ethical bounds. To this day, Carino still hadn't found anything that would prove otherwise—apart from this newly discovered relationship he had with Ramon.

Ramon was obviously here because Emerson needed him, but for what, Carino still didn't know. She hoped it wasn't because word had emerged that details of Emerson's business were being looked into. In fact, Ramon was so tight-lipped about his true purpose that, up until that day, she'd even wondered if she was on his radar somehow. She didn't even want to think about the many different ways that bothered her.

Abby's recent activities certainly had Carino worried; she was treading dangerous waters. She definitely regretted that she hadn't made the time to speak to Abby about the phone call she'd overheard, since there was no telling what kind of shit storm she'd managed to stir up. If Ramon had looked into Abby's background, Carino figured it was only a matter of time before he also realized she was looking into Emerson's files.

At least she's safe today, since Ramon is here with me.

Now there was a thought. Here she was, cavorting with the very man who could threaten Abby's life—and instead of being scared, she was thoroughly enjoying herself. Carino didn't know whether she should laugh about that or check herself into a mental institution.

What she did know was that things had changed. She had changed. No matter what Ramon was capable of or what he'd done in the past, in the span of mere days, he'd managed to shine a light on all she had sacrificed over the last few years. She had traded her personal life for a career, and now, what did she have to show for it? Barely any friends to speak of, no love life whatsoever, and she was accountable to more people than she cared to admit. Oddly, the only person she had never been accountable to was herself.

Carino could think of nothing more than loosening the ball and chain that had been hanging around her neck for so long. In fact, eliminating herself from Emerson's circle would resolve virtually everything in her life that she found troublesome. She just needed to figure out how she was going to go about accomplishing that, and how Ramon might factor into it all.

As they approached the front of his car, Carino began telling Ramon a little more about the castle they were going to visit and he took out his phone to pull up Google Maps so they could determine the best travel route. There was a woman parked next to him, and she had her rear door open, effectively blocking Carino from getting in the passenger side of Ramon's car. Carino couldn't see her very well, but could hear her talking to someone in rapid-fire Spanish.

Suddenly, all hell broke loose. Carino barely had time to catch Ramon's jacket and phone before they hit the ground as he dashed into the driveway and threw his arms around an older woman who'd wandered out in front of through traffic. A construction utility truck, loaded to the hilt with rubble, swerved at the last minute to avoid impact. The woman standing by Ramon's car let out a wail as he cradled the older woman tightly, spinning around so he could take the brunt of the impact from the glass and other debris that flew from the truck bed, due to the driver's evasive maneuver.

Carino was rooted in place, in shock by the scene unfolding in front of her. The other woman rushed out to Ramon's side, frantically waiving her arms and babbling unintelligibly the entire time.

A young boy followed suit, yelling, "*Abuela*!"

Amidst the chaos, Ramon's gaze remained fixated on the withered face of the woman he now held safely in his grasp.

As if in slow motion, Carino watched the woman slowly raise one frail, wrinkled hand to gently caress Ramon's face in one of the most reverent gestures she'd ever witnessed. Her lips were moving the whole time and Ramon's eyes were locked on hers, as he slowly nodded in response to whatever she was saying.

Then she patted his cheek, and Ramon released his grip to allow her to return to her now-hysterical family.

"*¡Mama! Gracias a Dios. Muchas gracias, señor,*" the woman exclaimed, over and over, while frantically looking her mother up and down, in disbelief that she was truly all right. "*Lo siento, a veces se confunde mi mamá.*"

"I…I don't understand." Carino hadn't realized the woman was speaking to her at first.

"I'm sorry, my mama gets confused." She looked back at Ramon, as she began helping her mother walk back to their car. "Thank you so much for saving her."

Even though the elderly woman was safely in her family's care, she kept her watery gaze fixed toward Ramon. And when he finally glanced in Carino's direction, the look on his face was hard to describe.

It was as if he'd seen a ghost.

Chapter 28

Ramon watched in stunned silence as the elderly woman's family took her from his arms and slowly walked her back to their car. He wasn't able to tell if she fully understood what had just occurred, as she appeared completely unfazed. But for him, time had stood still as she'd looked at him intently, as if she could see directly to the depths of his soul.

"*Mi niño, Dios tiene un plan para ti. Camino del diablo es peligroso.*" She'd spoken softly in her native tongue, which was a slightly different dialect than Ramon was used to, but he'd easily understood every word.

My boy, God has a plan for you and the devil's path is dangerous.

As she'd reached her hand toward his face, Ramon had only been able to nod his head. This stranger had just recited a phrase he'd heard countless times in his life, but not since he'd been a small child. She'd patted his cheek and Ramon had felt the tenderness in her touch, in spite of the leathery skin that covered her wrinkled palms.

"*Que la patrona Benedicto te proteja día y noche.*" *May the patron St. Benedict protect you day and night.*

He'd flashed to a memory of his mother, praying over him each and every night, without fail. She'd firmly believed Saint Benedict would keep him from being tempted by the sins of this world. Obviously, that hadn't worked out too well.

Ramon had stared into the strange woman's eyes, which were simultaneously cloudy with confusion and wise beyond measure. He'd known her words were simply a coincidence; nevertheless, they had pierced his very core.

Regaining his senses, he looked at Carino, whose face was as white as a sheet. He could only imagine her expression was a mirror image of his own: shock, fear, and relief.

Suddenly, he was surrounded by several men in coveralls smattered with white dust.

"Hey, man, are you okay? I didn't see her until the last minute, but I sure am glad you were at the right place at the right time!" The driver of the truck was visibly shaken.

"Dude, your shirt is ripped and you're bleeding pretty badly," said another man from the group.

Up until that point, adrenaline had kept his pain at bay. Now that the initial shock was over, his shoulder was screaming.

"Ramon, there's blood dripping from your left hand!" Carino rushed over to join the crowd, pointing at his wound. "We need to get you to a hospital right away."

"It's nothing—just a flesh wound." Ramon shook his head. A quick wash up and he'd be fine.

"Wait a minute, I think she's right, guy. We just finished demolishing an old workshop up the road and all that junk was in the back of our truck. Actually, there's pieces of glass sticking out of your arm," said the third man.

Ramon attempted to twist his arm around so he could see what they were all looking at, and instantly regretted his action; there were definitely shards embedded in his skin. And he felt every single one of them.

"Yeah, you might be right." His face scrunched into a wince; Carino seized the opportunity to lead him back over to his car.

"I'm taking you now, no question about it."

"I'm so sorry this has happened to you, señor. Can I please pay your doctor bill?" asked the woman, after safely securing her son and mother in their vehicle.

"Absolutely not. I'm just thankful that your mother wasn't injured."

"You're a savior. I don't know how else to thank you for what you've done for us on this day."

"There's no need, really." Ramon was uncomfortable with the praise.

"I'm sure whatever Mama said to you was nonsense; she has dementia and babbles sometimes. It's getting worse now—she just wanders off and doesn't realize how dangerous it is for her, and for others." She wrung her hands, grief apparent on her face.

"Ramon, we really need to get to a hospital." Carino's eyebrows were drawn as she bit her bottom lip.

"Vaya con Dios, señor." *Go with God.*

"And you, as well." Ramon allowed Carino to gingerly usher him into the passenger seat of his car. She waved at the men, indicating she had the situation under control and they could go on their way.

"I need to find the nearest hospital." Carino was now in the driver's seat, frantically rummaging through her purse. "Where is my damned phone?"

Ramon saw she still had his phone in her hand.

"Carino?" He attempted to get her attention, but she was entirely focused on digging in her bag.

"Where is that stupid thing?" She was clearly rattled.

"Carino!" Ramon's voice boomed throughout the car. Carino jumped. "You can just use mine, baby. You're already holding it."

She looked down at her hand then leaned her head back against the seat, closed her eyes and took a deep, ragged breath.

"Well, don't I feel like an idiot." She laughed, just a little.

"How about I look up the address to the hospital while you tear the sleeve off of my shirt? I don't think I could manage pulling my arm out of it at this point; there's too many splinters and whatever else sticking out of my skin. Plus, we need something to protect the seat. I don't know that the rental agency would be pleased to find blood stains on their leather."

Carino took a long, deep breath and exhaled slowly before handing him back his phone. "You know, if you wanted me to rip your clothes off, you didn't have to go to such great lengths—you could've just asked."

"I just thought it would be more exciting this way." Relieved she was showing signs of calming down, he turned his back toward her, causing the fragments to bite deeper into his flesh.

"Oh, Ramon, that looks really bad!" She carefully began tearing away the tattered fabric. "You might even need some stitches on the biggest gash."

Ramon hated getting sewed up, but definitely wanted the doctor to pick the splinters out. Every little movement he made seemed to work them farther into the wound.

While Carino gently removed his ruined shirt, Ramon clicked the home button on his phone, preparing to enter his passcode. There on the main screen was the preview of a text message from Raj.

"The cameras you put in her house weren't good enough to keep tabs on her? I wonder if she would've spent the day with you had she known your true intentions."

Prickles of fear crept up his spine and he shuddered, realizing just how close Carino had come to finding out about what he'd done. One single touch of a button and he would've been busted, and no amount of explaining could erase the major breach he'd committed by breaking into her home and installing the surveillance cameras.

I'm going to have to tell her the whole story about what's going on and why I'm here. It's the only way.

"Oh no, I'm sorry! Did I hurt you?" Carino quickly dropped her hands from his shoulder, mistaking the reason for his movement.

"Not at all." Ramon forced himself to ignore the gurgling in his gut and refocused on the task at hand by quickly searching for the nearest hospital.

"Penrose-St. Francis Emergency Room is only about five miles from here."

"Perfect. Now all I need are the car keys." Carino draped his shirt over the seat.

Ramon could feel the key in the front left pocket of his jeans, which was the same side as his injury. "You're going to have to dig it out of my pocket, because there's no way I'll be able to do it myself."

Carino's cheeks instantly turned pink, which was going to make the process so much more enjoyable for him.

"Um, okay—but can you lean back just a little bit?" She tried—and failed—to reach her hand into his pocket.

"Of course. Anything to give you—ahem—easier access." Ramon was struggling to hold back his laughter.

She narrowed her eyes and chewed on her bottom lip as she reached in again, carefully searching for the key that had buried itself at the inside corner of the fabric. Ramon could sense the awkwardness emanating from her body.

"Got it!" She grinned, pulling out a smooth, rectangular item. "Wait, where's the *key* part of this key? There's nothing to put in the ignition."

Ramon chuckled. "Oh yeah, I forgot this has a push-button starter, so you only have to keep the key somewhere inside the car."

Carino's mouth gaped open as she tossed the key into the drink-holder, feigning offense. The smile that broke across her face told him she was enjoying their banter just as much as he was.

"You play dirty, Ramon, or maybe you've just gone crazy from losing too much blood. I should smack you right now!"

"Please don't! I wouldn't want you to cut yourself on the glass sticking out of my arm, because then I'd be the one taking you to the hospital."

She shook her head at him and laughed. "Are you sure something didn't hit you on the head too?"

As she backed out of the parking lot, Carino tentatively placed her hand to rest on his leg. "You did a truly wonderful thing back there, Ramon."

"Ah, it was nothing." He brushed off the compliment.

"No, actually it wasn't. You probably saved that woman's life. And now you're the one paying the price for it."

Ramon nodded, swallowing the bile that suddenly rose up at the thought that Carino would someday discover the depths of his wickedness.

It's about time I saved a life instead of taking one. Only four more to go and I'll break even.

Chapter 29

As Carino sat waiting for Ramon to finish checking in at the Penrose-St. Francis Emergency Room, she had time to think about what they'd just experienced.

While she'd enjoyed their playfulness, she could tell he was covering for something. She didn't know if he was trying to minimize the extent of his injuries—which she knew were more severe than he let on—or if it was something entirely different.

On the way to the hospital, once she'd recovered from the sight of the toned abs and hard, muscular chest he kept hidden under his shirt, she'd finally asked what the older woman had said to him. He'd shrugged off her question, vaguely responding that she was merely talking nonsense. Clearly, there had been more to their exchange, as Carino had witnessed a dramatic shift in his entire demeanor.

Ramon had saved that woman—a perfect stranger—from a major, possibly fatal, injury; he'd thrown himself in harm's way without as much as a second thought. No matter what he had done in his past, or what the present held for him, there was good in this man; of that, she was now certain. An inherent goodness that needed to be nurtured and cultivated, so it could choke out the poison that had permeated his life for so many years.

She imagined that Ramon's regrets ran rampant through his mind on a daily basis; hers surely did. For instance, she'd never thought the consequences of her decisions would lead her to this place, yet here she was, hiding from the people in her life and free-falling down an emotional rabbit hole. Carino now recognized that her feelings for this man had taken on a life of their own.

When she had seen that truck swerve, barely missing smashing into Ramon, she'd been overcome with a panic so debilitating that, for several minutes, she could hardly function. She hadn't even registered that he'd been injured until she'd noticed the blood dripping from his arm. But it was in that split second, when she thought he was going to be stripped from her forever, that she knew she couldn't bear to lose him. Somehow, some way, she was going to have to figure out how to make this work.

Maybe they could just run off together. There was an airport in Colorado Springs, right? She could hire movers to pack up her meager belongings and ship them to wherever they landed. They could leave and never look back.

Solid plan. Except for, oh, pretty much all of it.

"They're going to take me back to a room within the next ten minutes. I also told them you were my wife; they weren't going to let you come back there with me otherwise."

Instantly, Carino's heart fluttered and her breath hitched in her chest. Mrs. Terrones. That had a nice ring to it.

You idiot, this isn't a marriage proposal!

"Oh, of course. That makes sense." Ridiculously, disappointment ran through her veins, flushing out her earlier euphoria. "And at least they gave you a clean bandage and something to cover up with in the meantime."

He'd put his right arm inside the hospital gown, but had kept his left side exposed. There was fresh gauze lightly covering the deepest gash, which had pretty much stopped bleeding on the drive over. Shame washed over her as she gaped at his nakedness; regardless of the terrible state his arm was in, it was virtually impossible not to stare.

"Well, this certainly isn't how I thought our evening was going to go." Ramon carefully eased himself into the seat next to her. He was definitely babying his injured side. "But I heard that the Salisbury steak at the cafeteria is second to none, so at least there's that."

"I knew you were just trying to get out of buying me a nice dinner!"

"You caught me." Carino loved the way his mischievous smile caused his dimples to reappear.

"How are you feeling? Can I do anything to ease your pain while we wait?" She was growing concerned about how long he'd been managing his discomfort.

"Actually, there is one thing you can do … " He grabbed her hand and gently pulled her into a kiss.

Carino's heart stuttered as her other hand landed on his chest. The feel of his naked skin detonated her desire, causing her belly to clench—as well as some other body parts down below. She could only imagine how overwhelming it would be to truly give herself over to this man.

"Emilio Sanchez?" The ER nurse's voice cut into Carino's lust-induced haze. They were the only ones in the waiting area and she hoped Ramon could get bumped in front of that guy, who hadn't even bothered to wait around.

Ramon broke their kiss. "Right here."

She fell slightly forward, reaching for the arm of the chair for support. She licked her lips, wishing Ramon's were still attached. It took another second or two before she even realized Ramon had given a fake name.

"Come on, babe." He was already starting to follow the nurse when he looked back, clearly noticing she wasn't beside him. "They said you could come with me, remember?"

"Yes, Mrs. Sanchez, you can sit with your husband while he waits for the doctor."

Carino cleared her throat and stood to accept Ramon's outstretched hand. She blared her eyes and pursed her lips together as soon as the nurse wasn't looking, trying her hardest to convey her question to Ramon about why he hadn't revealed his identity. And why he carried around a fake ID in his wallet, for that matter.

Where should he keep it? In a wall safe, perhaps?

· · ·

Once the nurse closed the curtain, affording them a small semblance of privacy, Ramon avoided her gaze; obviously, he knew it was explanation time.

"So tell me, Ramon—I mean, *Emilio*—what's going on here?" Carino's question carried on a fierce whisper.

"Okay, I know I should've told you that I was going to use another name, but there was no time."

"No time? You mean the entire drive over here wasn't enough?"

"Look, Carino, I just have to be careful about who knows I'm not in Denver right now." His answer did nothing but breed additional questions.

"Who are you talking about? And how would they know to look for you at a hospital anyway?" She was beginning to feel confined in the small space; there wasn't enough room for her, Ramon, and all their secrets.

"Just … people. Well, one person really. I don't know if he would look for me, but—look, it's just a really long story to go into."

"I think this is the perfect time, since I'm sure we're going to be here for a while."

He took a deep breath. "Raj knows we're together."

Oh shit. That wasn't good.

"I was on the phone with him back at the café and he overheard your voice. He's extremely angry because he told me to stay away from you—as if he has the right to do that—but now he's told Emerson too."

"And what did Emerson say about it?" She had been foolish, leaving her phone turned off all day.

"I don't know because I didn't take his call."

"You ignored Emerson's call? Was that such a good idea?" Carino's eyebrows nearly touched her hairline.

"I don't know that anything I'm doing right now is a good idea." She sucked in a ragged breath and he jerked his gaze toward her. Clearly he hadn't realized how that was going to sound. "Not with you! I just mean Emerson has certain expectations of me and I'm basically ignoring all of them."

"Expectations? Like what?" Although she pressed, she wasn't entirely sure she would be happy with his answer.

"Like, he expects me to keep him out of prison. And he expects me to do anything it takes in the process." He scrubbed his right hand over his face. Carino could tell her line of questioning was getting to him.

"Why would Emerson go to prison?" She wished she could suck those words right back into her mouth; even she could hear her phony tone of voice.

"Carino, I really do want to be honest with you, but I need your honesty in turn." She pressed her lips into a tight line, but knew he was right. "There's no way you could actually believe that Emerson is completely legitimate."

"Fair enough. Then maybe a better question is: *why* does Emerson think he's at risk of going to prison right now?"

He paused and tilted his head back, intently staring at the ceiling. For a tense moment, Carino didn't think he was going to answer.

"Because he knows—"

The curtain suddenly swung open, startling the both of them. Ramon grimaced, and Carino figured the motion had caused his pain to flare up again.

"Good afternoon, folks. Or I guess it's evening now, isn't it?" The cheerful doctor didn't look a day over twenty. "I'm Dr. Reed and this is my nurse, Kara. How are you feeling Mr. Sanchez?"

Carino crossed her arms over her chest and clamped down on her jaw. This was the most annoyingly efficient hospital she'd ever been to. They'd barely even been back there for five minutes!

"Not too bad, unless you count the glass splinters in my arm." Ramon again tried to make light of the situation.

"Well, let's get a closer look at what we're dealing with." Dr. Reed pulled on surgical gloves and gently removed the gauze from Ramon's arm.

Carino could tell, from the look on Ramon's face, that even the gentlest of movements were severely painful. She avoided his gaze, swallowing down her remorse at her selfish reaction to the doctor's untimely interruption.

"You've certainly got a lot going on back here. There's definitely glass and wood, plus a fairly deep cut—we'll be putting in some stitches, Kara—and that's just what I see on your arm. There are also a couple of areas on your shoulder blade that have already started to bruise and swell, but as far as I can tell there doesn't appear to be any splinters there. I'll need to examine those areas more as we go to make absolutely sure. What caused this anyway?"

"I managed to break the fall of some gnarly trash in the back of a construction truck." Ramon continued to minimize the bravery he'd shown in saving the older woman from harm.

"Your husband seems modest." Kara spoke quietly, leaning in close to Carino as she arranged the doctor's instruments on a metal tray.

"Yes, he sure is." Carino was once again reminded of her role as the dutiful wife. "He saved a woman's life today though."

"Better hang onto him then; there sure aren't many good ones left anymore."

Carino simply nodded, letting Kara's words wash over her as both she and the doctor began prepping Ramon's arm.

"I understand if you don't want to stay in here while they do this," Ramon said. Carino wasn't sure if he was simply concerned for her wellbeing or if he wanted to avoid continuing their previous discussion. And his face, as he spoke, gave nothing away. "Maybe you could go and get us both some coffee? By then, I'll be as good as new."

"Are you sure? I have no problem whatsoever staying in here with you." Truthfully, Carino was relieved that she wouldn't have to witness the pain on Ramon's face as they fished out the bloody debris from his skin.

"*Mi Cariño*, I would rather keep up the illusion that I'm a tough guy and not have you see me cry like a baby."

"We'll take good care of your husband, Mrs. Sanchez." Dr. Reed seemed to notice Carino's hesitation.

Smiling at Ramon's attempt to distract her from their unfinished business, Carino nodded at the doctor and approached the examination table.

"Okay, but I'll be back very quickly to check on you." She leaned in to gently kiss him on the cheek.

"I'll wait right here."

"And we need to finish our conversation." She spoke quietly.

His intense gaze met hers and she waited for him to nod in agreement before exiting the room.

As she walked down the hall, following the signs leading her to the cafeteria, Carino realized it would be foolish to leave this hospital before she found out what Ramon had been about to say; there was simply too much at stake.

Chapter 30

"That should do it." Dr. Reed completed the final suture on Ramon's arm and fixed his bandages.

It had taken over an hour just to pick all the glass, metal threads, and splinters out of his skin, not to mention the extra time spent cleaning the wounds and preparing him for stitches. But the worst part of the entire process, by far, was the tetanus shot; that hurt, plain and simple.

Carino had brought him some coffee earlier, but when he noticed her trying very hard to look away from the bloody fragments on the doctor's tray, he told her he didn't mind if she wanted to browse around the hospital until the procedure was finished; she wasted no time in doing just that.

Dr. Reed handed Ramon a script for painkillers. "We should have you and your wife out of here in no time, Mr. Sanchez."

Don't get too used to the sound of that.

"Thanks, doc. I appreciate you putting me back together again." He reached for his hospital gown, wondering if he would get to take it home. If not, he'd be walking out half-naked.

"You betcha. Off to see my next patient." Dr. Reed shook Ramon's hand before he left.

"You did a really heroic thing today, Mr. Sanchez." Kara beamed at him, assisting with the gown.

"Anyone would've done the same."

"Yeah, maybe. But it wasn't anyone; it was you."

Just then, Carino peeked around the curtain.

"How's our patient doing?" She looked relieved that his wounds were now concealed by clean bandages.

He hid a grimace as he twisted around on the examination table, drawing Carino into his open arms, as Kara moved away to tidy up the mess.

"Better, now that you're back."

"I bought you something." Carino handed Ramon the bag he hadn't noticed she was carrying.

"What's this?" Inside he found a black t-shirt, brandishing a small pink ribbon on the chest.

"Breast cancer awareness?" He was genuinely touched by her thoughtfulness.

"It's the only one they had in your size." She shrugged her shoulders. "And I figured if anyone would look good in pink, it would be you."

"You're very good to me, you know?" Ramon pulled her close for a quick kiss.

Don't get too used to kissing her all the time.

"How long have you two been married?" Kara clearly admired their affection.

"Not long enough." Ramon winked at Carino, causing her to blush, as usual.

"Well, it's always refreshing to see a couple like you two. I'll go and see if Dr. Reed has finalized your release paperwork, Mr. Sanchez."

Don't get too used to being a couple.

As soon as Kara left, Carino began carefully undoing the thin fabric strings Ramon had struggled so hard to tie mere moments ago.

"Let's get you out of this crazy thing." Carino carefully pulled his gown off without displacing the bandages.

"Really? You want to do this right here?" Ramon gasped, before shrugging his shoulders. "Okay, I'm game."

She laughed, but as her hands touched his bare skin, the humor in her eyes turned into something primal and the air seemed to thicken around them. Carino's touch caused goose flesh to break out from his head to his toes, and he would've given anything to feel her entire body against his at that exact moment. She leaned closer, reverently running her hands over his chest and up the sides of his neck, until she fisted them in his hair.

Ramon was still sitting on the examination table, so he spread his knees apart, reached his arms around her waist, and pulled her against him. Carino tilted his head back and leaned down to gently plant a kiss on his lips.

"Okay, you're all set," interrupted Kara. "Oops, I'm so sorry!"

Carino backed away quickly, wiping her mouth with the back of her hand. Ramon was simply frustrated; he wanted this woman all to himself for a while, and had long since grown tired of all the disruptions.

"Let's get out of here." He was anxious to be alone with her once again.

"Well, if you don't want a bunch of women swooning at your feet, you'd better put your shirt on. I can help you, if you want."

"Your compliments are extremely flattering." He turned around to grab his new shirt off of the table. Carino sucked in a horrified gasp as she saw the full extent of the abrasions and bruises that now marred his left shoulder blade.

"I'm so sorry, Ramon. Does it hurt very much?" Her voice was thick with concern, as she took the shirt from him knowing he'd need assistance.

"It's just a scratch."

"I'm just so thankful you're okay." She reached her arms up to position the opening of the shirt over his head.

Ramon swallowed deeply and nodded. Her nearness was beginning to be more than he could bear; they needed to get back on the road so he'd have something to focus on besides her alluring body and the delicate curve of her soft lips.

As they made their way out to the parking lot, Ramon told Carino that he could drive, but she insisted that he get some rest. Truthfully, he did think some time to relax would be helpful, so he didn't even bother arguing.

No sooner had she put the car in reverse did his stomach let out a loud rumble, reminding him of how long they'd truly been at the hospital.

"All right, I can take a hint." She eased out of the lot. "But since it's pretty late, how do you feel about pulling into a drive-thru somewhere?"

"You actually eat that crap?" Ramon clapped his hands against his cheeks and opened his mouth in horror.

"Of course. How do you think I keep my girlish figure?"

• • •

"How are you feeling?" Carino had just gotten back into the car after disposing of their fast food garbage.

His arm was beginning to throb, but he didn't want to waste any more time by stopping at a pharmacy; he wanted to spend every single remaining moment of the day focusing on Carino. And for that, he could handle a little pain.

"Definitely better." He hoped his lie was convincing. She didn't seem to handle seeing him in pain very well and knew she would never bypass picking up his prescription if she knew. "Plus, I've had enough food to last me for days."

"Tell me about it. I don't think I've ever eaten two burgers in one afternoon. It's going to take me forever to work off these calories!"

Ramon pointedly looked her up and down, immediately causing her to squirm under his blatantly appraising stare.

"Carino, I think it's high time you accept the fact that you're incredibly beautiful. Every single thing about you is perfect." He loved watching the heat rise to her cheeks.

"You must still be hopped up on whatever drugs they gave you back at the hospital." She was clearly uncomfortable with his admiration. "Plus, I think you're just trying to distract me from finishing our earlier conversation."

Ramon had known his reprieve would be short-lived, which was why he'd used his time in the examination room to prepare what he was going to say. Even though he wanted to trust Carino, he didn't know how she would take knowing he'd been investigating her and several others at Franklin Everly. And at this point, he simply wasn't willing to take a chance.

"In case you forgot, we left off before I could tell you why Emerson brought me here, and why he thinks his freedom is in jeopardy."

Carino shot him a sideways glance. "Oh, I didn't forget."

"Why am I not surprised?"

Am I going to be surprised at her reaction, if she ever finds out the truth?

He steeled himself against further self-depreciating thoughts, and began telling the lie he'd prepared. "Emerson recently started doing business with a new client, but began to suspect that the guy was stealing from him. Emerson figured, since he was going to be here signing the Costa Rica papers and it just so happened that the guy's primary residence is in Cherry Creek, that he could kill two birds with one stone—figuratively speaking, of course."

"So, how does prison time fit into all of that?" She was frowning, apparently trying to connect the dots.

"Emerson thinks the guy could be getting ready to double-cross him."

"And now he's angry with you because … "

"Because he expects me to *handle* the situation—and instead, I'm here with you."

Even though Ramon had prepared himself for her questions, he felt increasingly guilty as his lie continued to get bigger.

"Define 'handle.'"

"I'm sure you can imagine what a man like Emerson would expect of someone like me." Ramon was wary, knowing that he was skirting around information that could forever change her opinion of him.

"Ramon, I'm not naïve; you're very intimidating. And I know Raj is afraid of you for a reason. Obviously, you have certain … specialties, which Emerson clearly utilizes."

"That's a nice way to phrase it." He was simultaneously relieved and troubled that she could sense what he was capable of.

"But, since you're shirking your duties, what does that mean?"

Ramon breathed deep, taking a moment to look out the window at the darkening night sky; she'd asked a very poignant question, which he'd been pondering even more since he'd met her.

"Well, Carino," Ramon turned to face her, "that means I've decided it's time for Emerson and me to part ways."

Carino tore her eyes away from the road to quickly glance at him, and the look on her face was full of hope, with a dash of suspicion.

"So, you're telling me that you've suddenly decided, after all these years, that you're going to go your own way—and you expect that Emerson is just going to sit idly by and let you do that?"

"I really don't know what to expect. But the point I'm trying to make is that my life is my own, and this decision is long overdue."

At least that statement was honest.

"You do know there will be consequences, right?"

"Yes, and I'm prepared to deal with them. I've lived a life I'm not proud of, Carino, and I'm ready to make a permanent change."

Chapter 31

"Do you want to come inside for a minute?" Carino hesitated to get out, once she turned off his car. She didn't feel like they'd spent nearly enough time together and their day was already over.

"I'd love to." Ramon reached over and tucked a few loose strands of hair behind her ear.

She closed her eyes and leaned into his touch. It was so warm and gentle. She never wanted to forget the way his skin felt against hers. "I'm just not quite ready to face reality yet."

Ramon quickly pulled her in for a kiss, and Carino savored every last moment. It was becoming increasingly difficult to imagine a day going by when she wouldn't get to taste his lips or feel his breath on her face.

"Want to call in sick tomorrow and watch movies all day?" His offer was mighty tempting and she actually found herself considering it for a moment.

"If only." She heaved a big sigh and flopped her hands into her lap. Looking out the window at her house, she felt a sudden wash of melancholy come over her.

"C'mon, let's get you inside before it's any later."

As soon as she opened her front door, the absolute hollowness of her house hit Carino like a ton of bricks. It felt as if a lifetime had passed since the last time she'd been there, even though it had hardly been over twelve hours.

"Hey, is everything okay?" Ramon was instantly on alert, when she didn't immediately answer. With amazing speed, he whipped a knife out of his back pocket and stepped in front of her, instinctively protecting her from the unidentified danger. What he didn't realize was that he couldn't protect her from this, from the consequences of her own actions.

Nope, those I get to deal with all by myself.

"Ramon, it's nothing." Carino finally found her voice, although it came out squeaky from barely restrained emotion. She lightly grabbed his arm to capture his full attention, since he was still focused on the unseen threat. She eyed the weapon he was holding, noticing the sheen of the long, metal blade and the lethal stance he'd adopted like second nature.

After taking one last look around the room, Ramon retracted the blade and tucked it back into his pocket. "You scared me, baby. I thought someone was in here." She could see the veins in his neck pumping hard from the shot of adrenaline he must've felt. "I don't know what I'd do if anything happened to you."

Carino quickly wrapped her arms around him and drew him into a fierce hug. She'd come to feel the exact same way about him, which made everything that much more difficult from here on out.

"Sorry about that." She leaned against his broad chest. She could hear his heart beating fast and strong.

Ramon kissed the top of her head and then rested his chin on her. They embraced in silence for a long minute before he sighed heavily. "Well, I'd better get going and let you get to bed. Will I see you tomorrow?"

Probably not.

Looking up at him, Carino had a sinking feeling that things were never going to be the same as they were at this exact moment; they'd been existing in a bubble that was impossible to sustain.

She reached her hands around the back of Ramon's head and threaded her fingers through his hair, simultaneously pulling him down toward her. Her lips parted and she kissed him with all the fervor she could muster, searing the memory into her brain for all eternity.

Breaking away proved difficult, as Ramon closed in on her each time she tried. Before she knew it, her back was against the wall and she had nowhere left to go. Clasping each side of her face, Ramon's mouth crashed against hers, over and over, until they were both panting with pent up desire.

"Ramon," Carino pleaded, but he studiously ignored her as he sucked her earlobe into his mouth. "I want—"

Ramon silenced her with another searing kiss, his mouth hot and greedy. He grabbed her hips and pulled her toward him, grinding against her, wild with barely restrained need. Suddenly, he released his grip and backed up. "Baby, we've got to stop or I'm not going to be able to."

His words sent a jolt of desire through her body and she knew she didn't really want him to stop. But she knew she needed to get this out. "Ramon, I want you to know that this past week has been one of the best in my entire life."

He ran a hand through his hair and furrowed his brow. "But … ?"

Carino pulled completely free of his arms and stepped away. "*But* I know things could get complicated, and I just want you to know that I don't have any expectations."

"Yes, things might be complicated, but you're worth it to me. Carino, I'm willing to do whatever it takes. I just need to figure out a couple of things and then I'm free. For the next … I don't know, forever."

The heaviness of his words settled around her and Carino found that she didn't have a response. She kept her eyes trained on her feet, trying to figure out what to do next. She knew what her heart—and her body—was telling her, but it was completely at odds with her head and her responsibilities.

"I know it's a lot to think about and things have happened really, really fast, but please know that I'm telling you the truth. In fact," he paused to take a deep breath, "I think I've fallen in love with you."

Carino snapped her head up and looked him square in the eye. He'd just pinned his heart on his sleeve and was waiting to see what she was going to do with it. The sincerity that emanated from his eyes was overwhelming, and she could tell he was holding his breath, anticipating her response.

This is it. There's no undoing what I'm about to do.

She shut her eyes and breathed in deep. "Ramon, I don't—"

He took a giant step closer to her, holding both his palms out in front of him, as if he could physically block the words she'd been about to say.

"Please, Carino. Just think about it, because I know you feel it too. Please, don't shut me out."

Carino closed the remaining distance between them, and he loosely grabbed onto her waist, waiting patiently for her to speak.

"I wasn't going to. I was going to tell you that I don't want you to go."

He sucked in a breath and his eyes went wide. "You mean … "

"Yes, that's exactly what I mean." Carino confirmed the truth of her words—not only to him but to herself as well—by pressing her body against him once more and standing on her tiptoes so she could reach his lips.

Returning her affections with an unparalleled passion, Ramon picked her up and she wrapped her legs around his waist.

"Ramon, you should be careful! You're going to hurt yourself." He ignored her protests, and for a man who'd received six stitches in his arm less than two hours ago, he managed to carry her down the hall with ease.

"I. Don't. Give. A. Damn." He punctuated each word with a kiss.

They reached her room and Ramon gingerly laid Carino down on the bed. He hovered over her, merely brushing himself against her most sensitive areas, despite her shameless efforts to pull him closer. The muscles in his arms flexed powerfully as he deliberately kept his weight off of her, but the pure, unadulterated desire radiating from his body caused a shiver to run down the length of her spine.

"*Mi Cariño*, you are my world." He lowered his mouth to the tender skin behind her ear, causing her mind to go completely blank. "And you have my heart, forever."

After kissing a trail of fire down her neck, he continued his exploration until he reached the fabric of her shirt. "This has got to go. Now," he rasped, pulling her upright so she could maneuver it over her head.

Carino reached behind her back and unhooked her bra, thankful she'd chosen the one with pretty blue lace. Her breathing became more rapid by the second. As Ramon's gaze swept over her nakedness, a sexy smile spread across his face as he stood up, pulled a foil package from his back pocket, and slowly undressed.

"You are the most beautiful woman I've ever seen."

Carino couldn't even speak. She felt like she was floating on a cloud. Never before had she seen a man so glorious. He was all sinew and muscle, not an ounce of fat to be found. And he wanted her; that much was completely and magnificently evident.

Desire began to curl deep in her belly as he climbed over her once again. He lightly feathered his fingers over her body. His tongue was everywhere his hands weren't, and she quivered with anticipation, knowing this man was capable of inciting pleasure she had only ever dreamed about.

He began tugging at her pants, and growled as the button got stuck, causing him to stop his investigation of the tender skin around her navel.

"How fond are you of these jeans?" he asked, his voice so husky it barely sounded like his own.

"I can always get another pair." The sound of ripping material filled the room and then he was pulling them off. Her bare legs were fully exposed, but instead of feeling self-conscious, she felt like a goddess under his scorching gaze.

Carino felt his hot breath once again, only lower this time, and she gasped with delight. He knew exactly what to do to make her squirm. And when he finally brought his hooded eyes up to meet hers, she saw a hunger that surely surpassed her own.

...

"You're so beautiful." Ramon ran his hands through Carino's hair and trailed his fingertips lightly down her bare arm. "I could never get tired of just looking at you."

He was carefully lying on his right side, since he'd mentioned his other arm had started throbbing a little while ago. The blankets were heaped on the floor and Carino was beginning to get chilled under the thin sheet, but was too content to move. Her heart was so full that she thought it might burst right out of her chest.

"Thank you." She fought mightily against the urge to rush to the bathroom to fix her makeup, which was surely smeared by now.

"I'm going to get dressed and go find us something to snack on. Do you mind?" He leaned in to nuzzle his nose against her chin.

"Yes, I do mind. I want you to stay here with me."

"You've zapped my energy, woman! I've got to recharge."

Carino caressed his gorgeous face one last time, reluctant to let him leave the room, and he kissed the palm of her hand. "Okay, but hurry back."

She couldn't stop staring at his tall, muscular body as he began to get dressed. Of course, he busted her.

"Do you like what you see?" He slowly pulled on his t-shirt, mimicking a model's stance.

Carino threw her pillow at him and he caught it with ease.

"You'll do, I guess." She could still hear his laughter through the partially closed door as he walked down the hallway to the kitchen.

She flopped back down on the bed, completely stunned by everything that had just happened. Actually, the entire day had been overwhelming, right from the start. She and Ramon had reached a whole new level, especially after the intimacy they'd just shared. He was an amazing lover and she knew she was ruined against other men forever. She also felt like their relationship might actually stand a chance, since he'd trusted her enough to let her in—to know what he was dealing with and why Emerson had brought him here. And she was more than relieved that it didn't have anything to do with her investigation into Emerson, or with Abby or Franklin Everly at all, and that her suspicions about his true purpose had been way off base. His decision to give up the life he'd been living was enormous, since that was a hard limit for her. She would obviously never be able to carry on with him if he planned to keep doing Emerson's dirty work.

Reaching for her phone on the nightstand to see how late it was, she suddenly remembered it was still in the bottom of her purse. And it was still turned off.

The last thing I need right now is an unexpected visitor checking up on me.

Carino flew out of bed and hastily dressed, remembering that she'd left her purse somewhere in the living room. She should've turned it back on the minute they'd left the hospital, but had gotten so caught up in their conversation that she'd completely forgotten. Surely, there were plenty of colorful messages waiting.

As she began walking down the hall, Carino could hear Ramon's hushed voice coming from the kitchen.

"No, I haven't. Because I'm still with her. She's eating out of the palm of my hand. Maybe you are, but I'll leave the country before taking the fall for anyone—for you or Emerson, for that matter. Oh really, you're going to tell her about the cameras? What makes you think she'd believe you anyway? She trusts me, not you. Maybe I should just kill you too then. You're really starting to become a pain in my ass anyway."

"Ramon?" Carino was completely taken aback by his side of the conversation.

He spun around, guilt marring his chiseled features.

"I've got to go." He abruptly ended the call.

"Who were you just talking to?" Even though she asked, somehow she already knew the answer.

"No one important." He tried to act nonchalant, probably hoping she hadn't actually heard his conversation.

"Really? Because it sounded to me like you just threatened them. I'd say that puts them firmly in the 'important' category. So, who was it?" She was offering him one chance to tell her the truth.

"Carino, it's not what you think." He began walking toward her.

"Stop right there, Ramon." She held her palm out in front of her and her eyes were hard. "And do not even begin to tell me that you know what I'm thinking right now. Was that Raj?"

"Carino—"

"Cut the shit, Ramon. Was that Raj?"

He hung his head. "Yes."

"Where are these cameras he's going to tell me about?" She was angrier than she could ever remember being. "I mean, surely I'll believe anything you have to say since I'm—how did you put it? 'Eating out of the palm of your hand.'" Ramon's lips were turning white, he had them pressed together so tight. "Where, damn it?"

"In here. The cameras are here, in your house." He inched closer to her with each word of his admission.

"Who put them in here?"

"I did. Yesterday."

"Before you came to visit me at the office?"

He nodded.

No wonder Nathan wanted to talk.

"Why?"

"Because I was worried that Nathan was going to hurt you."

Carino rubbed her hands across her face, trying to figure out if he was even telling her the truth, since his betrayal had suddenly stripped her of her wits. She wondered how much of her private life he'd seen or heard. Did he know she was undercover? Is that why he'd seduced her—so he could get her to her most vulnerable state and then easily eliminate her for Emerson?

"You promised you'd never hurt me. Well, this hurts, Ramon." His face began to crumple. "So, what, am I disposable or something?"

"No, Carino, of course not."

"Well, what do you want from me then? What else aren't you telling me?" Her anger was quickly paving the way for the hurt she felt building up inside by the second.

"Nothing." He was content on continuing his streak of lies.

"Oh really? Is that why you told Raj you should kill him *too*? Who else do you plan on killing? Me? Was it your plan to screw me first? Well played, Ramon. Well fucking played. No wonder you had a condom in your back pocket."

"Carino, you've got it all wrong. I'm not going to kill anyone! I told you I've changed, and I meant it."

"Bullshit! Who are you here for, Ramon?" Carino's wrath was fueled by the fury flowing through her veins.

"No one!" The volume of his voice now rose to match hers. "I was supposed to be searching for a spy at Franklin Everly, because Emerson found out someone has been feeding inside information to the Feds. He wanted me to find and kill them, but after I met you, I knew I couldn't follow through with it. I'm getting out of the life, Carino. I can't do this anymore. I swear, that's the truth!"

Carino felt as if the floor was beginning to drop out from underneath her.

Oh shit, Emerson knows there's an informant. But he doesn't know who. He doesn't know it's me.

"Do you even know what truth is, Ramon?" She nearly choked on the hypocrisy that was beginning to bubble up inside of her. "That crap you told me on the drive home—was it all lies too?"

"Not all of it, but yes, I did lie about the real reason I'm here." He rushed over and grabbed her hands before she could pull them away. "I didn't want to risk losing you, Carino. I wasn't going to follow through with Emerson's orders anyway, and not just because Abby is too important to you. I wouldn't have let him hurt her. You've got to believe me. I'm done with it all, so I just didn't think it would matter in the end."

Abby? Oh my God. So Emerson did *find out she's been talking to someone outside of the firm and figured her as the informant. And Ramon was sent here to kill her. I've literally just slept with the enemy.*

Jerking her hands from his grasp, Carino crossed her arms over her chest in a lame attempt to protect her heart from further injury. "*You* were the one sent here to hurt her, Ramon. All the while you've been plotting her death at your hand. So how could you just act like everything was fine? Like you hadn't broken into my house! Like you haven't been spying on me! How could you brag to Raj about how you've used me? Was it also a lie when you said you loved me?" Carino felt the pinpricks of tears burning her eyes and she chewed on her bottom lip in an effort to keep her chin from quivering.

Ramon furiously shook his head. "Carino, I'm in love with you and that's a fact. I haven't been plotting Abby's death, I've been *protecting* her. Yes, I made a mistake putting cameras in here, and an even bigger one not telling you about them. You also should know I had a tracker on your car." Carino's mouth gaped open. "At first, it was because of the job I was doing for Emerson, but then everything else I did was to try to figure out why Nathan was stalking you. I was trying to help."

She blew out a deep breath. "So you have been watching me then?"

She wasn't as worried about him tracking her location, since lately she'd thankfully only been to home, work, and out with Abby. But she was concerned about the camera footage. She knew it was ridiculous to think he'd installed the cameras and then not looked at the feed, but she held out hope anyway.

"No. Okay, yes, but not—"

"You just can't stop lying, can you?" Carino threw her hands in the air. "You know, it's time for you to leave."

"Please, Carino, I'm trying to make you understand!" Ramon reached for her once more, a plea clear in his eyes.

"Don't you dare touch me, Ramon!" She moved out of his reach. "And I understand perfectly. Once a killer, always a killer, right?"

"No, Carino, that's not right." His shoulders sagged and he looked defeated; he could obviously tell he was fighting a losing battle.

"Get out, Ramon. Now. Please."

He searched her eyes one last time, but then grabbed his jacket that he'd draped over the stool. He took a small bag out of his pocket and laid it on the counter before turning to look at her; she immediately looked away.

"I never meant to hurt you or lie to you. I love you. If you don't believe anything else I've said, please believe that. One day, I hope you'll realize how sorry I am."

Carino didn't even respond, but instead stood in the middle of her living room with tears streaming down her face, while the man of her dreams walked out of her life.

Chapter 32

Throughout Ramon's life, he'd had to do some horrible things—unspeakable things that would drive weaker men to madness, but walking away from Carino was, by far, the worst. He closed the door behind him and stood on her porch, unable to bring himself to put one foot in front of the other. Moments later, he heard the deadbolt latch from the inside.

The entire day with Carino had been nothing short of incredible, with extreme emphasis on the last couple of hours. She was everything he could've ever imagined, and more. But now, everything was in ruins. Ramon hadn't been so naïve as to think his actions would forever go undiscovered, but he'd never imagined things would unfold quite like this. Just moments ago, he and Carino had experienced something truly life-changing; now, the polar opposite.

Devastation didn't even begin to define how he'd felt watching Carino break down in front of his very eyes. But he'd screwed up, and once again allowed his hatred toward Raj get the best of him.

He'd known Carino was deadly serious when she'd ordered him to leave, so there really hadn't been any point in trying harder to convince her otherwise. He could only hope she would have a change of heart after thinking everything through. Ramon doubted she would forgive him—at least not right away, but if she could provide him with even a tiny glimmer of hope, he could work with that.

He somehow ended up back at his hotel, but for the life of him, couldn't remember the drive. His mind seemed to have shut down, protecting him from a situation that was too traumatic to handle. But no matter how hard he tried, he couldn't seem to block out the last image he had of her, still standing despite the emotional ambush she'd just endured. Ramon knew the look on Carino's tear-stained face would haunt him for all eternity.

The valet had done a double take when Ramon handed him the key to his car, so he must've looked worse than he realized, but luckily due to the late hour, he didn't run into anyone in the lobby. It was after two a.m. and the lounge was closed, so Ramon trudged to his room and raided what was left of the minibar; there wasn't nearly enough to do the trick. Gulping down everything he could find, he sat cross-legged on the floor amidst an array of tiny, empty bottles, waiting for the alcohol to numb his pain. Or at least take the edge off.

Time had no meaning. He just sat, staring at a spot on the wall until he felt a slight warmth spreading throughout his body. He hauled himself off the floor, the weight of his despair making his movements difficult as he crawled into bed. He didn't even bother taking off his clothes.

• • •

His pounding headache woke him from a fitful sleep. Sitting up, Ramon immediately clutched his chest, certain that he was having a heart attack; there was no other explanation for that level of agony.

That's called a broken heart.

Inhaling deep, staccato breaths as he tried to breathe through the pain, he noticed the small alarm clock on the nightstand read 6:25 a.m. Less than five hours since "The Incident," as he'd now labeled what had happened between him and Carino. Ramon knew she didn't want to hear him out, but he absolutely couldn't bear the thought of her hating him. He had to tell her the things that she was too angry and hurt to let him say before, even if she didn't change her mind and forgive him.

Reaching for his phone, Ramon cleared his throat and dialed Carino's number. He tugged at his collar and bounced his leg up and down. His anxiety was becoming unmanageable. Instead of ringing, the call immediately went to voice mail.

"Hi, this is Carino. Sorry I missed you, but leave a message and I'll call you back."

He hung up quickly, before the beep; the mere sound of her voice had paralyzed his thoughts.

Suddenly, Ramon realized this could be his one and only opportunity to explain himself to her, so he should probably wake up a little more and plan out what to say, before he laid his heart on the line on a recording. She'd be able to play it over and over, so he'd better not screw it up.

Ramon went to the bathroom and splashed water on his face, barely recognizing the man reflected back in the mirror; it looked as if he'd aged ten years overnight. His eyes were bleary and his cheeks were hollow. He looked like complete shit.

Changing out of his limp clothes, he went back into the bathroom and brushed his teeth and shaved, all the while formulating something to say that would be compelling enough for her to give him another chance.

By the time he had his act together enough to try Carino's number again, it had been around ten minutes, and he was now worried that she might actually answer the phone instead of sending his call to voice mail; he *really* wasn't prepared for that. But, again it didn't even ring, and he was able to leave his message.

With the ball back in her court, Ramon now needed to focus on what to do about Abby. If Raj was right and shit was going down, he'd have to move quickly; the Feds wouldn't make a move against someone like Emerson unless they were ready to strike fast.

Ramon still didn't think anyone else knew about the information Abby had been compiling—and obviously sharing—on Emerson, but he couldn't be totally sure. He wasn't even sure of the extent of what she'd truly done, since he hadn't even confronted her about the specifics yet. He was certain, however, that if Emerson knew she was involved in anything that could lead to his incarceration, she was in grave danger. Even if her death wouldn't affect the outcome of Emerson's fate, he would see to it that she died, simply because.

Gearing up for the second difficult call this morning, Ramon dialed Emerson's number.

"So this is what a dead man sounds like?" Emerson picked up after the first ring.

"Let's just cut the bullshit, Emerson."

"Well, I just figured the only way you'd ignore my repeated phone calls was if you were face down in a ditch somewhere. But, according to Raj, you were just face down on some cooch instead. She must've been some piece if she could make you bite the hand that's fed you all these years."

"You need to be very careful about what you say to me. Don't forget what I'm capable of, and right now, it sure would make my life easier if you weren't in it." Ramon's mouth was fixed in a snarl as he began to pace angry circles around the room.

"No, *you* need to be careful, Ramon. I've already found out who the squealer is anyway, so I'll be taking things over. Raj overheard that bitch, Abby, himself, so a lot of good it did me bringing you here. You'd do well to remember your place, and that as easily as I made you, I can take it all away. Just like that! Gone. And you'll be rotting away somewhere in a hole."

"That's funny, from what I heard, it's going to be you who's rotting away. In fact, I think I'm just the one to make sure that's exactly what happens to you."

"ARE YOU CRAZY? DO YOU KNOW WHO YOU'RE TALK—"

Ramon ended the call before Emerson could spew any more filth out of his putrid mouth.

Springing into action, knowing he was now in a race against time for not just Abby's life, but his own too, Ramon grabbed the essentials and sprinted out of the hotel down to the lot where his trusty Camry was parked. Luckily, his GPS tracker indicated Abby was already downtown, so she must've gone to work early. That would definitely make a huge difference, since she wasn't very far away from him, but he still had to get to her before Emerson did—and he knew he'd be cutting it close.

Chapter 33

Carino didn't know how long she sat with her back against the front door. She might've even dozed off for a bit because when she finally tried to get up, her entire lower half was asleep. Her lips were chapped and her eyes were swollen. She aimlessly wandered into the kitchen in search of a drink of water to rehydrate all she'd lost from crying.

Deep down, she'd known Ramon had been a huge risk in so many ways, but that knowledge didn't soothe her hurt feelings even a little bit. But she knew that eventually, once the initial shock of their confrontation wore off, she would recognize how thankful she was that Ramon hadn't discovered she was working undercover. Which, she conceded, was a miracle considering how fully he'd infiltrated her life. What she couldn't get over was how quickly she'd become attached to him, and how much his betrayal cut her to the bone.

She took several deep gulps of water before setting the glass down on the counter, right next to the bag Ramon had left behind. Her first instinct was to throw it in the garbage without looking inside, but in the end, her curiosity got the best of her. Opening the bag, Carino pulled out a small item covered in white tissue paper. She unwrapped it, revealing a delicate silver cuff bracelet, with turquoise stones and what surely was hand detailing. It was very high quality and had definitely cost a pretty penny. She also loved it.

Clearly, she'd been wrong to assume her tears were all cried out because a fresh batch began free flowing down her cheeks. She put the cuff on her wrist and squeezed it tight; it looked beautiful.

She hated what had happened between her and Ramon. But what's more, she hated how much she already missed him. He'd taken her heart with him when he walked out the door, and now her chest felt painfully hollow. She wondered if he was feeling the same way right now.

Glancing at the clock, the time read 4:45 a.m.; she'd fallen asleep after all. Knowing there was no way she could go to bed now, Carino decided to take a shower. Her bones ached and her head swam as she trudged down the hallway, bombarded by the memories of Ramon carrying her to the bedroom mere hours ago.

Finally making it to the bathroom, she turned on the water as hot as it would go and began to examine herself in the mirror. Her face was wrecked and her eyes were nearly shut. She was pale as a ghost and there was an aura of sadness no amount of makeup would be able to conceal.

She undressed on autopilot and stepped into the shower, forcing herself to stand under the scalding spray until she couldn't take it any longer. She washed and scrubbed, trying her hardest to rid herself of Ramon's scent, but she could still smell him. It was as if he was a part of her very essence now.

Carino shut off the water, noticing her skin was beet red. She began her after-shower ritual, aiming for a look that would pass as presentable. When she finally entered the bedroom, she stopped in her tracks as a fresh wave of devastation washed over her; the rumpled bed was an unwelcome sight. She got dressed and immediately set about stripping the mattress and replacing the sheets with a fresh set. She loaded the soiled linens into her small washer before hauling out the spare comforter, which would get her by until she could make it to the laundromat to address the bulkier items.

At a little after 6:30, Carino sat down with a cup of coffee. Deciding she'd put off reconnecting with the real world for as long as she possibly could, she reluctantly clicked her phone back to life. Immediately, it began blowing up with notification alerts; she had four texts, five voice mails, and two new emails.

Well shit.

She decided to read the emails first, which turned out to be a huge mistake. Her heart sank as she read the first one, which contained a single sentence from the director.

"You'd better be in my office first thing on Thursday morning."

But seriously, what did I expect?

Her stomach turned sour at the thought of facing the next email, which, of course, was from Nathan.

"Are you crazy? How dare you go dark right now? You've seriously got a death wish."

Screw you.

The texts were all from Nathan as well, but basically said the exact same thing as his emails, so Carino quickly moved on to the voice mails. Four were from Nathan, but they were just hang-ups. The fifth message was from Ramon and the time was only three minutes ago.

"Please don't delete this until you listen to the whole thing. You have every right to hate me because I did lie to you from the start, but not about everything. Still, you deserved better than that from me—I mean, I don't know how I would handle it if our situations were reversed."

She closed her eyes and swallowed deeply, knowing full well that the skeletons she'd hidden in her own closet were just as bad as his—if not worse. Just as easily as she'd chosen not to include Ramon in her formal investigation of Emerson, she could've tricked him and taken him down too. She wondered how he would've reacted to that knowledge.

His message continued. "Yesterday, I wanted to tell you why I was really here in Denver, but it's just not that easy for me to trust people. I now know I can trust you, but it's hard for me since I've spent my whole life dealing with liars and criminals. I know that we can't have a long-term relationship if it's not based in truth, so I'm prepared to tell you anything and everything you want to know. I'm done hiding, Carino. I need you in my life. I need you to please forgive me and allow me a second chance. I won't disappoint you, I promise. I feel like my life had finally just begun and now I'm lost, all over again. We've got to figure this out, because I know we belong together. I'm at your command. Just name the time and place and I'll be there. Please, baby, I love you."

Carino was trembling when the message finally ended. No matter what, the fact remained that he'd lied to her. He'd made her feel used and had bragged about it to Raj, of all people. He'd invaded her personal space and compromised her privacy. In all of her wallowing, she hadn't even started searching for his hidden cameras, so for all she knew, he could be watching her right then.

But deep down, she reluctantly admitted that he was just doing his job, and not everything done in the line of duty was pretty. There were casualties—some physical and others emotional—and that's just the way it was. Besides, no one in their right mind would have trusted that kind of information to another person until they knew—for certain—that they were *the one*.

Exactly the same reason I haven't divulged my own secrets.

But now, hearing the desolation in his voice and knowing exactly how he felt inside, Carino knew she was going to forgive him. After she straightened out the mess she was in, she was going to call him and they were going to come together and air everything out. They'd start fresh and really give the relationship a shot.

Her phone suddenly came to life, the loud ring echoing through her empty house.

Nathan.

Carino took a deep breath. "Hello?"

"Holy shit, you *are* alive. I thought that maybe Ramon had killed you before he left your house this morning. I was about to come inside to check."

"I can't deal with you right now, so get to the point, please." She was beginning to buckle under the emotional strain.

"Well, you'd better suck it up, honey, because I'm just getting started."

"Goodbye, Nathan." She hung up, simply unable to muster anything more.

She immediately noticed there was a new voice mail indicator, which hadn't been there moments ago; another call must've come in at the exact same time as Nathan's.

Accessing her mailbox, Carino saw it was from Abby and pressed play.

"Carino! I really need to talk to you. I think I've seriously messed up! I never meant for anyone else to get involved, but then everything got really out of hand. I came in to work early today and there were men here. Official men, like the CIA or FBI or something, and they took Raj with them! I don't know what to do now, but I'm really scared. I don't even understand what's going on! Oh no, I've gotta go."

Carino didn't move for several minutes, as her sluggish brain attempted to process what was happening. She felt like she was going to pass out and couldn't seem to get her breathing under control.

Finally, her thoughts coagulated and the message was clear: if Raj was in custody, she needed to get to the office right away.

• • •

It was around 7:30 a.m. when Carino walked into the building, dressed in a dark, wool trench coat, complete with matching crocheted hat and scarf; it was chilly outside at that hour. But it was also sunny, so she had her aviators on as well. She was so bundled up that it would've been difficult to even recognize her, if anyone happened to be watching.

As she passed the guard station, she was immediately reminded of all the one-minute conversations she and Sammy had exchanged over the years. But, since she already knew what was in store for her once she got upstairs, she realized she'd probably never even see him again.

Carino pressed the button for the fifth floor and rode the elevator up, but probably should've run the stairs so she could've burned off the adrenaline that was pumping through her veins at the mere thought of being in that building right then.

Stopping outside the main entry doors, she stripped out of her extra clothes before walking in. She was already getting hot and knew it was just going to get worse, once they turned up the pressure.

Plus, she was stalling.

When she'd finally built up enough courage to walk in, Carino didn't immediately recognize the woman behind the front desk. She was on the phone, so Carino waited patiently while trying to figure out if she'd ever seen her before.

"May I help you?" the woman asked, as she ended her call.

"Hi, um…where's—"

"Oh, you're Carino, right?"

Carino nodded, as fissures of panic began to spread throughout her body.

"They're waiting for you in Conference Room D."

D for Dead. Fitting.

"Okay, thank you." She was so nervous she nearly choked on her words.

"Do you still remember where that is? I know it's been a while since you've been here." Carino barely heard her, as she had already turned down the long hallway.

She concentrated on the diamond pattern of the carpet. She focused on putting one foot in front of the other. Breathe in, breathe out. As she reached the conference room, Carino noticed the door was closed so she stopped and took a few deep, calming breaths. She counted to ten. She said a short, silent prayer. It had been several years since she'd stepped foot in HQ and she was trembling.

Myriad emotions were running through Carino's mind and body. Fear, anxiety, anger, relief. She knew that no matter who or what was waiting for her on the other side of that door, this signified the end of everything she'd worked so hard to accomplish over the past several years.

The door handle was cold against her sweaty palm and she paused one last time; once she entered that room, she knew everything would change. She would walk out of there a different person.

Literally.

Since they were expecting her, there was no need to knock; she opened the door and walked in. Closing it quietly behind her, she took a brief moment to survey the room's only other occupant, the director, and he was sitting at the far end of the conference table.

"Good morning." He pointed to the empty chair on his right. "Have a seat."

Carino swallowed the lump in her throat. She stiffened her spine and walked to her seat with strong, measured strides, waiting for the fireworks to begin.

"Sorry I'm late, director," called an all too familiar voice. The other attendee walked over and sat down in the chair right next to hers, leaning in close to say, "How nice of you to grace us with your presence."

She pressed her lips together in a tight line. "Hi, Nathan."

"This is a secure room, so you can address him openly," the director interjected. "But it has been a while since you've been out of deep cover, so I'll cut you a little slack, Agent Greyson."

Chapter 34

Ramon screeched to a halt in front of Franklin Everly's building and left his car against the curb, completely ignoring the "No Parking" sign; he didn't intend to be inside for long. He blew through the revolving doors and past the empty security station, his eyes peeled for Emerson's thugs.

Luckily, the lobby wasn't teeming with employees, as he'd gotten there after the early birds but before those on a more regular schedule; he didn't even have to wait for an elevator. As soon as he reached Franklin Everly's floor, Ramon could see Abby through the glass. She was talking on her cell phone and looked like she was in the middle of a total meltdown.

She ended the call as soon as she saw him walking through the door. "Oh no, I've got to go."

"Get your stuff and come with me." Ramon barked the order, looking about the office to make sure no one else was around.

"What? Why? I had to come in early today and I've already clocked in. I can't just leave!"

"Get your shit, Abby! We don't have much time. I'll explain in the car, but we've got to get out of here right now."

Realizing he was deadly serious, Abby grabbed her coat, tossed her phone into her purse, and rushed out into the elevator lobby on his heels. Ramon punched the down button repeatedly, praying one of the three sets of doors would open quickly.

"What's going on, Ramon? I don't even understand what's happening! Why did those men come and take Raj?" Abby was bordering on hysteria.

Things were happening much faster than he'd imagined, especially if they already had Raj. "Oh, spare me the drama, Abby. You know exactly why all of this is happening." She flinched at the harshness of his voice. "You can't divulge secrets to the Feds about one of the biggest international drug lords and expect that no one would find out—or care."

Her eyes went wide. "What? Ramon, I didn't—"

Just then, the elevator on the far right dinged and he held his finger to his lips, silencing Abby's denial. Ramon waited about three seconds to make sure no one was going to rush out when the doors opened, since the last thing he needed was to come face-to-face with the men who were here to take Abby to Emerson.

"Come on!" He pulled her into the elevator behind him. As they waited an eternity for the doors to close, he heard another ding, signifying the arrival of one of the other elevators.

"This way!" A man's voice commanded, followed by the sound of at least two sets of footsteps on the tiled entryway.

Mercifully, their doors closed and so began the longest descent of his life. Abby remained silent the entire way to the lobby, but all it took was one glance to see that she was already entering the beginning stages of shock.

"Keep it together, Abby. We're not out of the woods yet. Not by a long shot. Did you hear those men who got out of the elevator upstairs?" He waited for her to nod her head before continuing. "They're here for you. Do you understand what that means?"

She shook her head, but the look on her face told him she knew it definitely couldn't be anything good.

"That means Emerson sent them to kill you because of what you've done. So, if you want to live, you'd better do everything I say—at the exact moment I tell you to. Understand?"

She nodded again.

"Say it, Abby! Tell me you understand!" Ramon yelled, grabbing her roughly by the shoulders.

"Yes! I understand." Abby choked out her reply.

Ramon turned away from her as the car began to slow, wondering how many men would be waiting by the exit. "Stay behind me and try to act normal. I don't need you to panic and catch the eye of one of the guards."

"Sammy doesn't get here until 7:00 a.m."

The doors opened and a single man dressed in a black suit turned around as Ramon stepped out. He was clearly not expecting to see Ramon rushing toward him either. For all Ramon knew, the man could've worked in the building, but he didn't know for sure and wasn't willing to take any chances. The man didn't even have time to block Ramon's fist as he connected with his temple, knocking him out with a single punch. Abby let out a startled scream and covered her mouth with her hand as the man's body dropped to the floor like a sack of potatoes.

"Keep moving, we don't have much time." Ramon looked over his shoulder, making sure Abby was still following him.

The few other people he could see in the lobby were riveted in place, watching with their mouths gaping open as he and Abby ran toward the doors. Thankfully, no one tried to detain him and they made it to his car without further incident. Merging into rush hour traffic, several cars honked but Ramon didn't care one bit. His main concern was whether or not they were followed, which he believed they weren't.

"Okay, start talking." He weaved in and out of commuters until he felt they were thick enough into the mix to remain hidden.

Abby was clutching her purse to her chest so tightly that her knuckles were turning white. "I had no idea this was all going to happen. I just needed some extra help with my bills and they paid me really well for the information. I started off with some of the smaller clients, but once they figured out we handled some of the bigger players, they threatened to out me if I didn't start providing better information."

"Out you? To who? That doesn't even make sense." His eyebrows drew together.

Why would the Feds compromise their inside man?

"I guess to my boss. Or the partners. I don't know! I was too scared to find out." Abby was shrieking.

"Then why did you make calls to them from the office? Don't you think that was pretty stupid?"

"For a while, I wouldn't answer when they would call my cell phone, so they started calling me at work. They even threatened to come down there because I'd already taken their money. I couldn't lose my job, so I kept getting them the information they wanted, and sometimes they wanted it immediately."

"So, you're saying they wanted information on clients other than Emerson?" Ramon was struggling to make sense of it all.

"Yeah, but I gave them information on Emerson and his associates too. They ended up telling me they didn't want anything to do with him though because he was too heavily connected to the drug trade. They decided to focus on more legitimate clients to poach."

Poach clients? What the hell?

"Let me get this straight, you were providing confidential information to another firm because they wanted to steal Franklin Everly's clients?" Ramon suddenly pieced the puzzle together.

"Yes! That's why I don't understand how Raj got arrested this morning and why anyone would want to kill me. I messed up, but I don't think I deserve to die." The tears she'd been holding back finally spilled over and rolled down her cheeks.

Ramon was totally blindsided.

Abby wasn't the mole. But if not, then who was?

"Abby, did you ever hear anyone else using the phone in your firm's file room?" He began grasping at straws.

She wiped her nose and frowned. "Not really. Most people would either use their cell phones or the phones in their offices."

He'd known it had been a long shot, but had figured it was worth a try.

"Actually, come to think of it, there were a few times when I saw Carino hanging up the phone in the room, but I never heard her talking to anyone. Why?"

Ramon saw red and his blood pressure spiked. Suddenly, it all made sense. The lack of personal information he'd found on her, the unexplained connection to Nathan, the fierce drive to burrow deeper into Emerson's account, the overly-inconspicuous lifestyle, the story she had honed to perfection from years of practice—all part of a cultivated façade to keep people from getting too close.

And he'd bought all of it, hook, line, and sinker.

"Ramon! Watch out!" Abby's scream jolted him to attention mere seconds before he rear-ended the car in front of them.

"How much do you know about Carino before she came to Franklin Everly?" Ramon pulled over at the next available parking meter that appeared. "How much did she share about her life? Or what she did before she moved to Denver?"

"I don't know, not much. Why?" Abby was instantly wary.

He vibrated with fury, sick of her opposition. "Just answer my questions, Abby!"

She jumped, scooting as far away from Ramon as the small car would allow. "Um, she told me her parents and brother had died right after she'd moved here from Wyoming."

Completely unattached.

"Go on."

"Okay, she told me that guy, Nathan, had stalked her after they broke up." She closed her eyes, clearly searching the recesses of her mind for anything else Ramon might find useful.

"Did she volunteer the information about him or did you ask her?"

"No, I actually caught them together at the store a couple years ago. Come to think of it, she did act really weird about the whole thing too, but she was just so private that I thought it was because she was embarrassed."

Nathan, the perfect cover for an Agency handler.

Ramon slammed the palms of his hands against the steering wheel. Abby squealed.

"What's going on, Ramon? Where's Carino? Is she in some kind of trouble?"

"I really don't know, Abby. I just don't know what to think right now."

• • •

Ramon took Abby to her house, after instructing her to speak to no one and to leave town immediately. She said her mom lived in Idaho and really needed looking after anyway. She'd been planning a trip to visit next month, so he informed her that the visit just became permanent and the date had been advanced.

As he raced down the freeway toward his hotel, he tried calling Carino, but got her voice mail—again.

"Shit!" He threw his phone into the empty passenger seat and gripped the steering wheel until his palms burned.

Carino was the informant and she'd been under his nose the entire time. She'd had the nerve to accuse *him* of being dishonest, while he'd poured his heart out to her, after apologizing until he was nearly hoarse. He wondered if anything they'd shared had been real, or if she'd simply been doing her job. For that matter, he wondered what her real name was. Gnawing at the back of his mind was the thought that Raj had been right all along; his attraction to her had completely blinded him.

Well don't I feel like the fool?

Ramon ditched the car in the lot he'd been parking in for the last week, after wiping down the various surfaces for fingerprints. He hoofed it into the hotel, requested his rental car to be collected, and had his stuff packed in less than ten minutes. In and out before Raj—or Carino—sent the cops after him.

He had stashed a couple more passports in his baggage, so from this point forward, Ramon Terrones was no more. He was simply a figment of the imagination, easily erased. Forgotten. He was now Mateo Rodriguez.

If only it was that easy to forget my memories.

Compelled to try one last time to see Carino before he bought a plane ticket out of Denver, he sped east on I-70 toward her house, running sharp on a lean mixture of adrenaline and betrayal. Booting up his laptop en route, he tried to access the video feed from her house, but of course the screen showed all black. She'd obviously found the cameras. He shook his head, disbelieving that mere hours ago he'd been planning their future together and pledging his undying devotion. Anger coursed through his veins, hot and thick. He'd been such a sucker.

I guess the old cliché is true—there really is a thin line between love and hate.

Ramon chose a secluded spot to sit and wait outside Carino's house, but made sure he had clear access to see who came and went. Amidst his denial that he was holding onto a shred of hope that somehow he'd been wrong about her, he told himself he simply wanted to confront her, lay into her for all of her lies and double-standards, and walk away forever. But she wasn't home, which was obviously no surprise. In fact, she'd probably never set foot on the property ever again.

Resigned to wait a little longer, just to make sure, he switched on the radio in an attempt to distract his thoughts from his roiling emotions. Unfortunately, the stations were still featuring their respective morning talk shows, as well as frequent traffic updates to help the frazzled commuters navigate the best route to work. Quickly tiring of scanning the channels, he left it on the jazz station and sat back to contemplate his next move.

His mind suddenly filled with uninvited images of Carino's lithe body, writhing beneath him as she called his name. Of his hands and mouth all over her, caressing and tasting. Of her eyes as—

" … just released the name of the driver in the fatal, single car accident on E-470," the radio announced. "Twenty-five-year-old Carino Montgomery, a resident of Aurora, CO, was pronounced dead at the scene. There were no other passengers in the vehicle, and at this time, authorities have indicated a tire blowout may have caused the rollover. Commuters should exercise caution, as rescue workers are still clearing glass and debris from the roadway. In other traffic news, there is a disabled vehicle … "

Ramon's entire world shifted on its axis. His vision tunneled and he couldn't breathe. His heart jackhammered in his chest.

Carino is dead? No, that's impossible.

He still hadn't even confronted her about her involvement with Emerson's takedown. He hadn't gotten a chance to express to her how mad he was about everything she'd lied to him about. He hadn't even been able to ask her why.

But most of all, he hadn't gotten to tell her that—no matter what—he still loved her.

Chapter 35

Lindsey still couldn't believe everything had happened so fast. After Nathan … wow, it was hard to stop calling him that after all this time. After *Daniel* had joined her and the director in the conference room, she'd lost all track of time while being grilled and debriefed … and grilled some more.

Bottom line: her assignment was complete and she had hardly been able to wrap her mind around the concept. What had begun as a six-month stretch had morphed into nearly four years. She'd been living as Carino Montgomery for so long that she'd started to believe her own fake backstory. Her mom and dad might as well have died in a car crash because she'd been strictly forbidden from contacting them. At times, she'd even become distraught from having a brother who'd been KIA, even though that wasn't true either. But as she'd lived the lie, it had become increasingly difficult to decipher the truth.

Lindsey's parents hadn't been happy about her decision to go into deep cover at such an early stage in her career, but Daniel had assured her the perfect job had come along, and she'd be a fool to pass it up. She figured she could do anything for six months. But, as the months led to years—then additional years—it became harder and harder to deal with being alone.

Her parents had been anxiously awaiting their reunion at their property in Texas, and Daniel was supposed to drive her there after the debriefing was complete. While they were meeting with the director, Daniel had gotten his secretary to begin the process of having her belongings packed and shipped to a storage facility somewhere in Arkansas, and then again to another location in a different state—he wouldn't tell her where.

Lindsey was supposed to cut all ties to her secret life—all the way down to her wardrobe, so she was literally walking away with nothing more than the clothes on her back. But she couldn't wait to throw the damned contacts away and go back to her glasses, plus return to her natural hair color; she'd been a brunette for way too long. Once she settled in at her parents' house, they'd take her shopping for anything else she would need anyhow.

The director confirmed that Raj had already been taken into custody, and based on the information Lindsey had compiled on Emerson's whereabouts and actions during the final stages of the Costa Rica negotiation, they finally had sufficient evidence to arrest him—and their case was ironclad. Daniel figured Raj was going to spill plenty more details anyway, once they outlined the dossier of illegal activities they would be able to pin on him as Emerson's inside man; he would go into witness protection while the prosecutors readied themselves for a hearing.

Emerson had been detained while attempting to flee his hotel shortly after 7:30 a.m., and was being remanded into federal custody until further notice. It was doubtful he would ever see the light of day again.

Internal Affairs would be launching a full-scale investigation into who might've tipped Emerson off about the undercover operation, but were tight-lipped about anything they'd discovered thus far. Lindsey had made it a habit to never make calls to anyone connected with the investigation from inside Franklin Everly, but had let her guard down once. One time only. She hadn't thought anyone could trace a forty-five second call, but apparently she'd been wrong.

Carino was dead, both literally and figuratively speaking. She'd always known a car accident was how she'd go, which was to make sure if anyone caught wind of her involvement, they wouldn't have any reason to come after her—she'd already be dead.

Ramon's name hadn't even been mentioned, which had come as a total shock. Lindsey wasn't quite sure how or why, but she certainly wasn't going to bring him up on her own, considering how far from protocol she'd strayed by not reporting him—not to mention everything else she'd done. She would have to process her feelings for him later, because she was operating under her maximum capacity for stress. She had to focus her efforts on blocking all thoughts of Ramon from her mind, because as soon as she remembered the feel of his lips on her skin and the way she'd fully given herself over to him, she began teetering on the edge of sanity. Which was why, when Director Williamson began questioning her location during those last twelve hours, she'd clammed up.

"Why'd you drop off the map for half a day? For a minute, I thought you'd switched sides."

"Um, I—"

"Intelligence indicated one of Emerson's associates had come to town, and at the time, we hadn't confirmed if he was here on legitimate business or not." Daniel took over, once it was clear she didn't have a good answer. "Initial information seemed to indicate he was a threat."

"Is this the man you mentioned earlier last week? The same man I called and warned you about, Agent Greyson?" Director Williamson had looked back and forth between the two agents.

Lindsey had turned to glare at Daniel, but he was studiously ignoring her, further confirming her earlier suspicions that he'd gone straight up the chain, after she wouldn't respond to his warnings about Ramon. That was typical of Daniel's style—always operating by the book.

Daniel had cleared his throat and continued. "After I voiced my concerns to you, director, I continued looking into this guy's background. I wasn't able to reach a comfort level, so I made contact with Agent Greyson and ordered her to occupy him by any means necessary."

Director Williamson's eyebrows had shot up, but Daniel had pressed on.

"We were too close to wrapping up, and I wasn't willing to take any chances. She, wisely, took him out of town under the guise of showing him around the area, which helped us avoid any unforeseen, last-minute issues while we advanced on our marks."

Daniel had tapped his knee against Lindsey's leg under the table, signaling for her to go along with it; she had quickly fallen into step.

"Yes, Director Williamson, I felt it was best to go off the grid for a short time. I didn't know if I could trust him, and didn't want to leave myself open for any mistakes. Turns out, he wasn't a threat after all."

"Let me get this straight, Daniel. You made contact with Agent Greyson *again*, even after you were ordered, years ago, not to?" The director's face was pinched into a scowl. "That was a very big risk for you to take."

"Sir, I felt the operation was in danger of being compromised. I had no other choice." Daniel outwardly displayed the utmost confidence in his own lies.

Mercifully, Director Williamson had appeared satisfied and moved on from the topic of Ramon. Lindsey had answered countless questions before finally being dismissed with orders to take a ninety day hiatus to get her affairs buttoned up, and decide what she wanted to do next.

She had walked out of the conference room in a complete daze, and had followed Daniel to his office on autopilot. As soon as he'd closed the door behind them, he'd pulled her into a tight hug, which was all it took to unleash the waterworks. Lindsey had sobbed deeply, taking huge, gulping breaths as Daniel held her tight and smoothed her hair away from her soggy face.

"Red, look at me." Daniel called her by a nickname she thought she'd never hear again in all her life. When Lindsey had raised her head to meet his gaze, she'd been overwhelmed by the emotion reflected back at her. "I was beginning to think I was never going to get to hug you again." He'd struggled to swallow back his own tears. "But I knew you could do the job. I always knew you'd come out on the other side. I just want you to know that I'm extremely proud of you."

"I can't believe you busted me out to Director Williamson!" she'd managed to accuse him, in between hiccups. "Is that why you covered for me back there? Because you felt guilty?"

"That's where you're wrong; I don't feel guilty. I was looking out for you and I'd do the same thing again, if I had to do it all over." He'd reached over to his desk to grab some tissues. "I covered for you because that's what big brothers do."

They had stood, holding each other and crying like babies for who knows how long. But before long, they were being whisked across the city in a Town Car, heading for their parents' place.

"Take a look around because this is probably the last time you're going to see the skyline close up." Daniel looked thoughtfully out the window.

"I don't need to; I've had enough of this place for one lifetime." Lindsey had snuggled against his arm and allowed her overwhelming exhaustion to lull her into oblivion.

When she'd finally woken up, it was daylight and they'd been traveling all night. Daniel was giving the final instructions to the driver as she'd looked out the window, suddenly realizing they were already at her parents' house. She'd no sooner stepped out of the car to stretch her aching legs when the front door of the house had flung open.

"Lindsey? Is it really you?" her mom had shouted, blasting down the sidewalk past her dad. She pulled Lindsey into her open arms.

All Lindsey had been able to do was stand still and cry, overwhelmed by the love she felt for the family she hadn't seen in almost four years.

"Honey, we've been counting down the days until we'd be reunited. When we saw the news that Emerson had been arrested, we knew we were on the home stretch." Her dad had ripped her out of her mom's grasp into a massive bear hug. "I'm so happy to see you, baby girl."

"Mom, Dad, I've missed you more than I can even say." Years of sadness leaked out of Lindsey's eyes and rolled down her face.

"Have you been eating? You're so skinny! Let's get you inside and get some food in you." Typical mom behavior.

She'd turned to see her dad and Daniel wrap their arms around each other, and all at once she'd felt her invisible wounds, the ones that had festered for years on end, finally begin to knit closed. She had known it would be a while before she would recover from the emotional toll the assignment had taken on her, but she knew she would deal with everything one day at a time.

• • •

Swallowing the last bit of her ginger ale, Lindsey tried—and failed miserably—to settle her gurgling tummy. She focused her gaze out the window, but they were still too high up to see anything but the cloud layer below.

She was thankful for her solitude the last few hours; first class was the only way to fly on long-distance trips, and she'd been fortunate enough to have an empty seat next to her.

"Miss?" the flight attendant said to her, as he completed his final walkthrough of the cabin. "I need to collect your cup because we're beginning our final descent now."

She handed him her trash and buckled her belt tighter, afraid she would vibrate out of her seat from sheer excitement. Her legs shook and her teeth chattered; she was a ball of raw nerves. She was thankful they were about to land because she knew she couldn't stand the anticipation much longer.

It had taken her almost a week, after arriving at her parents' house, before she'd mustered up the gumption to confide in Daniel about her final days with Ramon. She had finally allowed herself to admit that she'd fallen in love with him and couldn't bear the thought of never seeing him again—or of him going through life thinking she was dead. Daniel absolutely disagreed with Lindsey's decision to try to contact him.

She'd called Brown Palace, but of course Ramon had long since checked out. She then used her new cell phone to call his number—repeatedly—but had received a disconnected notification every single time. Truly, she didn't know of any other way to get in touch with him, but knew she couldn't give up.

To her amazement, Daniel completely broke protocol and did some checking into Ramon's whereabouts. She wasn't sure what changed his mind—seeing her slip into the beginning stages of depression maybe?—but he provided her with some long overdue support. After a couple weeks, Daniel had followed the maze created by the multiple identities Ramon had used while traveling home. He'd left town the same day of Carino's "death" and had eventually ended up back in the Caymans, permanently under a new name, after stopping in multiple countries and purchasing various tickets under his numerous alter egos. Instead of moving back to his home on Little Cayman, Daniel had informed her he'd purchased a new home in West Bay, Grand Cayman.

While Daniel had been tracking him down, Lindsey had slowly been returning to her normal self—well, at least on the outside. She didn't know if she'd ever fully return to the girl she'd been before all of this; Carino had become a part of her, stained onto her very soul.

Honestly, she wasn't even sure if she wanted to fully give her up, but at least when she looked in the mirror, she'd stopped seeing a total stranger looking back at her. She was getting used to her glasses again, although she did miss her contacts more than she thought she would, and her hair was once again brilliant in its carrot-top glory. At her mom's insistence, she'd put on a couple of pounds, so instead of looking stick thin, she simply looked healthy.

But her life was nowhere near complete; Lindsey missed Ramon every minute of every day. When Daniel had presented her with the information he'd been able to track down, she knew right then what she planned to do during her hiatus. She wouldn't rest until she'd made things right between them.

"Ladies and gentlemen, welcome to Owen Roberts International Airport in Grand Cayman, where the local time is 8:25 p.m. and the temperature is a balmy 81 degrees. Thank you for flying with us, and may your trip be unforgettable."

That's definitely the plan.

As she retrieved her bags from the luggage carousel, Lindsey scanned the line of drivers, waiting patiently with signs identifying who they were there to pick up. She searched until she found her driver and walked over to meet him.

"Mrs. Sanchez?"

"Yep, that's me. And I'm ready to get out of here."

Chapter 36

He saw her everywhere, and not just in his dreams. It was pure torture. He was chasing a ghost and he knew it, but couldn't seem to help himself. He looked at the photos from when they'd eaten dessert in her office, as well as the ones he'd taken on their trip to Colorado Springs. If it hadn't been for those pictures, he might've thought she hadn't even been real.

What once had been an easy, restful life was now filled with a loneliness he couldn't shake. It followed him around like a shadow, ever-present. He didn't even have any friends he could commiserate with, since Ramon was no longer. He hadn't even returned to his home on Little Cayman, instead purchasing a new house under his new name in West Bay, Grand Cayman. The movers he'd hired shipped all of his belongings to a storage unit he'd rented on Cayman Brac in yet a different name, and he planned to leave the unit untouched until he felt confident he wasn't being sought out for extradition.

Outfitting his new place kept him busy during the day, but the nights were brutal. Visions of Carino's green eyes haunted him until he'd finally resorted to washing sleeping pills down with a few glasses of whiskey to get even a few hours of shut-eye.

On a whim, he'd bought a sailboat, desperate to find some solace from the anguish he experienced day in and day out. He spent as much time as possible at the marina, sometimes succumbing to exhaustion and falling asleep on the gentle waves.

Today, he'd brought his lunch, as he planned on going sailing later in the afternoon, once the winds really kicked up. He'd taken her out for the first time the week before, and was anxious to feel the salt water on his face once again.

Just as he was ready to set sail, he realized he'd left his satellite phone in his car. He contemplated leaving without it, but sailing by himself carried enough of a hazard that he figured it was better to be safe than sorry.

As soon as he reached his car and picked up the phone, he noticed several missed calls from his housekeeper, all within the last twenty minutes. Frowning, he dialed his home number and waited until she answered.

"Rosa? What's going on?"

"So sorry to bother you, Mr. Rodriguez. But the young lady, she came to visit a day early."

His heart rate kicked up a notch. "What young lady?"

"Lindsey. She said you were expecting her tomorrow but she came to town early, so I told her you were down at the marina. I hope that was okay, sir."

He didn't know anyone named Lindsey and was instantly worried that he'd been discovered. But even as he thought it, he couldn't imagine how that was even possible, since he had thoroughly covered all of his tracks. "It's okay, Rosa. Thanks for letting me know."

Ending the call, he got in his car and closed the door, surveying the area for anyone he didn't immediately recognize. Several minutes went by and the marina remained essentially deserted, so he decided to stop waiting around and get out on the water. Whoever was looking for him could wait, especially since he had no clue who this Lindsey person was.

No sooner had he stepped out of his car did a taxicab pull into the lot and a single passenger got out. He didn't recognize the woman with blazing red hair, but she was pretty far away from his vantage point. She walked down the dock, turning her head from side to side as she moved farther down the plank. When she reached his slip, she stopped.

He locked his car and began walking briskly toward her, wondering what could be so urgent that she'd sought him out at his boat. She must've heard him coming because she turned around as he approached.

As usual, he was seeing Carino everywhere; his brain had him convinced that this stranger was her, reincarnated. Blinking rapidly, he battled with his mind while his heart threatened to beat out of his chest.

"I wasn't sure I'd ever find you," she said.

Now his ears had joined the mutiny; the voice sounded like her too. But it couldn't be. Carino was dead.

"Who are you and what do you want?" His voice was harsh from the grief his memories incited.

She took a few steps toward him and pointed to his boat. "Rosa didn't tell me which slip was yours, but I kinda figured … "

He followed her finger to the words "*Mi Cariño*" stenciled on the hull before refocusing on her face once more.

It can't be.

"You look really good, by the way. A little thinner, but good." She took a few more steps toward him and removed her sunglasses.

His heart was thundering and his mouth ran dry. He tried to ask her again who she was but his words stuck in his throat.

"I wasn't sure you'd actually want to see me, but I figured I had to at least try."

She was standing an arm's length away. He could easily reach out and touch her, this stranger who looked so familiar yet so different with her tentative smile and flaming red hair. But there was no mistaking it—this was really Carino.

"Rosa said your name is Lindsey. I don't know anyone named Lindsey." He held his breath, waiting for the moment when his senses would clear and he'd no longer see Carino standing in front of him. At least that's what typically had been happening, although his visions had never been this clear or lasted this long before.

"Lindsey is my real name. But I guess we haven't been formally introduced." She held her hand out toward him. "Hi, I'm Lindsey Greyson."

He found his own hand reaching for hers, as if it had a mind of its own. Dazed, he said, "I'm Mateo. Mateo Rodriguez."

As soon as their hands met, jolts of electricity coursed through his veins. She took yet another step closer and looked directly in his eyes. He tried to look away but felt as if he were hypnotized.

"It's nice to meet you, Mateo. But to me, you'll always be Ramon."

He released her hand and rubbed his palms together, as myriad emotions wracked his body. "It can't be you. You died. I heard it on the radio and the newspaper had a story…"

"Ramon—I mean, Mateo—there's a lot I need to tell you. Can we go somewhere and talk?" She chewed furiously on her bottom lip, which he found still affected him exactly the same way.

He'd envisioned this moment over and over in his mind, practicing what he would say to her before he scooped her into his arms and kissed her senseless. Then they would forgive each other, forget the past, and sail off into the sunset together, content in each other's arms forever.

This was nothing like that.

He took a deep breath and blew it out hard as he shoved his hands into his pockets, still disbelieving this was really Carino, in the flesh. "You lied to me. You had me thinking you were dead for the past month."

She dropped her gaze and kicked at a small pebble on the dock. "I know I did and I'm sorry. Things just happened really fast and I didn't want to risk the Bureau coming after you."

"How generous." His words were laced with sarcasm and hurt. "I'm surprised you still cared, after the way you tossed me out of your house for lying to you. It's all a bit hypocritical, don't you think?"

She took a step back and crossed her arms over her chest. "I know and I'm sorry. I should've handled things differently, but I was too hurt to think clearly."

"Right. Well, I wouldn't know anything about being hurt, now would I?" His anger was rapidly mounting as he continued his barrage. "At least I didn't lie to you about who I was. But everything about you was a lie, straight down to the color of your hair." He reached out and touched her curls, noticing she leaned slightly toward his hand.

"Mateo, not everything was a lie. Not the way I felt about you, at least."

He ran his hands over his face, intoxicated by the scent of her shampoo that lingered on his skin. "Forgive me if I'm not buying it. For all I know, you're still working for the Bureau and you've led them straight to me. I mean, how else could you have even known where I was—who I was—unless you used official connections?" She opened her mouth to speak, but he held up his hands. "No, I don't want to hear it. My heart can't take any more. I need you to please leave now." His breath hitched as he saw her chin begin to quiver.

"Please, just hear me out." Tears filled her eyes and spilled over onto her cheeks.

Swaddling himself in all the hurt and anger he'd harbored for the past month, he formed a barrier around his heart. "Goodbye, Carino."

And with those parting words, he stepped around her and walked to his boat, unsure if he wanted her to chase after him or not.

• • •

He had no idea how long he sat on a small chair in the cabin with his head in his hands, trying like mad to comprehend what had just happened. However impossible it seemed, the woman he'd pined over had sought him out to make amends. And, in return, he'd ordered her away.

Why hadn't he just forgiven her, like he'd wanted to do all along? Why didn't he rush to her and smother her with kisses, like he'd dreamed of doing nearly every single night since they'd first met? Instead, he'd yelled at her and made her leave.

She'd looked so damn beautiful standing there with the breeze blowing her colorful hair around and making the gauzy fabric of her sundress cling to her gorgeous legs. Even though she'd looked different than he remembered, her eyes had still captivated him with just a single glance. He rubbed the palm of his right hand, still reeling from the way her skin had felt against his, just as silky as in his dreams.

He'd never stopped loving her, not even when he'd found out the truth. He'd also known, deep down, that she'd cared for him too, otherwise she would've tried harder to pinpoint his role in Emerson's dealings. She would have made sure he was taken down with Emerson's regime. But she hadn't done that at all. Instead, she'd come to ask his forgiveness.

Oh my god, what have I done?

He'd made a mistake. A huge one. He had to find her before she left the island, only he had no idea where she was staying. Dialing his home number again, his fingers tapped a furious rhythm on the table, impatiently waiting while the phone rang multiple times.

"Rodriguez residence."

"Rosa, did Lindsey say where she was staying while she was in town?"

"No, Mr. Rodriguez, I'm sorry. Why, is something the matter?"

He didn't even respond, as he'd already disconnected the call and was racing up the ladder and out onto the boat's deck. He climbed down and ran full speed down the dock until he reached the marina's snack shop, ripping the door open and startling the young man behind the counter.

"Can I help you, sir?"

Breathless, he managed to choke out, "Do you know the number for the nearest cab company?"

"I only know one, and you just dial all fours."

He began dialing immediately. When the dispatcher answered, he asked if they could research the pick-up address for the passenger who'd been dropped off at the marina on Yacht Drive. In short order, he was running to his car and driving like mad to the nearby Holiday Inn Resort.

Sliding into a parking space, he rushed inside to the registration desk and asked for Lindsey Greyson's room number. Of course, they refused to give it to him. He wasn't sure if it was simply hotel protocol, or if the crazed look in his eyes warned them against it.

"Please. I need to see her." He gripped the edges of the counter so hard, he was surprised the marble didn't crack.

"I'm so sorry, sir, but I'm not allowed to release that information." The woman behind the counter actually did look pained, but that didn't stop him from lashing out.

"You don't understand! She's the love of my life and I've just made a huge mistake." His voice rose several decibels as he pleaded his case, unsuccessfully.

"Sir, I'm going to have to ask you to keep your voice down."

He slapped his hands on the counter before running them through his hair. "What other options are there then? Can you call her room?"

"Yes, I can do that, but only if you calm down please." She shot a meaningful gaze toward a closed door behind the counter. "I want to help you, but if my supervisor comes out, he might not be so understanding."

He took a deep breath and nodded his head. "Okay, I get it. Please call her room."

She typed something into her computer, picked up the phone, and furtively punched in the number, obviously shielding it from his prying eyes. After several beats, she returned the receiver to its cradle. "I'm sorry, but there's no answer. I'm afraid you'll have to come back later, sir."

He pressed his lips into a tight line and nodded curtly. "Thanks for trying."

Turning around, he took one step and stopped dead in his tracks; she was standing a few feet away near the main lobby doors holding a takeout bag from some fast food joint.

"Mateo? What are you—"

He didn't allow her to finish her sentence, as his giant strides ate up the distance between them and he pulled her into his arms, sealing his lips over hers. All of his pent up emotion came flooding out and he couldn't tell if the wetness he felt on his cheeks was coming from him or her.

Pulling away, he planted little kisses all over her face, from her chin to her forehead to the tip of her nose.

"I should've done that earlier. I'm sorry for how I handled things and I'm so glad you're still here." He leaned his forehead against hers as he plunged his fingers into her hair and pulled her toward him for another searing kiss.

When he finally released her, she was breathless and smiling from ear to ear. "I wasn't about to leave before you came to your senses."

He returned her smile, his face feeling odd as he stretched muscles that hadn't been used since that fateful night back in Denver. Looking into her eyes, he felt the ice around his heart begin to crack and thaw.

"I know we've got a lot to talk about. How would you feel about dinner tonight at my place? Rosa made chicken enchiladas and she cooks up a mean sauce." He pulled her close, drawing her intoxicating scent deep into his lungs before slightly releasing his grip so she could have some breathing room.

"Well, it's no Burger King," she held up the bag, "but I suppose I could choke it down if I had to."

"It's good to see that our heated discussion earlier at the marina didn't spoil your appetite," he teased.

Pulling free of his arms, she opened the bag, revealing three chocolate sundaes. She shrugged her shoulders and smiled. "Ice cream therapy."

He shook his head and laughed, reminded again of the depth of his love for this gorgeous woman. "I know a guy who owns a sailboat out on the marina. I hear it's got a great view and I'm sure he'd let you on board, if you promised to share your sundae."

Lindsey stood on her tiptoes and kissed him softly on the lips, causing his eyes to close. When he opened them again, he could see all the love he felt reflected back in her expression.

"It sounds perfect, but I'll have to find another way to convince him to let me on board." She winked, as her eyes took on a mischievous twinkle. "I've only got one spoon."

He threw his arm around her shoulders, guiding her toward the exit. "I'm sure we can manage."

About the Author

B.B. Cruz currently lives in Anchorage, Alaska with her husband, two teenage daughters and two little doggies. She's a huge fan of romance, and loves to cozy up with a novel, which definitely makes the long winters and cold nights easier to handle. Visit her on the Web at *www.bbcruz.com*.

A Sneak Peek from Crimson Romance
(From *Inheriting Fear* by Sandy Vaile)

Her brown combat boots pounded the bike track as her eyes searched the shadows on either side. Mya had made the same short journey five days a week for eleven years, but at night it still made the back of her neck prickle. She could buy a car and live in fear. Not a chance. Fear could go to hell.

Intermittent puddles of lamplight dripped onto the tarmac. Laughter and evening TV programs carried through the open windows of weatherboard houses along the railway track, and she inhaled a waft of grilled chops with the rail grease. She pushed her chef's skull-cap into the back pocket of her jeans and wrapped an elastic band around her long hair. On the other side of the tracks, the Croydon Hotel emitted a bass beat that vibrated in the viscous humidity.

She glanced at her watch and picked up the pace. It was supposed to be her night off work, but the sous-chef wanted to leave early for a party, and it was Mya's responsibility to make sure the kitchen ran smoothly. It wasn't like she had a social life anyway.

An androgynous shadow ambled from the bushes ahead, hands shoved deep into the pockets of a hooded jacket. She moved to the opposite side of the track. As the shadow solidified it looked taller, broader, with a hairy chin protruding from the obscurity of the hood. A flickering fluorescent streetlight alternated the image of a man and an ominous silhouette.

They passed one another and he looked up. Red, glassy eyes devoured her from head to toe. A shiver ran up the back of Mya's legs to her scalp. One side of his mouth lifted in a half-smile, so she nodded a greeting but kept walking.

With her eyes ahead and ears trained on his retreating footsteps, she breathed easier as each second passed. Walking the bike track at night certainly had its hazards, but it just wasn't worth getting the motorbike out of the shed and donning all the gear to go a few hundred metres. Besides, she had as much right as anyone to be there, and she'd made herself a promise a long time ago to never let anything or anyone stop her from doing what she wanted. Fear was just an emotion and she could overcome those with steely resolve.

The footsteps behind her ceased and her heart flip-flopped into her throat.

Mya turned around slowly. The hood guy had turned around too, and his left hand held a beer stubby, but not at the base like he was about to take a swig. His long fingers were wrapped around the neck of the bottle, making it look more like a weapon.

A lump of panic stuck in her throat. Best to get the hell out of there, but it went against her training to leave her back unprotected. Her kick-boxing mentor, Ned, would clip her around the ear if she let anyone get the upper hand on her. When the thug finally took a long draught from the stubby, she hurried in the direction of the Croydon Hotel again.

"Whocha doin' out 'ere in the dark, Mya?" he slurred.

She spun around and narrowed her eyes at the blackness beneath his hood. "Do I know you?"

He swayed closer. "Nah, but I know you."

"Look, I'm going to work. I don't want any trouble."

"Oh, you're in a lotta trouble, love."

Something glinted in the faltering light; his other hand strangled the hilt of a long blade. Her pulse thundered in her ears, drowning out the crickets in the grass. The hood slid back as they sized each other up. He looked a bit older than her, maybe mid-thirties, half a foot taller and beefy—although height and weight didn't always mean much in a fight.

After a deep, calming breath, she drew on the long hours spent in the gym facing her demons. She wasn't the angry teenager Ned had taken under his wing all those years ago. Learning how to kickbox had given her courage. No longer a victim, but in control. Another deep breath. Her pulse slowed fractionally. She *was* in control.

The thug leered with a mouthful of mangled teeth. She'd seen that look before, and it meant trouble. Whether it was trouble for him or her remained to be seen.

"I've gotta deliver a message." He tapped the corner of a white envelope that protruded from his pocket, sloshing beer down the side of his jeans. "She says it doesn't matter if I mess you up a bit, s'long as you're alive enough to read it."

"What? Who says?" Maybe he was hallucinating from drugs. Unpredictable, but she'd been taught to deal with that. A long time ago she decided no man was going to beat her the way she'd watched her mother get beaten. She summoned an inner calm, relaxed her stance, and held his gaze. "You know, alcohol slows your reflexes. Be careful with that knife."

A crease formed between his brows, but any doubts he had appeared to pass because he clenched the knife tighter and took a step toward her. She took a step backward and waited with feet shoulder-width apart, knees soft. The rumble of a train built in the distance.

Hood-man lunged, but his depth perception must have been distorted, because the blade was half a metre shy. He looked at it with a confused expression.

It was probably a waste of breath, but... "You *could* just give me the letter."

"And leave a fine piece of tail like you alone?" He lunged again.

This time she lifted onto her toes, raised a knee, and snapped the ball of her foot into his gut. He grunted and dropped the stubby in preference of clutching his stomach. Brown glass shattered and latte-looking foam pooled on the tarmac, circulating a yeasty smell. She was relieved to see the knife had slumped downward with his shoulders.

"I told you it was hard to concentrate when you're under the influence." With one finger she hooked her undie elastic out of her arse. Jeans weren't ideal for kickboxing, but her boots were solid. Old faithfuls, with years of stains slopped over them and frayed stitching.

"You're gonna be sorry for that, bitch."

"I doubt it," she muttered.

She'd spent too many years living in fear as a child. Now she was in charge of her own destiny, and no man was going to dictate to her. His eyes were wider now, and the whites were yellow with red capillaries tangled like a mess of string around the irises. Definitely drugs. Dark hair flopped across his face, and he pushed it back with a twitch. His weight shifted left and he feinted right.

Mya stood her ground.

"Why don't you give me the letter and we can call it a night?"

The sounds of crickets and a baby crying were swallowed by the rumble of the passing train. As he thrust the knife again, she pinned his wrist in her armpit, and elbowed him in the gut. He hunched over, and she snapped her arm back. Knuckles connected with his nose. *Crunch*.

He yowled and stumbled back, dropped the blade to better clutch his bleeding nose. Quickly, she snatched up the knife— cheap army disposals crap—and tucked it through a belt loop.

"Message delivered," she told him as she grabbed the envelope from his pocket.

He remained bent over, nursing his nose, as she jogged along a strip of moonlit track to the footpath. The envelope felt like a hot coal in her hand. She glanced over her shoulder. No hood-man, so she slid the blade up her sleeve, cupping the hilt in her palm, and crossed the railway track.

It looked like local band Shamrock had pulled a big Saturday-night crowd. Windows vibrated in time with the thud of the bass. Party-goers leaned against the faded blue pub front, and she held her breath to pass through the haze of smoke drifting in the warm air. She stepped through the back door of the pub and … breathed. It felt safe here, almost like home. She'd worked her way from apprentice to head chef at the Croydon and was practically part of the furniture.

At the back of the store room, she stashed the knife behind a sack of rice, then wiggled a finger into the back of the envelope and split it open. Inside there was a lined page with a jagged edge, like it had been torn from a spiral-bound pad. The handwriting had a backward slant, but the note wasn't signed.

She could just throw the letter in the bin and pretend she'd never seen it, but whoever this woman was, she had gone to the trouble of paying off a druggie to deliver it, maybe hoping Mya would get roughed up some. The guy had said "she," and he didn't look in any position to improvise, so the author must be a woman.

More worrying, the woman knew her by name. That took motivation, and Mya needed to know what kind of person would go to those lengths. Sure, she'd pissed off a few people over the years—especially in the boxing ring—but an enemy? She couldn't think of anyone who hated her enough to bother.

After a fortifying breath, she read the letter.

You're good at running and hiding, aren't you, Mya? But I know who you are. I bet you thought I'd forgotten about you and your retarded mother. Thought you could hide from me, but I'm coming for you, bitch.

I'll be watching … sleep well.

Something slimy slid down her throat and into her gut: familiarity. There was no way it could be who she thought it was, but the note gave her a sense of panic from a long time ago. It felt like when she was eighteen, standing in front of her government-appointed housing with a thirty-something redhead yelling at her.

The conversation had started civilly. The woman wanted to know about Jack Roach, but Mya's father had been dead a year by then, and good riddance to him. But carrot-top wouldn't leave her alone, insisting Jack had another family, and wanting to know things about Mya. Things she wasn't ready to share.

Bloody Jack had been the one who tore apart everything she knew and devastated the only person she cared about, her mum. There were only tatters of her life left, but they were hers and no sham relative was going to turn up for a hand-out and stop her from taking care of her mum.

It couldn't be possible for Rhonda to have tracked her down. Mya had changed her name and moved. It wasn't feasible. She forced short breaths out of her tight lungs. A shudder started at the crown of her head and made its way down her spine. She glanced at the darkness beyond the hotel's back door and then hurried to the bright kitchen. Service was in full swing and the din of the exhaust fan, crockery, and sizzling food soothed her raw nerves.

She'd left Jack behind, but the prick was still tormenting her a decade after he died.

"Hey, Mya, you look like you saw a ghost." Jilly tucked a pen behind her ear and dropped an order pad into the pocket on the front of her apron.

"You okay?" Marion, the sous-chef, stepped away from the grill.

Even the dish pig had stopped feeding greasy plates into the commercial dishwasher to stare.

"I-I'm fine. Just had a run in with a punk on the bike track, that's all."

Marion nodded knowingly. "Why you insist on walking along there in the dark is beyond me. It's not safe for a woman."

"I'm not scared of any man," Mya snapped a little too forcefully to be convincing.

Marion shrugged. "Well, thanks for covering for me tonight. I just put a medium-well rump on the grill and a salmon in the oven."

"Sure. You're still okay to work tomorrow?"

"Don't worry, I won't get smashed at the party. I'll be here at ten a.m. Enjoy your day off." Marion tossed her tea towel at Mya and circled her hand at the kitchen. "Have fun, peeps."

"Enjoy the party," everyone called.

With a shake to clear her head, Mya tucked the tea towel into the front pocket of her jeans, slid the white skull-cap onto her head, and familiarised herself with the dockets clipped beside the grill.

Worrying about the letter would have to wait until after service. God knew she'd lived through enough bad news to last a life time, but she wasn't the same girl now. Whoever sent the threat would have to wait their turn and, when the time came, she'd face them head on.

In the mood for more Crimson Romance?
Check out *In the Shadow of Vengeance by Nancy C. Weeks* at
CrimsonRomance.com.

www.ingramcontent.com/pod-product-compliance
Lightning Source LLC
Chambersburg PA
CBHW010857100726
47905CB00011BA/3246